The Grey

Lady

Thomas William Dulaney

Dedication

I want to dedicate this book to the following people, my dad Don, grandfather Barney, grandmother Earlene, uncle Pat, mother Julie, brother Steve, sister Kerry, my godmother Angie, all of my relatives, fellow shipmates, those I've served in the military with, my dearest friends Stephen, Boon, Shank, Doc Nancy, Riley, Big James, Lilly for the cover, Salena for the editing and guidance throughout this journey. Also, to anyone else, I did not mention.

Preface

This story was inspired by the hardship of war and strife in our own world. The author, having witnessed the harsh realities of war, found solace in crafting a world both fantastical and familiar. A realm steeped in magic, became a canvas to explore themes of courage, duty, and survival.

Tayg, the protagonist, embodies the disillusionment many soldiers face. Uprooted from his life and thrust into a strange land, he grapples with the weight of his past and the uncertainty of his future. Yet, amidst the chaos, he finds purpose in protecting Aethel and its people.

This story is for those who yearn for escape, for those who find strength in unlikely heroes, and for those who believe that even in the darkest of times, hope can endure. The author invites you to step into the world of Aethel, where magic clashes with steel, and courage knows no bounds. Prepare to be swept away by a tale of unexpected alliances, unwavering determination, and the fight for survival.

Introduction

This book comes from a special place in my heart, this has been a goal of mine since I was a teenager. This book is a marriage of many passions together, brewing, medieval cooking, medieval research down to clothing, and applying the historical method of what would logically exist in the universe this book has created. Each culture has had to have its attention and love to bring it to light.

I have had a blast going through historical sources, archaeological sources, old stories, and music. To me music is a must for writing, I got it down to some of the characters having favorite genres of music. Many sailors during my time in the navy and while on the ship would have their favorite songs and there would be just about every type of music covered.

The ship itself is similar to one from the Gator navy, they would take marines where they needed to go, then switch over to humanitarian aid. This ship was based on the ships that were around in the Vietnam era. These ships were not quick, but they were good at what they did.

The crew and other people you will interact with all come from special places, everyone's known a Tayg or two. Someone who can do more than they thought, one that tries to live by an honorable code. I was able to interact and work with many from many parts of the States and sometimes even the world. I hope you enjoy your time onboard the ship and with the crew, I know I had fun with them as well.

Contents

Chapter 1
The Quartermaster

As a Quartermaster, I am usually not supposed to be at a loss for words and how to write things down in the order they happen; writing smartly and succinctly is part of what I do. I can still remember the adage rocks and clocks. We mind the rocks and clocks. We get the ship where it needs to go, on time, in one piece. The saying about our Rate or military occupational skill for you non-squids is, "Trust your keel to those who wear the wheel." Our Rate has a ship's wheel, one of the original six rates. The others are Signal men (we call them skivvy wavers; skivvies are tighty whities {We usually joke that they are waving underwear on the bridge wings, with or without skid marks}, they do the ships communication via flags and Morse code with lights). Messmate (Cook, but many are apt at making messes of food) Boatswain mate (the derogatory term is Deck ape, just don't tell them I told you) Gunners mates. Oh, I forgot you're reading this, and I didn't say who I am. I happen to be Quartermaster 3rd class

Tayg MacDermott; everyone calls me QM3 for short or Seamus. No, Seamus isn't my middle name; my last name gets slaughtered, and well, our weapons officer said I looked like a Seamus with the green flat cap I always wear.

I am stuck in the chart house trying to make sense of the fuster cluck we are in; I can be a bit more candid since Commander Alvarez wants me to just get the information down. We can keep our short logs, but he wants the full story down here. He's given me full reign. To be honest, it's not as stuffy and congested as the deck logs usually are unless you count the first entry for the year. Only at that time we get to have some mandatory fun. I swear, whoever thought that was fun, taking it very seriously, is probably having some sort of ulcer linked to an aneurysm.

Now Cmdr. Alvarez is the skipper or old man you want. A charismatic badass built like a Victorian strong man. He could tell us we are going to sail for the lost continent of Atlantis and take a pit stop to go kick Loki's ass in Hel, and 95% of the crew would say, "We got your back, sir; when do we deploy and whose attitude needs to be adjusted?" This was supposed to be our last deployment for the Ashtabula LSD 37 (landing ship dock). We are basically an Uber for Marines, and we only do beach pick up and drop-offs. Please do not forget your crap and give us 5 stars and let big navy know we did a good job. Once we do that, we turn into the official UPS ship for that section of the world or offer humanitarian aid.

Now, how did we end up here? I am not sure exactly where it is. I know it's Earth, and the northern hemisphere, possibly Europe, is about as far as we can get. Thankfully, our Chief told us to keep the charts for the weird places. We've been correcting stuff like mad; we really did not have any way to get new charts. We normally use GPS, but it usually craps out as much as it did before coming here. I think I heard a cash register ding with dollar signs on the display every time it broke; it would either read out weird latitude and longitude. I remember QM2, my lead petty officer (LPO for short), humming the Russian national anthem, not the new one, the menacing one. The last time it happened, the GPS had declared we were in the middle of landlocked Russia.

Now this entire suck fest started off the coast of Indonesia. We were headed near the island of Bali. I've heard it is rather nice; it's got wonderful surfing, scuba diving, beaches, and friendly people. I don't know because we never made it. We got diverted off course due to a rogue out of the blue Typhoon. Now, Typhoons do happen in the area between 15 and 25 latitudes, both north and south. They always go north in the northern hemisphere and south in the southern. The wind near 5 degrees North and South cancel each other out and create for me one of the creepiest places in the world. The water is like glass, with no wind, birds, fish, dolphins, whales, or anything. Ships just seem to float on glass. Distance is all weird and hard to tell. The naked eye can see around 14 nautical miles. For the non-nautical types, there is a difference between land and nautical miles, it's all because someone decided the equator was at a slightly different latitude. So, a nautical mile is 6080 ft, and a land mile is 5280 ft.

We diverted course and radioed the other ships in the task force, wanting to link up after the storm cleared. After our brief port stay, we were supposed to stay a few weeks in Bali, then head back to the US, pick up our marines and deploy all over again. Our loved ones thought we were coming back after a diplomatic tour. Let me tell you the flared tempers after that one. We didn't fault the old man; it wasn't his call. We had about 50 marines in total. Not our full 350, just their field gear armaments, and that's about it. The seas towards Okinawa were a lot rougher than normal; the peaks and swells were about 18 to 30 feet. The Ashtabula LSD 37 is a flat-bottomed ship; we have a stern gate, pretty much a giant truck that has a hydraulic tailgate. Thankfully, we got ours fixed. I'll have to tell you about that later. Now, we did not cut through the water like the Coast Guard cutter and Destroyer we were attached to. Instead, the Sea punched us hopefully in the direction we wanted to go - meaning we felt every wave. The stabilizers can do only so much, and the bottom of our hull, the part of the ship in the deepest part of the water, can have boats and other amphibious vehicles drive into it and park.

The sea started getting really dark blue, very different from the normal light, almost crystal-clear blue we'd take note near Okinawa, then out of nowhere, the seas started churning, developing into a whirlpool. The inner diameter could easily swallow an aircraft carrier or 3 in one gulp. I was on the bridge wing holding on for dear life, opened up the water-tight door and grabbed onto the o crap bar.

The o crap bar went through the middle of the bridge and was there to grab onto. Since I was on the right bridge wing, I walked past the skipper's chair with him in it. He gave one glance at me; thankfully, I did not fall overboard, and said, "QM3, grab the bar and hold on tight. Don't go back out there. "I responded with an aye, aye sir." and held that bar with all the force I could. As we spun through the void for what seemed to be an eternity, it felt like we were on a bucking bronco, who was a lower enlisted getting drunk and high off of 5-dollar Goldschlager shots at the off-base strip club. The collision alarm went off, and thankfully, BM2 LeBlanc grabbed the green alarm, the one for collisions, and yanked with all of his might. He yelled over the 1MC (our announcement system), "Brace for impact" With a final few bounce, we ended up steaming comfortably with the sky in the air. It was clearly night, and with a land mass to our east, something looked way off. We noticed that the latitude and longitude had zeroed out entirely; the unit was screaming like a banshee. We thought the GPS was wailing for broken parts like it normally does. It would not quit. We had to unplug the unit to get it to stop.

The ship was dumped out into the ocean, then broke out all the old books and the sextants. Now, nautical navigation has come a long way, and the old ways, even being over a thousand years old, still work. Thankfully, the night sky was mostly clear, but we did not appear to be in the right location. I had to consult Publication 1 to finally figure it out. Publication 1 is the ordering catalog we would use to see what charts we needed. If I ever hear someone calling a map a chart and a chart a map, I will deep-six them (throw them overboard, you get one warning, and this is it). There is a huge difference between the two. Charts are focused on making the water more accurate than land, and Maps are focused on making land more accurate than water.

When the sun rose for the day, the surroundings were way different from before; it was blue. There was a rich emerald island with almost slate grey rocks near the shore in the distance, with a rock to its northeast that seemed to slump with its back away from the island as if the island wanted to try to get away from the larger one. The island came up to a peak facing away from the island; it was entirely slate grey and did not seem to match the larger island. It looks as though it was placed there like a chess piece. With no docks in sight, we figured instead of continuing to steam, we would anchor off the shore of the larger green island. There is an old trick that was used even in the days of sail. The Captain and officers would take a stale piece of bread and throw it off the ship. They did this to see how the seas would move the piece of bread; it would do the same to the ship. Perspective makes it easier to see how the ship would handle the waters. It took us a while to figure out how deep the ocean was below us. We had to hope and guess it would be the same near where we were trying to figure it out a rough prayer to anyone who would listen allowed the anchor to catch on the sea bed and stay. With a more modern chart, this would be easy. We had a British admiralty chart from around the time the ship was built in the '60s. Those charts are the bane of many Quartermaster's existence; the chart scales are not displayed in the bottom right-hand corner but on the latitude lines on the right-hand side.

When measuring distance with any chart, you only need to use latitude. The latitudinal lines are based on the equator and are the same exact distance no matter how far north and south you go. Now, normally, you can use the scale of any chart or map to measure distance. The Admiralty charts do not include distance on the scale, and you have to remember that each tick on the chart is part of the distance. It is always hilariously ironic that these charts are from England, and this is how they still use the English customary system. I'll save the rants about the metric system, for the sanity of both of us.

Now, the trouble my division has is keeping track of where we are. With nautical navigation, we can only determine where we are 4 times a day. The chart we had covered the entire British Isles, and we were off the Coast of Ireland somewhere near Kerry County is the best we can tell. To be honest, I am glad I am not in charge of communications or trying to reach out to any allied units to see what is going on. I just have to bring the news to the old man on where we are, the adage of rank has its privileges comes to mind. That and I am off of watch, so I pretty much have to start collecting data to help keep the chart updated. I do not wish to have our ship become an addition to the islands we see in front of us.

The old man's cabin is probably the best real estate on the ship; it has carpeting and looks like a real professional office. He even has windows where the sun can come in and warm the office. Cmdr Alvarez was there with a cigar in one hand and a nice rock glass in the other. The whiskey was fragrant, I could catch notes of fruit, possibly raspberries, vanilla and hazelnut coming from the glass. I could tell the price point was way above my pay grade. I noticed that the cigar had a smooth fragrance as well. I could smell the earthy tones, and both smells combined to make an unworldly aroma in his cabin.

He looked at me at the entrance and said, "At ease, QM3, please come in and let me know what you have for me."

"Sir, so far I can tell we are still on earth; our GPS unit, both military and Civilian, are confused about where we are. They are not syncing up with any satellites. Thankfully we have a chart that does sort of line up with where we are, after using celestial navigation. However, sir, we only have a British admiralty chart that shows the entire region, and there are no other replacement charts or scale charts. I know the ICs are trying to figure out what is going on and trying to reach out to any allies. I have already started taking more detailed logs on what is going on."

"Outstanding QM3, please keep our logs updated and ensure that you are keeping our charts updated."

"Thank you, sir; the biggest challenge I see in our department is ensuring we have proper depths recorded. With all due respect sir, our ship is not equipped with the ability to provide this information."

"Qm3, thank you for your honest input. I'll see what we can do to implement that. Carry on, please get some rest; glad you are still with us, and we have the o crap bar."

With that, I did an about-face and proceeded to leave the room.

The commander said in his rich, baritone voice. "Oh, one more thing before you go, I want to give you this; you've earned this already." His giant hands reached out to hand me his commander coin.

The brass-looking coin had the ship's crest on one side. The crest for the city is rather interesting; it has a lot going on. There is a train, a log cabin, a canal boat and an old plough from when horses were used. On the other side, it has the commander's name and rank. On the commander's side, it has two eagle feathers. Inscribed on the other side are the words "*Acta non verba,*" which translates into English as "actions, not words."

"Thank you, sir; I'll let the others know what we need to do before heading to sleep. Did you want me to close the door behind me?"

"Seamus, please do. I'll be up on the bridge wing soon to get some air and to think."

With that, I left the Commander to his thoughts as I saluted the commander and shut the false door behind me (a false door is what we call any door that is not watertight). After leaving the commander's estate, I went to the ship's store. This place was a proverbial rumor mill that also happened to carry all things such as junk food (Gedunk, a word that everyone knows what it means, just not where it comes from), rumors (scuttlebutt, also the same name for drinking fountain), lighters, the ship's ball cap (part of our working uniform), T-shirts and other miscellaneous items. I still remember the time they put the Milky Way candy bars next to the laundry soap. No one told anyone that happened, and imagine my surprise biting down into my favorite sweet and tasting laundry soap.

Now favors are a sailor's favorite commodity; depending on the order of cigarettes or even dip, the favor could fluctuate. Also, one must take into consideration the E-4 mafia. I am not saying it exists; if it did, it would probably somehow involve the ship's barber shop or store.

As I walk into the store just around from the General Mess, the IT shack, and the Dragon. (The dragon is where you put your mess gear - plates, cups, and silverware - to be cleaned. It is a huge dishwashing station called a dragon because it looks like steam is being exhaled when it is opened a lot like a dragon's mouth). SH2 Wayne was the person who usually manned the ship's store. He was one of the guys on the ship you could rely on and a good source of information on what was happening. He was a bit of a bigger guy compared to me. Everyone is a bit bigger. I am a bit on the taller side, 6 ft 1 inch and a rather slender build.

SH2 Wayne: "Seamus, what the hell is going on? That was one hell of a bump we hit. Luckily, I got everything stored back and didn't get knocked out by the lighters."

"SH2, you didn't hear this from me, but I don't think we are near Indonesia right now. My best guess with using the stars is off the coast near Ireland. I think we got sucked down a whirlpool. I have no idea what we are going to do next; I just let the old man know. He told me to go get some sleep."

"Seamus, then I'll let you go. Get some sleep; I have a feeling this is going to get more than a little bit weird."

I kind of had to let him know; he looked out for me more than a few times. He got me a ship's hat after mine got stolen and one of the ship's lighters when they were sold out to send back to my grandad, who liked to collect lighters. The hats were part of our uniform; you had to wear a hat outdoors.

I trudged back to my bunk thankfully, it was the bottom one. The bunks in the navy are stacked 3 high and go up past 6 ft. There were about 30 or more beds in our sleeping area or berthing. I was smart. I got one of the racks towards the back at the bottom; I was not going to let that rack go for all the gold in the world. The problem with our berthing is we had people who never had to stand watch; they worked a normal 40-hour work week and would come into our berthing all hours of the night slamming the thick water-tight metal door, shutting off or turning on the AC unit (our only source of air) and turning on the lights without warning. Thankfully, I got really good dark-out curtains for my rack, and most of the light cleared out. The other bad thing about our berthing is it was right under one of the 50 caliber machine gun mounts.

So I crawled back to my rack, pulling the curtains as tight as I could and getting music ready so I could sleep. I would have to have music to sleep due to the noise on the ship; the AC unit would make a loud bang and heavily breathe out cold air. I would also hear the thud thud thud of the 50 caliber machine gun above or the distant gear grinding of CWIS or, more affectionately known as R2FU (it looks like a robot from a certain space movie involving wars in the stars).

As I fell asleep, the songs I heard were not on my mp3 player, nor songs I ever heard before or since. All I can remember is it was a heavenly woman's voice singing in a language I never heard before. Instruments I heard in the most traditional Irish songs. I fell into a trance-like sleep. Around me, the seas became land, and hazel trees sprang from the ground around a pool of water. In the middle of the pool, there was a fish whose scales contained all the colors that could be seen by the human eye. With a whipping sound, the curtains opened, and the brightest light on my face, the trance ended.

A voice I had not heard before grumbled, "Dude, you got the next rover watch."

"Wrong bunk, guy. I'm a Quartermaster; I only stand watch on the bridge when the ship is at sea."

With that interruption, I could not go back to sleep; I jotted down what I could remember. I went to the bridge and to the Chart house. This was my rate's center of the world, our domain. We stored all of the charts we had for the regions we had been to or expected to go. I went there to get caught up on the special project I was tasked with. Getting an accurate account of what is going on on earth. I mentioned earlier that the way we record ships' logs is wildly different, and it still has to be recorded in that way if we ever find a way back. I think if we do, we are all on mandatory drug tests for the rest of our lives, even after getting out of the military. Who is going to believe us that this actually went down?

Anyway, the logs should look like the ones below:

0800 Reveille was played over the 1MC; we are near the coat of Bali on a training exercise.

1200 Lunch has been called over the 1MC.

1300 Ensin Brown was the Officer of the deck, and he relieved LTJG Smith.

Not like:

0630 The Ashtabula off the coast of Bali has been sucked into a whirlpool into Davy Jones' locker to who knows where.

0730 LTJG Smith is now surfing in the well deck, battling mutant Squids

Every entry needs to have some military bearing, and records have to be entered in a short, sweet, and concise manner. So inside the Chart house, we had pretty much at least one every current gaming console. We had one TV hooked up to the Ships TV channel that would host The Military network TV shows. They were terrible at best, and I remember hearing the legends about how terrible the training they put out was. The old timers (usually the first classes) would talk about seeing better class plays written and directed and costumes created by 2nd graders. By comparison, the 2nd graders' content would be considered Oscar-worthy material compared to what the military network put out. However, I cannot get too mad. We could see movies sometimes 4 to 6 months before they came out on video. I guess you need to take the good with the bad.

The chart house is a classified area that lives behind a cipher lock. On the other side of the door, our coats for sea and anchor detail are hung. But our most prized possessions were our coffee pot, coffee and creamer, sugar, and cups. There is a fine naval tradition of not washing your coffee cup, and some followed that honored tradition. If you washed their cup, you might be deep-sixed (violently thrown overboard). At the worst of the best, you might have to sweep the rain with a broom on the main deck outside. Our coffee pot had velcro on the bottom of it and on the chart table. It was not going to move anywhere, along with enough bungee cords to keep it stable in the worst of seas. I think the Navy runs off of caffeine, sarcasm, hatred, and profanity. The order in which any of those appear is purely situational.

After getting a fresh pot of coffee started, I dove back into the records I was working on while looking at what data we have on the area. It is not too much previously; we would get the information from NOAA (National Oceanographic and Atmospheric Agency). Apply them to our publications on board the ship and make corrections to the Charts as needed. Now, it was up to us to figure out the depth, currents, and materials that make up the sea bed. We were lucky that the chart we had was partially correct, as we've noticed so far. We do not know if it is truly off the coast of Ireland or not. Part of what Quartermasters do is remain calm in scenarios like this. I can still remember my instructor from Quartermaster school QM1 Velazquez saying you need to remove the four-letter L word from your vocabulary, and I am not talking about love. He explained, "It's alright to not know exactly where you are, but narrow it down until you can." For example, we knew the stars were similar enough to work, so we guessed that we were on Earth, in the northern hemisphere, and somewhere close to Ireland and Europe. Now, when we are is a totally other thing that is outside my rate and above my pay grade.

The heavenly earthly aroma of coffee with that silky smooth scent and flavor of Irish Cream had brought me back to reality. Sadly, we cannot have alcohol for most of the time; if we are on the ship, beer day is the only scenario that can change that. The mention of those two words strikes dread, fear, and vomit in the mouths of most sailors. If we are stuck at sea for 45 days without the opportunity to go ashore in the next 5 days, we can request a beer day. I heard the last time this happened on the ship, they hit 3 beer days; the last one, the XO, said no to the last since they were going ashore in the next 7 days.

As I pour the coffee, I only pour half of what I need, then put in the creamer, then sugar, and finally fill in the rest. It is a lovely trick I came up with since we have no stirring sticks and cannot have spoons in the chart house. Doing it this way avoids burning your finger and allows a perfect coffee creamer and sugar mixture. After I had poured the coffee, I went to the bridge and the starboard bridge wing to admire the view of the ocean. I have always loved these moments; seeing the sunrise at sea with a hot cup of coffee will always be some of my fondest memories at sea.

I was supposed to take the morning watch; when you relieve the previous watch standard as quartermaster of the watch, you are supposed to get a proper turnover. If anything crazy is going on, where are we going? If the chronometer report is in progress, who is doing it? The person I was relieving was QM3 Davidson. Now, Davidson was a rather selfish man; he wasn't bad at his job unless it was counter to his benefiting from it. He had the deck logs at an awkward angle, covering up part of the chart.

Davidson: "MacDermott, there is nothing special going on; it's just another fine navy day."

Myself: "Roger that, thank you. I'll take the watch."

Davidson to the officer of the deck LT Jorgenson: "Officer of the deck, I am being properly relieved by QM3 MacDermott."

As he left the bridge, Davidson said, " By the way, MacDermott, we have a man overboard."

I asked him, "Can you let our chief or anyone else know?"

Davidson: "No, I got to go to chow."

With that, he left the bridge to go to chow; now, with a man overboard, a few things have to happen. Thankfully, under the deck logs, the proper mark was put on the chart with the time. Davidson never entered the deck logs or told the officers when the person fell overboard. A real dirtbag maneuver, if you ask me. So what he gave me is a 3 to 5 person job. This is also part of my rate; if someone is reported overboard, we treat it as if this is the real deal; it is a real person until we find out otherwise.

The positions are one person on each bridge wing, we have a gyrocompass on each bridge wing, and we have an item that goes on top of the bridge wing that allows us to have a line to the degrees both true and relative. When we are close to land, we use that device to see what degree the landmark is from the ship with relative degrees (relative degrees will always have 0 degrees at the front of the ship, and 180 degrees will always be at the back. However True degrees will rotate depending on what direction we are going). Don't worry; you'll pass QM A school if you keep reading and paying attention! There should always be someone at the chart table, someone recording in the deck log and remembering the time, and possibly also making the decisions. You can see where one would get stressed if one had the time. That was a luxury I did not possess.

I quickly spoke up as the horror was etched on my face. "LTJG Jorgenson, sir, it looks like QM3 Davidson did not bring to your attention that we have a man overboard. "

LTJG Jorgenson was a prior enlisted built big guy who looked like a personification of a bulldog tough as nails, looked mean as hell, but a dang good officer. He knew how to have fun and crack a few jokes, but he knew when the nose hit the grindstone and did everything to get the job done.

LTJG: "Thank you, QM3, BM3 Sanchez, please make the announcement on the 1MC."

BM3 picked up the boatswain's pipe, and the sounds coming from it and going into 1MC could be described as a blood-curdling scream from a dying tea kettle who found out their Camaros had been totaled by their stripper ex-wife. Also, their insurance will not cover the value left on their 49% loan.

Sanchez: "Man overboard, man overboard reported over the starboard side."

LTJG: "Helmsman, please execute a WIlliamson turn, Seamus; please keep an eye out for our man overboard and let me know how we need to rescue him."

(The Williamson turn is basically a wide turn around the area the man overboard is reported to be. We do this to not run over the man overboard and allow the waves produced by the ship to not push away the man overboard or drown them).

Myself. "Sir, I think using the Captain's gig (boat) or the XO's skiff is our best bet. We don't have a helo, nor do we have the right equipment our SAR needs."

Sadly, we were not given the rescue equipment; it was on backorder from the supply department, and MR2 was swamped with other crazy metal fabrication products. I think, at times, we are expected to move a mountain with a spork from a fast food restaurant.

LTJG: "Roger that, wheels, can we launch the Gig or the skiff? It doesn't matter; it's just whatever crane is available to do so."

Given the age of our ship, one of the cranes was usually a little more temperamental than the other. You have to understand that navy ships are made of steel that is dropped in salt water. We have special paint to help, but that only works so much.

As all of this was happening, I was racing out to the starboard bridge wing to get a bearing on the man overboard, racing back in to update the deck log, reporting out recommendations, making sure the Williamson turn was being executed, and providing adjustments. Luckily, the rescue swimmer made it to the crane; both cranes wanted to be in the Navy today. They launched the XO's skiff. As our SAR swimmer (search and rescue) jumped off the boat to swim to the man overboard, the skiff slowly crept up to where the swimmer and man overboard would meet up.

BM2 LeBlanc was driving the skiff. Normally, he was the one driving the Captain's gig. The difference between the boats is the captain's is a bit more fancy and has a bit more brass bells and whistles. The boat was almost an extension of BM2; he drove it like a professional driver. As our SAR swimmer GM2 (Gunnersmate, they maintain the firearms and some weapons systems for the ship), Schroder was built like a professional football running back. He didn't swim; he punched the water out of his way with extreme violence. GM2 was going to get the man overboard; the ocean, gravity, and temperature were not going to get in his way.

This all seemed to me to take an eternity; GM2 made it to the man overboard. The man overboard seemed to fight GM2. I do not know who in their right mind did. I witnessed the dude's workout routine. GM2 got the guy into the boat. Now, here is where it went sideways. As he did, two birds swooped down, and the man overboard was turned to stone. I did not get a good enough glance at what happened, and I thought I needed to get some sleep. I could not see the situation clearly, and I might have been delusional. I raced back inside the bridge.

Myself: "Officer of the deck (LTJG), sir, GM2 was able to rescue the man overboard."

LTJG: "Good job, everyone, we saved him. Wheels that were out freakin' standing, I am amazed at how you did that alone."

The rest of the watch went off without a hitch; I was able to get the logs corrected and updated. The end of my watch was at dinner; my turnover was QM3 Gilbert. Gilbert was even thinner than I was, with red hair and sky-blue eyes. He was always a very happy and chipper guy. He was usually rather shy and soft-spoken, too. His favorite thing to do after watching was to hum the victory song of a Japanese RPG game, something about finality and fantasies. After evening chow, I went to my bunk to read and fell asleep again. I heard normal songs and could finally get some sleep. No dreams this time.

Chapter 2

Metal Turtles

I was awoken to a sound over the 1MC it sounded like the trill of a bird singing while trying to escape a garbage disposal, then the words "All hand heave up and trice out, breakfast for the crew."

I stumbled to the head (bathrooms and showers), woke up, got my shower, shaved, and headed to the general mess decks. Got in line, and the only thing good seemed to be omelets (somehow, the messmates did not screw it up too much). The rumors were wild on the mess decks, and some of the crew were getting yelled at for socializing in the general mess rather than eating. I quickly scarfed down my food, climbed it up to the chart house to get my coffee, and went through the same rituals, almost like a prayer to the coffee and navy gods to hopefully have a good day. After that, we were to muster and be briefed on what was going on. I already had a good idea.

Above the bridge wings is the signal shack, and at the back of that is the O5 level, which is five floors above the main deck. We were supposed to have our department meeting with the Quartermasters and Signalmen. Interestingly, we both had chiefs. And SMC Woodward was supposed to be leaving the ship, and QMC Morrison was supposed to be taking his place. We were told there was some news at our next meeting that we all need to be at. The funny thing is all those meetings were mandatory. When attending the meetings, we must be attentive unless told to relax and stand at ease. I quickly enjoyed my coffee, gave the last parts out to the sea, ran to stow my cup in the chart house, and got in formation.

The sea was a bit on the colder side. So I grabbed my sea and anchor coat.

SMC Woodward was a thin guy like me; his brown haircut and build made him look like he had escaped from the 1960s movies. He even had the black horned-rimmed glasses from basic training that earned the lovingly named Moniker Birth Control glasses (they made anyone look so ugly no woman would want to sleep with you). Make no mistake, his jokes would normally get people laughing. Now, QMC Morrison was the polar opposite; he looked like a very fit and buff Doctor Evil (yes, the Dr. Evil from the Austin Powers movies). If Dr. Evil laughed, you knew you were in a lot of trouble. However, you knew exactly where you stood with Dr. Evil. If you knew your job was a rockstar at your rate, he would back you up. Dr. Evil pushed you to your limits. Somehow, that man knew what we were capable of.

SMC: "OK, we just got out of the Chief's meeting, and well, this deployment has obviously been extended. That's the bad news. The good news is that the rumor you heard about our rates being merged is not happening. Commander Alvarez said it was one of the most boneheaded maneuvers he had heard in a while. However, considering the situation, it would not hurt to try to learn about each other's jobs. The old man wants people to try to cross the train as much as they can. That does not mean we need you to learn the engine plant; we just need to be able to help around if things get crazy. I am not going to expect you to learn all the flags and semaphore (the skivvy waving language of spelling out things with two flags) and certainly not the flashing lights with Morris code. He also said we are not dressing out the ship for the foreseeable future. " (Dressing out the ship is putting all of the signal flags out in a certain order that goes from the mast down to the fore and aft parts of the ship.)

QMC: "We just want to let you know what's going down the pipeline. Remember what I told you: you will never know all the answers, but it is more important to know where to find them."

SMC: "Right, both QMC and I are going to work together for our department; the admin department is going to split off and help out with the Corpsmen, and the OSs are going to do their own thing."

QMC: "And that leaves us working together; I do not mind nor does SMC if you use cheat sheets, and we'll make sure there is always an SM on hand or QM on hand for the things each person does not know or is having nothing but trouble with."

SMC: "If you have any questions, please let us know, and before you go, you all have done a fantastic job keeping the ship going. It takes many people to keep this old gal running. We were supposed to decommission after this last deployment. It is nice the old gal is able to get in at least one more deployment."

QMC: "Dismissed, QM3 MacDermmott. I need to talk to you in the chart house. "

I thought, *oh, what did I do? How did I screw up this time?* I said, "Aye, Aye, Chief," as I followed him into the chart house.

QMC was already in the chart house making coffee. As I entered, he said. "At ease and sit down, son."

I took a seat as he sat in the other chair we had.

QMC: "It was brought to my attention that you are rather knowledgeable about many different things; you did hunting, fishing, tracking, and reading a lot of history, especially where we might be. Is that correct? "

I told the chief, "Affirmative, with all of those things."

QMC: "We'll need to figure out where we are. We need to figure out how we are going to get more supplies; fuel doesn't magically appear, and there arc no other ships we've been able to communicate with so far. This is coming from the old man. I certainly do not want to part with you, but the old man is right; we need someone to go ashore who has a good idea of what might be out there. You are not going out there alone; we are getting some of the Marines and a corpsman assigned to them to go out with you. They'll be at the well deck. I think they want to train you before heading out, and you'll be working with them until you all head out. I dismissed QM3. Good job rescuing the man overboard. I'll talk to Davidson; what he did was not right."

I responded with an "Aye, aye, Chief," and with that, I headed to the well deck.

The well deck can be a very busy or dull area, depending on what is happening. If we are taking craft on or the craft are leaving the ship. We would take on everything from hovercraft (LCACs)to amphibious assault Vehicles (AAVs) and even boats. At one time, we had basically a barge the Seabees drove on our ship (think construction workers with automatic weapons) in our well deck with plenty of space to spare. The bottom of the well deck is flat with wood and holes that one can fasten down equipment with. There was a ramp that went up to the gym. We had a meeting area in that place. It was typically used to plan when we would have ships or anything else come in through the well deck or land on the helicopter pad. Some people played games with books, paper, and pencils in the same room.

I was supposed to meet the Marines in the Gym Area to begin training with them. I had the option to be a corpsman but thought against it, and to be honest, the Marines scared the hell out of me prior to joining. So let me explain why: I am from a small town in the middle of nowhere, Ohio. The recruiters all had offices in one part of a strip mall. You had to go into the door for all of them, and each had their own personal office carved out of it. There was a hallway that connected them all. I had initially made it to the Marine office, and inside, they had Metallica playing with multiple pyramids of Mountain Dew cases. The suite looked like a gym out of a 1980s high school movie. The wood paneling mirrors and the hand-painted mural of a bulldog wearing the top part of the marine uniform with the drill instructor campaign cover with the angriest face I've ever seen in art. This was a nope, out-of-here situation. The Navy guy was a lot more upfront about things, so they were not as scary. I still remember my recruiter, PH2 Doubek, who was very honest about most things. Annoyed I didn't get the college fund, but I don't think the GI bill would be accepted where we currently are.

Anyway, on to the Marines, their sergeant was a bit of an interesting, charismatic leader. He comes off as a hard charger, and his knife hand is something to be feared. I think it could bend reality. Their Corporeal (E4, same rank as me) was an interesting person who pretty much looked like a clean-shaven dwarf. I later realized this guy was probably one of the main sources of mayhem, destruction, and craziness out of the entire bunch. He was akin to a professional athlete at his craft. Both had interesting moral patches, but now, those were rather strange to me until I got used to them. They are usually funny patches people were "allowed" to wear when away from command. Considering that their Gunnery Sergeant is the highest-ranking officer and non-commissioned officer, they were allowed to wear them all the time. Commander Alvarez had no qualms with this for the Marines.

The Sergeant wore a patch with a goose with a knife in its mouth, saying peace was never an option. The Corporal he picked had a different patch: "Warning, I cause safety briefs." Prior to this deployment, my experience in the field was super limited at this time; I had only done nature trails and car camping with some youth programs. I learned about tracking and edible plants, but I was a Boy Scout compared to these guys. Yes, as an aside, their sergeant hated puns as well.

Now, their Corpsman was almost a literal giant of a man; the dude was built like a professional wrestler at what felt like 6 feet 25 inches. He could fireman carry around two or so marines at a time if needed. His quiet demeanor was something different once you got past that; his mind was just as warped and twisted as the Corporal. His combat patch was sneak attack sasquatch. Apparently, this was his nickname, and he was very good at somehow sneaking up people half his height. That and not being afraid to throw a marine into an ambulance or sit on them if needed. Doc was someone you never messed with. I knew this being on the Navy side.

My training with them went over as best as it could, and I had to see if I could hang out with them before we headed out. I learned the very basics of firearms maintenance. This is a skill I think every sailor should have; it might help with keeping up maintenance on the ship. I got more range time, something I think more sailors need rather than once a year before our current deployment. I would not be as good as the Marines going into the field, but I might be able to handle my own and assist for a few moments. I was not taught clearing a room and other such lessons. Those were promised to be taught later. This was more of a recon mission. Luckily for us, we were supposed to be picking up recon marines; however, we only got a few of them. The rest of the crew stayed on the ship to man the 50 cals and set up shop for their gear, other than the sergeant, Doc and Corporal, and a few lance corporals. Sergeant Buford got to pick the ones he wanted for this forward mission; he was initially not happy with squid babysitting his words, not mine. I totally understand taking someone who has never been out to the field for recon work. I surprised him a little about what I knew already; he must have figured he could work with that.

Sergeant Buford loved his insults, and some of his favorites were getting new people reporting to him to apologize to trees for making them work so hard to produce the oxygen they wasted doing dumb things, saying Mr. Rodgers would be disappointed by their actions. He had a gift with insults; they were 359 degrees away from being a compliment. It was so close you thought it was a compliment. He was tough but fair. I learned a lot in the two-week Marine crash course. I knew it would not be enough, but the on-the-job training would happen later. I think that's the military for you, though.

Thankfully, not like right out of the boot, our A schools would train you wrong (I'm not sure what other branches called your basic Military occupational skill schools). You had to unlearn all the wrong ways to do stuff and learn the right things once you got to the fleet (what people preferred to call the real navy). Perfect example: Quartermaster school was six weeks, and each week, there was one subject and a test on that week. You could fail two subjects, if you failed more, you went in without a Rate (MOS for non-navy types). I bombed the celestial navigation school for a good reason. I only knew two things about Trigonometry (the type of math used), that it is a real word and that it is complicated math. I bombed that segment, yet did rather well on every other one. I passed but got to pick from two different ships in the same town on the east coast.

Anyway, back to the Marine accelerated scouting class, I was doing alright, or at least I thought so; being thrown into the deep end of the swimming pool was not something unfamiliar. We had one more week; the other stuff was going to be aquatic stuff, basically driving the boat up to the beach, hiding it, and that sort of stuff, for our Mission, though BM2 LeBlanc was going to be driving it and driving it back. We could not spare another boat at this time. Lucky for me, one of the marines did not show up; I guess he was missing movement. I got my newly issued Marine-style camo for the forest region (the guys' old uniforms; I still had to transfer some of my name tapes from non camo uniforms to the camo's). To be honest, I did not know Marines had so many different types of camo. I got issued a ruck, thankfully, it was well-balanced, with the proper gear and weapons; it was weird carrying around a battle rifle and a Beretta pistol.

With that, we loaded into the boat, and BM2 was blaring music along the way. I swore I heard Detroit Rock City by kiss playing on the boombox he smuggled into the captain's gig. The volume was cranked as loud as it could. He had a cigarette in his mouth that bounced while mouthing the lyrics to the song. The pedal was touching the deck of the gig. At the aft of the boat, a 50 cal was mounted. This was the old man's idea, he was taking no chances. We had one of the gunner's mates, a corpsman, and BM2 on the boat in addition to the 6 of us, counting the sergeant; he had his wrecking crew, including Doc. I was the tag along in this mission, the intelligence, I think. When the car crash part of the song came on, a rather scaly-looking monstrosity jumped out of the water right behind us. The 50 call roared with a thud thud thud, turning it into scaly, chunky red salsa. Another flew out of the water and was turned into pink mist when it got domed.

Surprisingly, no one on BM2's boombox played music perfectly fit the insanity next to follow, *Motley Crue's Kickstart My Heart* was now joining us, and a rather wicked smile was slowly etched on the gunner's mate's face. He started showboating with the 50 cal by shooting it to the drum beat as LeBlanc tore up the ocean to the shore, all while lighting up another smoke without taking both hands off the wheel. He pulled a Williamson turn, dropped us off at the beach, and tore off back to the ship, swerving along the way, hearing more rounds in the distance.

Upon getting out of the boat in a quick fashion, I noticed first the shore; the beaches had a very light brown sand, and it quickly gave way to grass and then to trees. The trees cover the horizon, shielding the land from the sea and the ship from the land. The trees are clearly old and most likely ancient. We were clearly not in the world we knew. As we followed the beach upward to the closest path, noticing the shade those guardian trees provided; it clearly made it around 10 degrees cooler. The path we found must have been a hunting or deer trail at best; getting used to the ancient smells of the forest, we noticed the smell of water, which was akin to well water. When you come to get a closer look at the pond, there is no algae, and you cannot see the bottom of the pond. The pond itself, looking at the trees, was surrounded by hazelnut trees. I recognized them very well; they looked similar to the trees in the forest around my grandparent's home.

The pond itself had a stick tied to a line planted into the ground; the line itself was tugging the pole, threatening to snap it in half. The pole itself had remarkable bend and give. I instinctively grabbed for the fishing pole; there was a look of *what the hell are you doing* from Sergeant Bradford. I grappled with the fish in a fight to the death; the thing must have weighed about 5 lbs as it tore through the water. As I grabbed the line and fought with the fish, getting it closer to the surface, the line cooperated, and the fish broke the surface tension of the water. Up came the most beautiful salmon I have ever seen with colors I have no words for. I have never seen them before and will probably never see them again. I reached to grab the fish. It then stabbed me with the dorsal fin, drawing blood as I stabbed the fish out of instinct and frustration. I got some of the fish's blood on my tongue and down my throat. With this exchange of violence, I dropped the fish; it snapped the line and vanished into the depths of the water. Doc Humongous cursed in my general vicinity and raced towards me in almost slow motion. The world started to spin for me; colors seemed to bleed and wash away as the ground started to rush up to meet me. The last thing I saw was his gigantic hand grabbing me as the ground offered its hard embrace.

With the world blacked out, colors started to come back, starting with the color green; words and letters flew by, and many B's and H's. Those letters started to take shape and started to make letters, words, and other phrases. Context and slang started to show up, as well as everyone's favorite little brother's profanity. Stories formed, cultural norms and laws, a history of kings, customs, and culture grew before my eyes in the colors of the salmon that got away.

I awoke to a campfire, someone perpetually pissed off, using insults I had never heard before. I think they accused me of being so mean I would steal the alcohol out of beer. There was shouting. I could hear both sides; the one flinging the insults had more of a sing-song tone to their very melodic voice, and he was trying to communicate with Sergeant (yes, that's his first name since he outranks me). Both were yelling and could not understand each other, yet somehow I could hear both. Corporal Mcgee noticed my eyes opening first.

Mcgee: "Sergeant, I think sleeping beauty is now waking up. I am sorry your princess is in another castle, and we regret that these are the best accommodations we could provide for you." He ended the last sentence, almost laughing in his Southern accent.

I woke up to my right hand bandaged and a dirty look from Doc. I interpreted it as you screwed up badly, bud. No fun time with the guns for now. The sergeant gave me the annoyed drill instructor combined with a disappointed dad. When I started to talk this confused the hell out of everyone, including the man by the fire yelling. Below is a rough translation. The best way to translate is to try to throw close words together instead of using apple and orange; try using fruit, and hopefully, you get the point across. This is as close as I can remember this conversation and translated back.

The old man rattled, "Why did you steal my fish? This was my entire life's purpose?"

Myself "I had no idea whose fish it was and whose line it was. I was only trying to ensure the person did not lose their fishing equipment."

Cranky Old Man: "But I was foretold to catch the fish and get all of the knowledge."

Myself: "What legend, what knowledge?

Cranky Old Man: "Clearly you are not from here; I have never seen people dressed in such a way, talk with such accents, almost rough like a boat that has never been carved smooth. The prophecy is that a man with dark hair and who lives with a metal turtle will inherit the fish of the holy pool of Maclir."

Myself: "I live upon a metal ship that moves like a turtle, and I have dark hair."

Cranky man: "Curse my luck, the fish was for you, well get out of my site, come back here never again, I wish to not see your face unless it is judgment day."

I had relayed our conversation to the sergeant since the cranky old man had harrumphed us out of his camp. We rucked (I think I got the marine lingo down) another two clicks I think in, along other trails. The trees still protected much of the interior. We set up camp in a defensible spot. I did what I could with the nods of the doc here and there. Trying to set up camp with just my left hand was a pain. I felt like the broken spoke on a wagon wheel. We were told no fires for now and to be careful, we do not know if we lost the cantankerous old man, who knew what he could do or alert. With those thoughts, I slowly fell asleep.

The dream that night came to me; I relived the moments of the man falling overboard. Overhearing the rumors of the statue and how difficult it was to get it off the captain's gig. I remember the rumors of owls being involved; owls at sea made no sense at all. Why on earth would an owl who lives near forests or buildings be anywhere near the ocean? Another question tossing around in my REM sleep-addled brain is that it's not normal for a written and spoken language to be instantly downloaded.

Not to forget stories, history, customs, religion, and law just like I have always known them, neatly compartmentalized like it has always been there and filed away by professional librarians. This does not happen in any form of reality. I think we left reality back in Kansas after leaving the coast of Bali. I know this makes no sense, but that's what is happening.

The scuttlebutt, I heard before leaving the ship, they placed the man overboard on the O3 level (this would be two levels above the main desk). Also, I found out the man overboard was Fireman Moore. He was placed outside what was lovingly referred to as the ET Shack. The Electronic technicians kept all the radars and other similar equipment aboard the ship in working order. The interesting thing about the Navy is we have a lot of specialists, and there is not really a chance to cross-train into other things. So, instances like mine are shaking up the structure of the crew and the usual routine. The ETs were on the case to figure out why the GPS looked like it should be working yet not picking up a single satellite. The OS's were pretty much doing the same thing by looking for contacts around us.

I later learned that Fireman Moore was not having a good deployment; he simply wanted to go home after getting the Red Cross message about a loved one. I had talked to the guy a few times; he seemed like a good kid (I understand the irony of calling someone lower ranking and about four years younger a kid. The military ages you a bit with the insanity and craziness).

Now, knowing that I wanted to figure out what the heck caused him to turn to stone, why their owls were, who could help with it, and what our initial orders were from the old man himself. Figure out where the hell we are, how we can get fuel, allies, and possibly all things willing to get home. We were given a signal, and thankfully, the Marines knew Morse code. I could not learn it; I kept getting told that a dot is slightly longer than a dash with light, and you'll know it when you see it. To be honest, I know the crew might read this but that is the absolutely worst way to train someone. It's never you know it when you see it. No, that won't work; sometimes, you have to break out the purple and green suit, and some of us are so dense we need it. I was slowly getting it with the Marines, but nowhere near understanding the letters other than the standardized SOS; some think it means something like save our ship; others think that it is just the two easiest characters to do in a row that look wildly different. It could be both, but no one seems to know.

So, moving further inland, we finally get to a clearing. In this clearing, we start to see buildings. Now, these buildings were made of wood thatch, and the fencing looked to be made of reeds. Each building was a round house made of thatch, a clay-like substance on the outside painted white, possibly lye, and wooden inside. They looked rather cozy and simple, like farmer's houses. They looked rather huge and could fit an entire family inside, and we heard singing and music from a distance. You could smell the cooked pork sweetened with honey and the freshly baked bread in the distance.

Chapter 3
Banshee

Upon reaching this small settlement at night, we noticed a lot of statues. There was joy, yet somber was nearby like a low-hanging fog that refused to lift. As we got closer to the small village, it had dogs. There were so many dogs; they were there to alert and possibly protect the village from any upcoming presences. Even being with those who go bump in the night makes it very difficult to hide from man's oldest friend. The only way I could describe their howling is to imagine a department store having a wall of alarm clocks and some psycho path set every single one to go off 5 mins later; imagine that happening in an entire village, and that is pretty close to how it sounded.

The village quickly raced to action, out of the conical houses. In a quick fashion, it went in the direction of the barking army of dogs. I think each house had at least 2 or more dogs. The dogs were huge Irish-looking wolfhounds; if they were any bigger, an average person could ride them into combat. Their long, lanky legs with wiry, thick coats raced in our direction. Their owners were trying to calm them down and see what was happening. Most of the people wore one or two colors in their clothes, and they came out brandishing farming equipment as weapons.

The farmers made it to our location, wondering why someone was out this late at night. Our gear was not helping in the slightest. I ended up being voluntold to translate.

An elderly-looking man is wearing three colors in his tunic (think of a baggy long-sleeve sweater that goes down at least to the mid-thigh. Now, in Irish culture, the more colors the person wore, the higher they were of status. Status is something that can be earned and lost. The most common ways are deeds and wealth. However, one can lose prestige by being a total jerk and refusing to pay fines. It is believed that this is where the term blood silver comes from. You had to pay the families if you killed another rather than being ostracized. The fine was based on the offending party's station.

The man had black and pepper grey thinning hair that came to a point. He held a rather beaten-up sword in a death-like grip as he approached our group. His colors dictated he was a merchant by trade and probably the one who unofficially ran this village.

Merchant: "Are you messengers?"

Myself: "Yes, we are; we are friendly messengers."

Merchant: "Well, you can call me Sean (pronounced Shawn; I know Gaelic is not pronounced how it is spelled)."

Myself: "Thank you for your hospitality, Sean; my name is Tayg MacDermmott; this is Sergeant Buford, Corporal MacKay (Causes Safety Briefs) Doc Bosko, Private First Class Williams, and Private Murray. We are travelers from far away."

I was thankful for the weird download of ancient knowledge to my brain. I was able to figure out that hospitality is something freely offered as long as it is for a messenger. They must offer us a place to sleep, clean our clothes, food, and water. Politics, messages, and means of war could not be brought up until the messenger had time to rest. I pondered how fascinating this culture would be to an outsider.

I translated back to Sergeant Buford. He gave me a look that translated to we needed to talk 3 years ago yesterday, and I might need a drug test followed by a Captain's mast. XO's mast means you royally screwed up, and the Chiefs are pissed as well. So the order of this is if you screw up badly enough, your LPO, in this case, would be sergeant, then Gunny, then the Old man. If you were to go see the old man, the worst of punishments are in store for you because you screwed up big time.

The punishments can differ because the Old man gets to dole out the sentencing. I have heard of people having to clean out the bilge (it was a space set to prevent the ship from sinking and arguably the most disgusting place on the ship with a toothbrush) to solitary confinement and rations of bread and water for 45 days. I have known people who get ordered to clean the ladder wells; you might call them stairs, ours were pretty much ladders with the incline. The metal steps were ridged; now if you had a broom or a dustpan, you could do it quickly, but one guy had to clean one four times for the entire day. He had nothing but a toothbrush, and they picked the one that went to the general mess.

After I had been advised of the sleeping arrangements, it was in the merchant's house, and I politely excused myself. I quickly went over other things that could offend our host and made my way to Sergeant Buford.

Myself: "Sergeant, you wanted to speak with me."

Buford: "Yes, MacDermott, let's head outside for a brief moment."

Myself: "Roger that, lead the way, sergeant."

He took us outside; the farmers were still trying to calm down their dogs, the noises of night, the chirping of insects, and the glow of fireflies.

Sergeant Buford: "How did you learn to speak with them? How did you learn their culture so fast? This makes no sense. It takes linguists 6 years at best to be that fluent. What the hell happened back there with the old man? Why did you pass out like that? I am glad we had Doc Mongo with us."

If Mongo must be explained, it is a character, big and not too bright, from a Mel brooks film called *Blazing Saddles*. To paraphrase the line, people tend to remember Mongo is a pawn in the game of life or something like that, guys known for brute force, and he's usually got a wind tunnel between his ears. Kind of ironic calling Doc Mongo, but hey, nicknames in the military can be brutal and funny if they are an oxymoron.

Myself: "Sergeant, this is super weird. I am equally confused; I think it was that fish. Something about it was really weird about how it moved, and I think it happened when it stabbed me. After that happened, I think everything blacked out. I had an almost fever dream. I woke up with being able to understand the old man." (At the time, my adrenalin spiked, and I could not remember the blood as I wrote before.)

Buford: "What was the old man in the camp yelling about? Why was he so pissed off?"

Myself: "I took his fish; he said something about a prophecy about a man who lives with a metal turtle and is destined to eat that fish."

Buford: "So the old man was pissed, ok, not our problem, unless it is later. What about this village?"

Myself: "Sergeant, permission to speak freely."

I needed to speak freely about this; this is something that normally saves your backside if something is weird or you need to use your opinion and expertise in a way that shouldn't get you in hot water.

Buford: "Permission granted, Petty Officer."

Myself: "Ok, so I think this is also linked to the fish; I know things about their culture, their religion, history, and other things. It's like I grew up within a dual language and culture household, and that fish I do not think was a normal fish; I think it was a fish of knowledge."

Buford: "It sounds like you are talking about that geeky dungeons and dragons game."

Myself: "Sergeant, I do not think we are technically on the earth that we knew. There was a story about this with Fionn mac Cumhaill. He burned his thumb and then ate the entire fish; he got all of the knowledge of everything, even his own life, including when he would die. However, the stories are a bit different from having to suck his thumb down to bite his thumb rather violently. There was an old man with him teaching him the magic and holy arts. He was disappointed but understood the prophecy. I think we might be back in that time or something influenced by that time. The Village: I understood the culture a lot more. I was able to convince the leader of the village, who was a merchant, to let us stay for the night. Now, they have to let us stay if they think we are messengers, and that's what we technically are. In their culture, they cannot press politics or force a messenger to deliver the message until they have had food, a change of clothes, and a chance to get clean. Their cleanliness standards are on par with ours.

Buford: "So you are going to translate what I am saying to the leader tomorrow. This town is rather odd, though; there are no defenses or walls that I can see. Something seems wrong about this place. I will tell the men to sleep with one eye open and at the ready. "

Myself "Understood, I will do my best tomorrow."

Buford: "You better, we are counting on it."

With that, he entered back into the merchants' large house, leaving me to smell the night air and hear the sounds of the night life, seeing stars for as far as the clearing allowed. I shuffled back into the house and passed out, of all things, a couch carved from a tree trunk. It was lovely, layered with reeds and furs, keeping it warm and inviting. You thought you were sleeping on a dream bed out of a mattress commercial. The house itself was open and roomy yet comfortable and warm. The biggest problem my marine cohorts complained about and, after a few seconds of explaining to me. I understood the problem. The house only had one door. I slowly drifted off to sleep, no dreams, no music, just uninterrupted sleep.

The morning greeted us with the cacophony of barnyard animals. It was like all the animals played the notes. Differently some played the same song backward, others from the middle, and others just jumped around. One of the junior marines jumped off the couch and nearly hit his head on the ceiling brace and face-planted into the soft dirt that was on the floor of the house. I woke up under the furs and made sure my uniform was as clean and presentable as It could be. As a Quartermaster, our uniforms always had to be on point (Not even a hint of a wrinkle or other unauthorized crease. We liked to call the uniforms with excessive wrinkles summer wrinkles; some are here, some are there.)

I was able to get some freeze-dried coffee before departing, but no creamer, though. I had made some of that with the hot water we had asked for in the morning, and the Marines joined me in my morning ritual of coffee. I just need my two cups to get the day started. I'll sink to the terrible navy coffee if I have to, and freeze-dried coffee works as well if enough creamer and sugar can be used to salvage it.

After that, sergeant Buford and I started talking about what we would want to do and the best way to handle the situation. I told him I was still getting used to the knowledge that had been neatly packed away. To me, it still felt weird that someone else had organized memories for me, and I could not seem to get down to their organization method. The best analogy I can give you is someone breaking into your house and rearranging dishes; they put in new ones that you had no idea where they came from, what some of them did, or even how to clean them. That is what the fish did to my brain.

The meeting itself went rather well; all of the marines, the sergeant, and myself were fully given the customary hospitality. We were brought to the Merchant after our meal. I will do my best to translate between the Merchant and the sergeant.

Merchant: "What brings you to the fair village I look after for the king."

Sergeant: "We are travelers from a far-off land. We are trying to get the lay of the land and find out who we can trade with. We want to work with those around us and build relationships."

Merchant: "Well then, deeds speak louder than words. To see if we can trust you must complete a worthy deed."

Sergeant: "What do you have in mind?"

Merchant: "There is a well we used to be able to use generations ago; it is important and has clean water nearby. It used to belong to a minor noble."

Sergeant: "Anything else you can tell us about the land belongs to the noble."

Merchant: "The house has fallen into disrepair. There is something there; I have no fighters, just farmers. The only thing they can slay is a wolf or two if they are lucky. They are better off slaying rodents and dirt clumps in the fields."

Sergeant: "I see you have no trained fighters; we happen to be fighters. We will check out this land belonging to the minor noble. Do you know anything else?"

Merchant: "It is rumored to be haunted by something fierce. The noble disappeared, and the house and family died with grief. The house was considered cursed."

Hearing the cursed and haunted had me trying to remember something at the back of my mind. There was something important about that phrase, but I could not remember it. It felt like it was on the tip of my tongue. With that, we were given directions to the location.

After that, I gave the sergeant the look that we needed to talk.

Myself: "Sergeant, something does not sound right. I think we aren't being told what is going on."

I could hear Corporal (Causes Safety Briefs) whisper, "Winning the sharts and dimes from people." If you barely paid attention to him, one would instead hear him winning the hearts and minds of people.

With that, our meeting concluded, and the merchant left his house to attend to the day's affairs. Before his parting, he motioned that we could take advantage of his hearth and home for our next plans, and he gave us general directions to the abandoned nobles' home.

Sergeant Buford was making plans and drawing a map of the surrounding area. He motioned to the others to gather around.

Sergeant: "Listen up, everyone, we have scarce details on the area; we need to scout the area. MacDermott, I need you to get any knowledge you can on the land we need to investigate, problem makers, anything you can get."

Myself: "Aye, Aye, Sergeant."

Sergeant: "I am going to give you a few hours, then come back; we should try to check out the area during the day."

With that, we were dismissed to start planning; the marines were checking out their gear, getting it ready, and talking amongst themselves. Doc gave me a nod as I left the merchant's house.

The town looked different in the daylight, with many sleeping dogs lazily lounging in the sun as their owners slipped out to the fields. It was one of those lazy summer days with that bit of humidity in the air. You just wanted to go back to sleep and sleep until right after noon. The outside smelled of earth, plants, and animal dung. The plants were being cared for, and there were men outside tending to the land. They seemed idle and at work at the same time. Some were repairing the tools of their trade, and everyone was talking.

The first thing I noticed was the most realistic statue I had ever seen. It looked like it was holding onto its tools and trying to walk back home. You could see the sorrow defining the face and body. It was like the statue was carved for this purpose. It held a rather realistic scythe in its hands. The entire thing looked off. I approached the farmers.

Myself: "Good morning, good sirs. I would like to ask you a few questions; my cohorts and I are trying to find out about the well near the village. Can you tell me something about it and anything else about the surrounding area? We are travelers from a far-off land."

The farmers looked amongst themselves, and an uneasy laugh began to trickle through the group.

Then, one looked at me with thinning hair and dull blue eyes. "If you want to talk to someone, you will want to ask Barra for information. He should be in his house, and he seldom leaves unless he talks to our friendly leader." He pointed towards a rather modest and small house.

I provided a polite nod and thanked the farmer for the information. As I headed in the direction that the farmer had pointed. I noticed a few more statues, others in faces of anger or sadness. One was holding a broken tool.

I made it to the old man's hut, which was small and simple. As I knocked on the door, I heard a shuffling and a muffled call to patiently wait.

The door had creaked open, and a man who had seen a lot of life was in front of me; he wore his life on his face. However, his eyes remained the grey of a razor-sharp sword. He walked with a cane that thumped along with his steps.

Barra: "Well, you must be the outsiders that everyone has been talking about."

Myself: "Yes sir, we are; we have been asked by the Trader to look into a problem the village is facing."

Barra: "Oh yes, that land; let me think, I have been around for a while." His eyes seemed to sparkle almost with a hint of sadness. "Oh yes, the land you mentioned, I was but a young boy; if I remember correctly, it was a noble household. The houses we had were ones that worked for him. There was something tragic that happened. I wish I could remember, but I was very young then. I do remember having to flee the lord's house. The house fell into disrepair. The king wished not to have the house lived in and allowed the merchant to build a humble house there. I wish I could provide more information, but that is all I can remember."

I nodded with respect and allowed Barra to speak uninterrupted. If this was the best information I could get, it was more than we knew before and probably slightly more. I moved back to our meet-up point. I thought the sergeant would be disappointed with me for not finding out more.

I approached the merchant's house, where the other marines were gathering their gear. Doc was getting his bag organized and inventoried. Sergeant Buford looked at me.

Sergeant: "Did you find anything useful?"

With that question, a book was checked back into the library, the gears were turning upstairs, and information was being accessed in the force that placed the information in my brain; it could be many different things, ghosts possibly, but something still sounded off I could not place. It was at the back of my head, literally with everything else I knew. I relayed the information I got from the village elder Barra. I added that it could be a ghost; it could be anchored to something. It could be something else. Barra was not sure what had happened when he was very little. I noticed that the Sergeant hung on to every word I had relayed to him, including what I thought. He took the entire conversation seriously. When I finished, he simply nodded like a librarian receiving a book to be checked back into their library.

I could see a brief flicker in his eyes, a bit of calculated mayhem. He motioned to get our gear set up to head out. He grabbed his gear and took a drink from his camelback. He looked eager to find out what this was and how to make it a distant nightmare.

I gathered up my gear; it was not too much, thankfully. I just had the standard gear and tried to put it in the same way I was quickly trained. We all met up outside the merchant's house in the village of Clonboi, named for its meadows and harvest of wheat and other richly yellowed grains.

This language was getting fun, especially with the names of places. They were rather logical and descriptive. The place names and people's last names were generally where they came from. Only people who had a nobility background really had a last name. It was almost always a descendant of someone who had the last name as a first name. For some, their last names were descriptive, such as descendants of their mother; for others, their father.

With that, we headed to the west of the village on an old, overgrown road. You could tell that the road was used at one time, but it had been many years since the last it was used. The grass grew really tall along this road. The birds slowly stopped singing the further we made it from the village. We made it to what remained of the house as the sun was starting to set. The stars were waking up for their watch, yet not shining as brightly as they normally do. Also, the moon was mysteriously absent from the sky.

The house itself must have been magnificent at one time. You could still see the wonderful handcrafted wood adorning the corners, and the door looked like it was thrown off its hinges outside the house. The earth slowly took back the house; however, you could still see some of the paintings inside. You could not make out most of the art, and you could see burn marks on some of it. However, there was one detail, a giant bee. This bee was painted on the side; it held three different items: a hammer, a sword, and what looked like a machine gun. It was a bit different, but there was no mistake in this symbol. I knew I had to bring this up to the sergeant's attention. I motioned to the Sergeant with the hand signals I was taught, then pointed to the bee I had noticed. He simply nodded.

The rest of the team scoured what was left of the house, almost everything was broken. Weeds growing through the middle of the floor. An earthy smell lingered inside the house, no welcoming nor warming feeling inside. The faint glow of the stars of the nights tried to go through the windows and holes you could see through the roof of the house. An eerily calm set the ambiance inside, there no sounds were to be heard.

Suddenly I could faintly hear a wind start up, there were dead leaves and branches that started to rustle. This wind was something not possible given the remaining walls. The winds built up into a violent crescendo. The leaves spun into a tornado, with that there was a hum of dread that seemed to come from the walls. We had worn our hearing protection, thankfully it was automatically set for anything above what a normal person could hear. This was to make sure we could hear each other over gun fire. These were fancier than what I was issued on the ship. They had to be customized to each person. It took a while to notice how much higher the sounds were being reduced or eliminated.

With the whistling wind a bony hand reached out of the floor boards, it had a dress that clung on to the skin that stretched tight over its dried husk of a form. The hair was wispy and seemed to blow with the magical wind. The wail that came from the skull with the stretched hideous grieving frown. The entire being emanated grief, sorrow and primordial rage. The next keen caused the private to crumple over in pain, I could hear the pain coming from him, sheer blinding pain. Doc Mongo sprung into action, slung him over his shoulder like a sack of potatoes and booked it out of the house in what seemed to be one action. The sergeant told us to open fire, our bullets just went through the being, even the ones hitting center mass did nothing.

Corporal Causes Safety Briefs, maniacally laughed, threw a small chunk of C4, and ran out of the building. He yelled "knees to chest"and ran, and hoofed it out of the building. We ran toward the ditch and he tried to use the clicker, yelling "Stupid piece of government crap."

He then clicked it a few times, nothing happened. He then threw it to the ground and violently stomped on it with his boot heel. This caused the building to vaporize. I started to wonder when did it start raining? A gentle rain of dirt began to sprinkle over our heads. We simultaneously surveyed and admired the carnage, the entire building was gone, just empty rubble. The others had no idea how he avoided the well.

Causes Safety Briefs "Sergeant, at least it's no problem now."

Sergeant: "I see. Was that a bit of an excessive use of explosives?"

Causes Safety Briefs, "Sergeant, there is no kill like overkill, and at least we know it's dead now." He looked at me and said with a grin ear to ear, his voice oozing with sarcasm." Petty officer, welcome to the Corps."

Sergeant: "We need to head back to the village and let the merchant know what happened, then head back to the ship."

With that we gathered up everything and headed out, we split up Private Murray's gear amongst ourselves to help Doc since he was still carrying Murray. With that we trudged back to the village.

As we were walking back to the village it was unearthly quiet, no dogs, no animals, not even a sneeze. I hated moments like these, you knew something bad was going to happen, it was like being in the middle of a violent storm. The animals knew what was happening but were unable or unwilling to tell you what to expect.

As we made it back, Doc set down Murray. With that a fluttering sound came from the south, groups of owls flew towards us. It was odd seeing the owls flying in pairs. They somehow had something hanging from their claws. There were about 6 pairs of owls. Two flew closer to Murray. The other 5 paris flew throughout the village. Doc Mongo, had gripped one in a giant meaty hand almost making it look like a small song bird. The other he punched full force. With that I made a mental note to not mess with doc ever.

The owl took his punch full force and flew in a crumpled mess violently colliding with a building 30 feet away. The owl in his other hand quickly had its neck snapped. I guess we will never know how many licks it takes to get to the center of a sucker.

We quickly went into hand signals, looking for other owls. We all saw Doc's quick lesson on how to deal with the threat. with that we moved as one unit throughout the village, towards the center. As we got closer to Barra's hovel we noticed that the door was wide open, quickly we went into formation to enter the building. My job was to slowly open the door. The door eerily creaked open making the only sound we could hear. With that we heard a soul wrenching scream of the deepest sadness coming from inside. It was pitch black. The scream slowly faded from reality rather than increased in pitch and volume. We got the signal to flick on night vision, it was so quiet you could hear it whine into existence, that green glow permeated the void that was Barra's hearth and home. A statue was standing in the middle of the room, the owls had jars that glowed with a swirling light. We had raced to attack the owls, I had riffle-butted one, missing the owl but connecting with the jar. The jar exploded into smithereens, with that the energy swirled back into the statue,as it seemed to come to life.

Barra exaggeratedly exhaled. "I err aaaaa!"

Myself: "Barra, please remain calm, what happened?"

Barra: "Thank the gods you young men showed up. I was overtaken with sadness at the loss of my daughter this morning. I did not want to function, I was trying to deal with my grief and everyone here was supportive."

I listened to him and relayed the information back to the sergeant. He just nodded with the same look as someone taking the pizza order. I told Barra, he was welcome, we ensured he was alright and guarded him until the sunrise. We slept in shifts, keeping watch over the old man. The only thing that had interrupted our watch was the sun rising. The village and animals slowly awoke from their nightly slumber.

We made sure the door and house for Barra was in working order, I politely excused ourselves and made our way through the village, we were greeted with welcoming smiles from the farmers. The birds greeted us with their song as we made it to the door of the Merchants house.

As we entered the Merchants house our nostrils were wafted with meats, cheeses, baked breads and beer. We could feel the warmth and safety of a hearth in the house.

The Merchant: "I heard a loud thunderous roar, and the ground shook from where the old manor was. I feared the manor's inhabitants killed you."

Myself "Good Merchant we were able to take care of the manor, the "Guest" should not be bothering you again."

He looked over us and our gear rather curiously as I described what we saw, his face drained of all color as we described it. I could see that he mouthed the word banshee. That word had unlocked part of the weird filing system in my brain, I was able to understand that word and the significance of it. I had muttered a few silent curses on not knowing this when it could have been needed. Maybe Murray would not have been injured and possibly permanently lost his hearing. I could understand the merchant's shock at how we were still alive and how we could hear him.

The Merchant "I am glad to see all of you, in one piece and of good health I assume?"

Myself "Good Merchant you are mostly right, one of my comrades has been injured, we are thinking of heading back to our ship for medical attention."

The Merchant "The King who rules this land might be able to provide assistance. He lives in the city of Kildun. If I can point you in the right direction and send you with someone who can provide an introduction, I need to be here for my next shipment of goods and anything else that may require my direct attention."

An introduction would provide an invaluable resource for a mostly oral culture in their traditions, legal procedures, history and stories. The Merchant had introduced us to his own son to have him go with him to also relay a message from the village to the local king. The Merchant Sean introduced us to his son Connal.

Connal was an average-looking man, just shy of our own average height, with blue eyes and black hair. A beard was starting to form on his face. His blue eyes you could see more than a flicker of intellect and a passion for adventure. He quickly gathered his things and met us outside. He warned us along the way the road is protected by the king and not to stray off the trail no matter what.

Chapter 4
Kildun

We made our way closer to the woods, the farm fields slowly disappeared and the forest was rather dense. This was an old growth forest, the grass and other plants slowly disappeared, a bit of leaf litter stayed on the main path that was wide enough to fit two wagons comfortably. As we made it to the main road the branches of the ancient trees reached from both sides of the trail to touch each other. They shaded both sides of the trail, you could see the sun's rays dyed green through the forest leaves. The trail itself was clearly lined with stones of great artistic effort. Warriors equipped with spears, slings and swords all seemed to look around as you walked. There was what seemed to be a holy man wearing a robe with a staff he pointed in the direction Connal was taking us. Connal seemed to be a man on a mission, he moved at the same pace never slowing or stopping.

Myself "Connal, how far is it?"

Connal: "It is a day's travel. If we keep this pace, we should be able to make it by nightfall. What I would not give for a horse to be there by mid-day. Good thing father let us leave first thing. "

Myself: "Well, what happens if we go off the path? You see, we are visitors from afar away land."

Connal "Well that is obvious you are, so there things worse than being dead, things not as nice or pleasant as what you interacted with last night."

I relayed this information to the sergeant and the rest of the squad. Then I thought about what could be worse than death as I took a drink of cool water coming from my camelback. That cool, refreshing water was almost gone. I think we would get halfway there, and most of us would be out. We never thought of filling up at Casa de Banshee. We could see old buildings off the path that seemed lost to time and memory. The stones seemed to beckon to the curious parts of my brain, but Connal's warning and the hairs on my neck seemed to staunch my curiosity for the moment.

We kept moving, time seemed to move weird here with the trees blocking the sun. It seemed the birds sang oddly to, not the normal happy chipper tunes they would sing, but some sang backwards, some hit discordant notes that seemed to not be on any scale notes between ones that should exist. I tried to check my watch, the watch I picked up from the ship's store, it seemed to be running slower than normal, the second hand seemed to get stuck every 15 seconds or so. I promised myself this was my third and last watch from the ship's store. The first one's hands just fell off in a few months, the second the alarm got stuck, I could not shut it off and it made a wail that I thought was the worst I had heard until last night, I ended up deep sixing it when no one was looking. (Deep Six means to toss overboard with abandon). I might buy a new watch from the ship's store once we get back, with the hopes of the forth watch would be the charm.

I let my mind wander for a brief moment, just enough to let the past few days sink in. We were in another place, possibly another time, maybe another world?. It was hard to say. We were obviously not on point for the initial mission; what would our mission be, and would our enlistments still stand? A new start sounds great, but well I do not see too many other prospects. Do I reenlist? Who or what is my enlistment to? I still got 3 more years, stupid bonus.

An arm violently grabbed my collar and gave a sharp yank; the sergeant yelled, "Petty Officer, what is your malfunction? You told me we need to stay on the path no matter what?"

Luckily, my feet never left the trail, so I broke into a cold sweat and was jolted back to reality.

Myself: "Sergeant, my mind must have escaped from me for a brief moment."

Sergeant: "Thanks Captain oblivious, you made a quick left face with your eyes glazed over and started to walk slowly towards the end of the trail. Don't do it again."

Myself: "Aye, aye sergeant."

I did my best to be in charge of my faculties from then on.

Connal cleared his throat "We are pretty much almost there, just a little while longer."

Sure enough he was right the trees started to spread further apart, their branches still trying to reach the other side of the trail, some of the branches did and others did not, the sun seemed to be setting and the forest started to get darker, weird ominous orbs danced far off from the trail. It was like club lights in a lost forest club with a dj of doom, his mix was personally tailored to be the last thing you experienced.

We reached the end of the forest, the fields here seemed to stretch further, methodically stacked stone fences easily reached about hip high, the stones were solid, roads were carefully worn, we could smell the earth, not a dirty smell but one of welcoming one of care and warmth, peat the early form of coal was in many of the fields. I know my family usually burned this on special occasions such as the end of the year, in honor of our ancestors. Here this seemed to be burned a lot for heating and cooking. In the distance cooked meats and freshly baked breads wafted in our noses. A welcome scent to the MRE's we brought. A stomach could get used to eating this way.

Connal's stride seemed to never slow, he seemed to walk with a purpose and a mission. We walked past many horses, dogs and chariots. These chariots were made of wood and reeds. The reeds were woven artistically, the wooden parts finished and painted in many different colors. Each one a masterpiece, as unique as a custom car. The things they all shared were the almost solid wheels and how they hooked up to the horses. They used what I could describe as a gooseneck trailer hitch. Ingenious if you think about it, the yoke rested around the middle section of the horses. This allowed for a tighter and more maneuverable vehicle.

The shields were just as immaculate; I could see that the marines gave looks of respect. A warrior can respect another and can judge a lot on how well their kit is maintained. I was just as flabbergasted by the attention to detail, how beautiful and unique each shield and each chariot was.

We found out the city's name was Kildun; it pretty much means a forested fort. It was the biggest city for miles from what Connal told us. It was the gem of the kingdom where the king lived. Where his warriors would live if it was a time of peace. If not, they would spread out in units throughout the kingdom.

We made it through this small city; this was a bit bigger than the village I grew up in. The streets seemed to lazily wander around with a purpose. The roads seemed to be just as organized; you could get to where you needed to, but there always seemed to be some sort of magic behind it. We made it to the king's house; my expectations were blown away here. This house would have made any Hollywood actor's house look like a ramshackle shack made of balsa wood. The outside of the house seemed to be similar to the ruins of the house we found last night. The art was wildly different. There were warriors fighting various things, and the house's main color was a very bright bone: white. The accents were preserved, and polished wood, a very rich and deep brown color, and bronze, and red stones were also incorporated. You can tell this person just oozed fame and money.

I quickly caught everyone up on what was expected of us; no business tonight; food and a place to sleep is promised. It would be good food, the best possible place to sleep, and the promise of clean clothes.

I then asked our Messenger, "Connal, how will we get back? Will you take us back to your village or the coast?"

Connal: "No, I cannot do that. I need to head to the next village tomorrow; after my news to the king and your introduction, you can see if you can convince the king to be a guest for a few days. Who knows, he might pay you for the interaction with the banshee. I will make sure he knows that you and your friends did it."

Myself: "Connal, we cannot thank you enough for this. It is odd being in a place where no one knows you, and the culture can sometimes be difficult to understand."

Connal simply nodded, herded us towards the entrance, and said we were with him to see the king. The guards stepped aside, and Connal had opened the door. We all were still a little bit on edge, and Murray was still in rough shape. We had to kind of guide him on where to go. His hearing was gone, and our hearing protection was obliterated after that blast from what we thought was the Corporal Safety brief's proper usage of c4.

I relayed the information to the sergeant, and he nodded and gave the look that he wanted to talk after our meeting.

We followed Connal into the king's residence. The inside of the estate was just as ornate as the outside. It was well-designed. There was art inside, rooms, and a welcoming oasis exuding warmth. The walls were bright; there was ornate wood, gems, and metals worked into the walls, the paintings, and overall decor. The interior was well-lit, warm, welcoming, and luxurious. The air of freshly cooked pork, cheeses, breads, and ale wafted into the doorway, challenging our nostrils. The pork was cooked with plenty of spices, and all sorts of fruits, butter, and other drinks littered the table.

A man approached us. His brown beard was salt peppered, his face worn by wars and combat untold, his face creased in smiles and with military bearing. Clearly, he was sizing us up to see if we could or couldn't. It was something I did subconsciously when training new people or learning firefighting, ship repairs, and even security if unauthorized people came on the ship. I think professional soldiers do it subconsciously. At least the good ones do. He wore a wonderful tunic full of rich blues, greens, reds, yellows, purples, whites, and even a little bit of black. It was all placed together very well; this clearly, with the memory being accessed in my brain, is the king; only a king is allowed to wear that many different colors.

Being a king is not forged by lineage, they are by deeds and actions. They must prove themselves to their people and not just once, they need to continue to do so. They are supposed to be slow to anger yet wield it with supreme authority. They are supposed to care for the weak and protect the innocent.

Connall approached the king. "My king, these soldiers from a far-off land were the ones that helped our village get back the well that had the old manor house. They also protected our elder Barra. They put themselves at risk by doing this for us without us asking. One of their own warriors was injured. Would you be able to help him?"

He pointed at each of us and tried to say our names as best he could.

The King's brows were furrowed in thought. "Good Connall, of course, I would be happy to help these warriors. They aided my kingdom without knowing how much that would mean to me. The least I could do is to assist warriors who put their lives on the line to aid someone they did not know. They will be taken care of during their stay here, and we will help them with aid and payment for their deeds. I think we will retire for the day."

With that, I sighed with relief. Meeting someone who did not want to take credit for another's actions was refreshing. Those kinds of people annoy me because they want the credit without the work. That has happened to a lot of people; those who do this tend to want to step on anyone on their way up the ladder.

The king then motioned for those in his service to show us our rooms. The rooms were spacious and well-designed. The walls were lined with art, tapestries, and a table with water. The beds were made of metal, and each leg had ornately carved interlaced knotwork, including the room I was staying in. Hidden in the work were boars, foxes, wolves, humans hunting, and even what looked like deer interlaced. It looked like the foxes, wolves, and humans were hunting other things. On top of the bed were possibly the softest of furs, along with the softest of clothes. The tunic and pants waiting for me had 5 colors, symbolizing an experienced warrior. We were also provided with new shoes. These shoes laced up along the upper calf and were almost as sturdy as our boots.

I forgot to mention the significance of the colors one could wear; only the king could wear 7 colors, druids wore 6, warriors wore 5, and bards wore 4. Merchants were 3, farmers wore 2, and servants wore 1. You could go either up or down the ranks of society based on your actions. If you committed crimes that injured people, it was based on your station, not the position of the person you had offended.

We had baths waiting for us, the tubs were also ornately designed, and the metal was specifically casted and designed to retain heat evenly. After that, we were welcomed into the kings hall to feast; the food was amazing, pork perfectly seasoned with nuts and herbs. The honey drink around the table was to die for. It had a hint of raspberries. The cheese and bread were also very good.

The king's house was a fortress, it was as well protected as it was lavish. Someone clearly knew how to do both at the same time. The guards were alert as we were. They were armored and had their weapons easily accessible.

We slowly made it back to our rooms; the music floated throughout the house up to our rooms. However, when the doors were shut, the music could not be heard. The rooms themselves had incense of turf and other fragrant herbs that helped me to drift off into a mystical slumber.

I dreamt of the past, of my trip right before heading to the Ashtabula. I left from my last command. I was part of the Decommissioning crew (this is when you try to fix up a ship to retire it. It was my first command; just before leaving I had found out the love of my life had left me a letter. A dear John letter, basically for those who never served, those letters are always nasty, brutal, and usually delivered at the worst possible time.

After the ship was stricken from navy service, I took a flight to Las Vegas, the city of Sin, for my leave, no, I did not go home; I needed to get this out of my system. I frequented the bars during the day, worked out like a madman in the morning, and went to a metal show one of the nights. A metal band called Hollow Point Molly was playing. This band was something else; they had no drum, but they used a 50-caliber machine gun as their drummer. I remember the concert; I was annoyed that the band did not have their music at the merch stand. However, I do not remember getting back to the hotel.

I woke up in my bed in a cold sweat, I tried to yell, but no sound came out of my mouth, my throat was dry. I drank some water, realizing I was not in Vegas or on the ship. I was in a faraway land, unsure if it was a different time or space.

My door was violently yanked open, and one of the guards looked at me and started talking."Are you alright?"

I nodded and tried to say yes, but the words failed to leave my lips.

The guard nodded back and shut the door.

I tried to sleep again, but after an eternity, I drifted off. This dream was different. I could see the coast, a chariot I was driving with a woman who was beyond beauty. Curves in all of the right places, full lips. Her skin was the purest of snow, her eyes were polished steel, and her hair was red like a roaring fire. There was a smile she had that made the coldest winter feel like summer. She held onto me tightly, smiling with stars in her eyes, looking at me. She looked like an Irish A-tier Hollywood actress or a model.

I woke up in the morning, and we huddled around the table with meats, bread and cheeses, porridge with honey and raspberries in it. I could get used to this type of diet. To be honest, we needed the calories. I could overhear the guards talking about birds attacking the house.

I started talking with the sergeant about Murray, our next steps, and what we wanted to talk to the king and his healer about. How best to start forging an alliance, and what information we wanted to return to the Commander. Sadly, the only thing missing from this table was coffee. For me, that was the only way to start the day off right. I dug into my pack and found an unopened freeze-dried packet from one of the MREs. Thankfully, hot water was pretty easy to get, but coffee was rare. So, freeze-dried coffee would have to be done.

After the table was cleared, we were advised that the king wished to talk to us, so we motioned and used hand signals to roughly communicate with Murray. We went to the king's royal area. His throne was well designed, and it looked like it was carved out of one piece of wood, yet the armrests were of lighter wood. It was oak and ash well put together and well preserved, and it looked like the varnish was a clear coat so the wood could speak with its own beauty. The king sat upon the throne with all of his majesty. His torc was wonderful. A torc is typically made up of finely entwined brass strands twisted around each other. Usually, the ends have ornate decorations. His torc ended in bears with their mouths open in a raging snarl. Their eyes were adorned with rubies.

Connal had long ago left on his next errand. The king was at a loss on how to communicate until I had opened my mouth.

Myself. "Good morning, your majesty, you called for us."

The King, "Yes, you can call me Donngal Mcgregor. I am sorry to hear about your comrade. I wish to see if my healers can help ease his pain. My best healers are at your disposal to see if they can help."

He was amazed and put at ease when he realized he could understand me, and I could understand him. The king motioned to the cloaked figure to his left. This guy was the polar opposite. The cloaked man had a long beard that was pepper and salty; it was mostly grey, with some flakes of pepper. He looked like he had gone grey before his time and had given off the aura that he had lived for several lifetimes. His voice was enriched with wisdom and weight. It was akin to listening to your grandpa tell stories in his favorite rocking chair. He wore 6 colors in his clothing. He was clearly a druid of some renown.

Wise man: "You can call me Ronan. I am one of the king's personal advisors and healers. Let me take a look at your injured comrade. I think I might be able to help."

Murray came up closer to Ronan. Ronan took off his hood and took a closer look. He had taken out a brass device and looked inside Murray's ears, asking me to have him stay calm and breathe like he normally would. We had to write the instructions since reading lips and talking were unreasonable. Murray had calmed himself and allowed Ronan to look.

Ronan went about the normal hmms and brow scratching any modern doctor would do. He looked amazed at Murray's general health. Ronan scratched his beard.

Ronan: "What did this was some awful loud sound. Is this commonplace in what weapons and equipment you use?"

Myself: "We do have loud sounds on the ship, but not what caused this; think of thunder striking the same location many times. We do have equipment that is supposed to protect from it due to the screaming ghost, or something I have heard called a banshee."

Ronan: "It seems his hearing is badly damaged, as far as I can tell. He is lucky the banshee did not kill him, and you are lucky as well. Those are some very tough ghosts to deal with. They have killed many seasoned warriors. I can make up something that will bring back his hearing; it will take time, and he must be in places that do not have loud sounds. It might be best if he stays here for one cycle of the moon."

Ronan sat up from his chair; he went behind him and grabbed a mortar and pestle. He started rummaging through pouches and vials near him and mixing things. Combining them and chopping them up, he mixed up a dry powder. He then put them into a silver metal container. It had a snake on the outside, and the snake was ornately entwined and adorned with many oak leaves. Ronan handed the tin to Murray, but told me

Ronan: "He will need to take this 5 times a day until it is completely empty. He is not to be around any loud sounds until at least one day after this is empty. What I mean by loud sound is anything over normal conversations. He is under my protection and care until we get him back to you."

Ronan motioned back to the king.

And with that, the king said, "We can take you back to the shore, however, we were told of a prophecy of a silver turtle that would come to our aid in our darkest hours, when even the earth is still with sadness. I think your people might be the ones prophesied."

I nodded in respect to the king. He talked to the servant near his throne, then motioned to the warriors near the throne.

King Mcgreggor: "Some of my finest warriors will take you to the coast and help you look for your people. I think there might be a bit more to you Seamus, than even you know. I find it interesting you show up and in a few days, you are speaking like you know our language. Maybe we can talk over the cups about our stories the next time you are here. Before you go he handed us a sack with gold and riches."

Myself "Your majesty, I would greatly appreciate that honor."

WIth that, we split up the payment, then left the king's house with the soldiers, and they moved to their chariots. These were the same ones we saw on the way into the city. We loaded our gear into the chariots and and then stepped in. Each chariot had a driver and a warrior. We were going to be friendly for the trip, but it was better than walking. The wheels were sturdy, and the chariots were pulled by two horses. They were deceptively fast and maneuverable. We raced toward the shore.

The Chariot I was on was painted with very rich blues and greens. The Warrior looked like a Robin Hood from a Hollywood movie. Feathered hair, green eyes, that smile that showed white pearly teeth.

Warrior: "You must be the one who can understand us, and we can understand you."

I nodded. "You can call me Tayg MacDermmott. There are some that call me Seamus for short."

Warrior: "Nice to meet you, Seamus; my name is Artur Mer MacDonnal."

We had a quick handshake; his shake was very strong, and it returned the same strength to him. It is good to know that they use a farmer's handshake. The way to tell it will be a farmer's handshake is their hand will go directly in front of them and not from the side. Handshakes that go wide outside the person tend to be softer. It is worth noting and remembering that if the person gives you one shake, you must meet with that same handshake and not the other; both will be annoyed or think less of you if you do the wrong one.

Artur's driver was one with the road, and I could let my mind wander a bit. It's nice to let your mind stretch and take a break from focusing on just what is in front of you.

I had no oath to him or his people. My oaths were to the ideals of my nation, to the ship, and to my crew mates. I thought of the flag we flew, those areas of the US we could never see again, those family members we would possibly never see again. However, there was no time to dwell on that. We had people counting on us, the farmers who could not defend themselves. We could make a decent living here. We'd have to adapt and work on our own, but we'd get all the credit and blame. The Gator navy tended to be one that had no frills and hardly ever noticed.

Artur poked me and pointed at the beach, "Seamus, look, those are the types of horses you need to leave well alone."

The horse he pointed at looked majestic, out of a fairytale movie, with a perfect white coat hair moving like it was in a shampoo commercial.

As the horse majestically trotted along the beach, it slowed down like that beach TV show, with the lifeguards running.

A man greedily looked at the horse; he thought he had won the most beautiful horse in the entire land.

The horse had bent down as if to bow in respect and allow the man to climb aboard to claim him.

When that happened, the man could not move. It was like he was glued to the horse. The horse's eyes grew wide, almost lizard-like; they went from brown to a laser-red color, and razor-sharp teeth grew in place of molars. The horse then bolted off for the water faster than they normally would run. The rider screamed, trying to get off the horse. It had swum far enough off the shore and dove under the water with such force and anger the water came crashing up with one-third of a whale's force. The water in the area was dyed a strawberry red.

Arthur looked at me and said, "That was a nucklaveve, a nasty beasty. They disguise themselves as horses in hopes of catching prey. Many are always on the lookout for the most beautiful and fastest horses possible.

"

I thought, well, that puts the saying don't look a gift horse in the mouth, on its side. Also, without danger, there cannot be any adventure. At that moment, we made it to a clearing. It was not quite a beach, but there was grass, and the trees were few and far between. We could see the ship in the distance. As I walked, my boot struck something solid, and I almost fell. I held up my hand to hold so I could investigate the clanging sound. I knelt down to get a better look. It was a metal handle going into the ground, almost a cast iron handle. It was very sturdy and cold to the touch. I was able to dig out the handle up until it ended into a pot; this was like a tiny cauldron, about the size of the small gifts you get for friends for the holidays. As I tried to clean it, I started to notice all sorts of knotwork with boars and deer on the sides going down to the corner. It would have only made a cup of soup if you used it for its true purpose. Sergeant Buford gave me a weird look when I pulled it out of the dirt.

I told the others as I put the cauldron in my ruck, "This is pretty unique, I think we should take this with us; I am not sure where this came from?"

I got a nod from Sergeant Bufford, and then he took out his polished mirror and used his light to signal the ship. About an hour later, the captain's gig arrived with BM2 LeBlanc at the helm.

He pulled as close to the shore as he could, with a smoke in his mouth, and he joked, "Well, took you long enough. It was not a picnic before picking you up. I think we lost one, eh?" He gestured at our current number, 4 clearly being lower than 5.

Myself: "Murray got injured, I'll have to tell you about it later. It was crazy, and we are going to need to do this over a beer or 12. He's getting medical care from where these wonderful people live."

LeBlanc: "Please tell me we sailed onto some stupid cheesy historical movie? Please tell me it's *Brigadoon*, that Wallace guy 3 movie, or something like that.

Myself: "I wish it was BM2, I really wish it was."

We piled into the boat, waved at the warriors, and sped off to the ship. Upon getting closer, I could see that there were some repairs going on, some welding, and people waiting to apply paint.

Myself: "What on earth happened?"

LeBlanc: "This is when you just need to pinch yourself or punch, but I'm not sure which. We got attacked by some giant squid and had to use all (the gun) mounts to get it to stop. The FCs (Fire control man, they maintain and fire all the fun big weapons, stuff us mere mortals who only want to push the red button just once) went a little trigger-happy with the CWIS. The old man was pissed and grabbed his blooper (The mark 79 grenade launcher, and yes, we had a gun rack behind the Quartermaster's chart table for him with his blooper and M14) and started shooting."

I could just imagine that carnage, and well, a good leader isn't afraid to roll up their sleeves to do the work, too. Not sure if the old man could also get a gig doing leadership motivational speeches. I can see it. I slayed a giant squid monster, and you can too. Another best seller; 10 steps to inspire your workforce by slaying mythological monsters.

Chapter 5
King and Crow

We made it to the gangplank, got off with our gear, and trudged up the 30-degree incline of the steps. We were still expected to salute and introduce ourselves with our IDs. After that, I moved back to my rack, got a shower, and put on the spare set of cammies. My bunk on the bottom had a coffin rack. As I was getting back from the shower, QM2 Moreli approached me; he always had an annoyed look on his face.

Moreli: "QM3, where the hell have you been? You were supposed to have a watch."

Myself: "QM2, I was told by the Captain I was assigned to the Marines, you can ask Chief."

Moeli: "I do not care what you were told; your orders were to be on watch."

Myself "QM2, I am not sure what to say about that. I was following my orders."

Moreli: "Your orders come from me, and you are to get out of that uniform; you aren't a Marine, you aren't attached to them, and you are to stand Quartermaster of the watch since you are a Quartermaster!"

Myself "Aye, aye, QM2."

With that, I got into my coveralls and raced to the bridge. I got some weird looks from those on the bridge with my turnover. I started looking back at the chart. I looked out at the ocean after adjusting our 15-minute position update. It was a nice, calm night, and the waters were rather smooth.

There was a tap on my shoulder; I turned around and saw that it was QMC.

QMC: "Son, we've been looking all over for you; this is the last place we thought you'd be."

Myself "Chief, what can I help with? I was told to stand watch."

QMC: "Who told you to stand watch? You were supposed to report in with the skipper. We've been waiting on you. The Marines are waiting on you, too."

Myself "QM2 Moreli told me to do that."

QMC: "Go, I'll handle this." With that, the chief took the watch.

For those playing the home game who do not know the subtlety, if an E7 says they got it handled, it will be done. For those who do not know, chiefs really run the navy. The good ones will go to bat for you. With that, I left the bridge, and thankfully, the skipper was still awake, so I walked past O country. (Officers quarters. They all had Estate rooms, 2 people in one room vs the 30 plus at times the enlisted had.)

As I walked to the Old man's estate, it was one of the few with windows. His estate had that dark navy blue carpeting; his office was perfectly new, with the ship's seal in the middle. (to me, it was a habit to never walk on the ship's seal.) It was regal in its own way; he had two bottles of whiskey nearby in decanters. The door was only open almost all the way. Protocol dictates you always knock and ask permission to enter into any space, especially the old man's estate.

Commander, "Enter."

Myself I rendered a salute "Thank you, sir, I am very sorry for my tardiness."

Commander: "Excused; what happened after you made landfall? And where is the missing Marine?"

I told him the entire story, including the fish stabbing me, the others we met along the way, what happened to Murray, and how he was getting medical attention. I left out my dreams about my Vegas trip, the visions of the redhead from my dreams on a chariot ride. Not sure why; I felt ashamed, and those felt personal and irrelevant to the current intel needed. I had also brought with me the currency that the King had provided me for rendering aid to both Barra and well taking out the Banshee and what a banshee is.

Commander: "So you are saying, when this fish stabbed you, you learned how to speak with them. If this place wasn't so weird and what we dealt with a few days after you left, I would have you drug tested until you ended up in Captain's mast."

Myself: "I understand, sir. The people we left Private Murray with are an honorable bunch. They are very hospitable and welcoming. Their leader feels honor bound to right an injury to one of our warriors. He sees us as warriors, and in their culture, warriors are nobility."

Commander: "Well, that is very interesting, I will need you to sit down with our ICs (Crypto nerds) and do a data dump with them and the other marines. You are going to be assigned to the Marines until further notice by me. Also, here's a bit of good news: We got news of advancements a few weeks ago. I wanted to let you know you made QM2. I wish I had better news."

Myself: "Sir, thank you for letting me know. I am doing my best to help in any way I can. Sir, this is what the king said: our payment for helping out the old man and their village with their water problem. Also, here is this little caldron I found before we were picked up." I handed him my share of the money, which the king paid us. It was not light at all. The cauldron was gently set on the commander's desk.

Commander: "This will be helpful to keep the ship afloat. Thank you for offering it instead of keeping it for yourself. As you say, this little device is quite unique. I am not sure what we'll do with it. You've given me a lot to think about. I will want you to be in the next navigation brief. This is after I had time to think about this and you've talked to the chiefs. They want you in their mess next. If you can track down Sergeant Buford, I will want to get his input, too."

Myself: " Aye Aye, sir, is there anything else I can help you with?"

Commander: "QM2, please keep the news of the promotion secret. We will have an awards ceremony at our next formation, and you will be dismissed."

I swelled with pride knowing I had been promoted normally; this would have been a really big pay bump and extra duties. I would probably be resigned to another ship while on deployment, but that was not going to happen now.

Myself "Aye, aye, sir, and thank you."

With that, I about-faced and walked out of the commander's estate room. I saw MR2 outside the captain's estate room. He knocked, and I heard the same thing being said.

MR2: "We are starting to get low on metal for making parts, sir. We'll be fine for now, but we cannot keep this up. Especially after that squid fight. Even my tools are starting to get long in the tooth."

Commander: "Understood."

As he said that, I could see for a split second the cauldron started producing a green bubbling smoke, sort of like dry ice. Towards the top of the lid, a wrench started to appear out of the bottom of the cauldron.

I then made it down one deck and past the general mess decks, where people were playing cards. Two different games were being played, Spades and Euchre. If I were to play, it would always be Euchre, never Spades. However, a few gathered around a table with a mountain of books and dice. I think they were playing some sort of game. I had no time to talk nor the ability to see what the other game was; if one was smart, you never let the chiefs wait for anything.

I knocked on the door to the chief's mess. It was more of a fine dining area set up cafeteria style, with nice wooden chairs attached to the tables like the old fast food style chairs in the 1980s (The general mess was similar, just not as nice); the walls had wooden paneling and a few TVs. To be honest, it looked like any VFW; maybe it was the same person who did their interior decor. As I said before, it is known that chiefs run the navy, and this is where business goes down. I have heard rumors that there is almost always a chief here; if there isn't, then you are wrong. With that, most chiefs were in here save a few from Engineering. They were all talking about what would happen and how we would keep the ship running.

One of the chiefs I was unfamiliar with said, "QM3 is here to talk about what happened, and Sergeant Buford is on his way."

Inside the mess, there was only one Gunnery Sergeant. He looked like a military action hero with the evil Bert haircut and blue icy eyes that could knife-hand your DNA. Gunny then looked at me and said, "Son, you missed a lead-slinging party."

Another chief I was not familiar with piped up, "Gunny Hull is right. It was a bit of a situation. A giant squid tried to wrap around the ship; the DCs are bending out parts of the ship damaged by the squid."

I relayed that my experiences concluded with returning to the ship, leaving out the two dreams for the same reason as the captain. Partway through telling them what happened, there was a knock on the door, and I paused.

Sergeant Buford could be heard saying a muffled " Permission to enter."

One of the Chiefs said, "Enter."

Sergeant Buford entered and stood at attention.

Sergeant "Gunny, sorry I am late."

Gunny: "At ease, sergeant."

The door was quickly closed, and the chiefs nodded at me to continue. Sergeant Buford had added in things from his perspective, and that complemented the story; with both perspectives, it helped to build a complete perspective.

The collective E7 mess had nodded along with the story. You could see the military bearing, but their eyes were quickly calculating the next steps and the resources the ship would need and could obtain from this intel drop. They asked questions along the way on how I could remember some things but not others. I had to try to explain how the knowledge worked to the best of my ability and how it was weird trying to access something I could not remember; sometimes, the memories did not want to cooperate. They thanked both of us and reminded us that tomorrow would be a beer day and a steel beach picnic for our holiday routine and to enjoy ourselves tomorrow for our hard work. I could smell that coffee brewing even at this hour. Any sailor loves their coffee. I think the obsession started after the Navy went dry.

Now, by dry, I mean no alcohol for the most part. It used to be a ration of rum every day, but the drink of choice was switched to coffee afterward. I often think of one of my favorite signs at a beloved coffee shop. It had the slogan Drink coffee and do stupid stuff faster with more energy. Now, my own Chief spoke up first,

QMC: "That is a lot to take in; we will need to think about this and talk with the old man on this. I think it's best for both of you to get some sleep and relax tomorrow. You are going to be our eyes and ears out there. We have no idea where we are, and it seems when we are too."

With that, we were dismissed; I wanted to get some air at night. It was something to take in the salt air. I looked up to see the American Flag flying, knowing that those stars might only mean something to just us.

The people out there might never have heard of those stars and what that flag meant. Positive note: beer day tomorrow, I thought as I trudged back to my rack, crawled in, and was rocked to sleep by the gentle caress of the ocean punching our ship.

We would get a beer day if it was 90 days since we've last been on land and not going ashore within the next 7. There were rules, of course. You could not chug or trade the beers. Also, if you were standing watch in the next 6 hours, you could not have them. These were always tied to Steal Beach picnics (think a big old grill out.) However, every Steel Beach picnic was not a beer day. We would have seagulls and sliders. Seagulls were what we called BBQ chicken, and sliders were burgers that were so greasy they would slide right through you.

With the steel beach picnic, there was always music playing. Now, here is the interesting thing: this ship has its own band. I kid you not; the guys brought on their own personal drum set, guitars, and gear. They practiced in their spare time and let me tell you they were good. They played mostly country, rock, and blues. They knew a ton of songs, and I heard rumors that they were working on some of their own. That day, they played some Johnny Cash, then switched to a bluesy cover of Metallica's *Ride the Lightning*. I secretly think they liked to mess with our heads. The covers they did were amazing, and it was interesting to see how long it would take to figure out what song they were playing.

I went to get my food, spend time with my friends on the ship, shoot the crap with some of the Marines, and just relax. As I got my food, I was in my camies, wearing the green undershirt and pants like the other marines. I was just chatting with others, talking about what it was like going ashore and how pretty the trees were. I was in the middle of describing them, and a familiar face showed up. He was a bit taller than me, one of the few OSs I got along with, and a bit on the taller and average build side. Think of an Anglo-Saxon knight turned surfer.

Myself "Hey, OS2 Culbert, how is it?"

That was the phrase he used when greeting people. I remember our shenanigans when I first got to San Diego. I remember having to jump into his moving car, or I would have to walk, I remember the trips to LA. We went up to concerts, shows, and even a few shadow cast performances of *The Rocky Picture Show*. The actors would perform the show while the movie was playing in the background. There were more than a few attractive girls there, and I loved going there. Sadly, they were flirty and nothing more.

Culbert "QM3, not too bad. We had that squid attack us, and I was on the bridge when it happened. Let me tell you, Combat was not happy."

He and I often stood bridge watch together; he would stand at a scope near the Quartermaster's table. He would be wearing a sound-powered phone that went back to combat. Combat was responsible for tracking all of the ships, and they were all considered contacts until we identified them as friends or foes. They were also secondary navigation. Their courses in navigation were rather brief. Some of them were way better than others.

They always had to work on targeting solutions to the contacts near us in the event they would be needed for a firing solution, and some made a game of it.

Myself "That must have been crazy; it was nuts being off the ship for about a week, I think?"

We would have the same food each week (many of us counted how long we were deployed off of the food schedule) - typically, it was messed up in one way, shape, or form, undercooked, burned to a crisp, or ruined in many different ways. I remember one time we had a choice of Turkey ala King and Pork Adobo. The Turkish ala King looked like wet, dry dog food, and the Pork Adobo looked like canned wet dog food. I have seen burned dry rice and burned watery coffee (I am still amazed at the talent that it takes to both burn and make watered-down coffee in one go).

Culbert: "Pretty much, it's about a day shy; tomorrow is supposed to be fish, but I think I heard one of Gunner's mates joke saying 'Squid's back on the menu, boys'."

I opened my beer and clinked the can, saying, "Cheers."

We drank the beers and continued to chat about nothing for a few hours. The rest of the day was relaxed, and it went without trouble. The food was surprisingly good. The BBQ sauce was well made, and they made a nice one with tomato; I like BBQ sauces made with vinegar just as much, so I might have to share the recipe I learned as a kid. The band played on as the sun started to set. They packed up their instruments. As that happened, Sergeant Buford looked at me. We moved a bit away from the crowd. We went under the ladder well by the flight deck and underneath it. Most people avoid this part of the ship. He then motioned for us to have a seat.

Sergeant: "Petty officer, you did good out there for a squid. We are going to need to go back out there, though. I want to make sure Murray is doing alright and see what else we can find out there."

Myself: "I understand. I also cannot sit idly. I hope Murray is doing better; he seems like a good kid."

Sergeant: "Yeah, he is, I feel off about him being in the hands of people we hardly know; I know they are soldiers, and they seem honorable. But that's one of ours, and we don't leave anyone behind."

Myself: "I can see how that is troubling. We need to get back out there to see what we can do about the fuel problem."

I looked out to see the sunset, and I saw my first green flash. I had heard about these and was unsure if they were true or if everyone could see them. A green flash happens when the sun sets. The effect seems to happen when the human eye is overloaded with colors as it sets. With all of those colors being seen, green is the most common. We just nodded, taking in the salt air.

The sergeant looked at me and said, "QM3, get some sleep; we are going to need it; we are heading out after formation."

Myself: "Roger that. I thank you for your guidance and mentoring."

With that, he left, and I was there alone, holding an empty plate, a beer can, and a full stomach. I took care of my trash and headed to my rack. I made it back with no problems, no weird dreams, just normal music. The waves gently rocked me to sleep.

In the morning, I went through my normal morning routine, had coffee and breakfast, and headed to the mezzanine deck. This is where most of the crew who were not actively standing watch would go when we had an all-hands meeting.

All of the workout equipment was on the mezzanine deck. A ramp went down to the well deck where if we had any ships, tanks, or other equipment would be stored.

I ended up standing with the Marines, since they were officially unofficially part of my chain of command now. I kept getting angry and dirty looks from QM2 Moreli, during the formation.

With that, the head honcho, Commander Alvarez, walked in.

Commander: "Shipmates and Marines, we find ourselves in a difficult and dangerous situation. We will need everyone to come together as you have in the past to keep this ship working. We have to look out for her, and after her, she depends on us. Our mission has drastically changed; we obviously do not have all of the marines we are supposed to have, and we are not headed to our initial goal. Your Divos (Division officers) and

Chiefs will keep you in the loop on what we know. If you have any suggestions or know how to make things more efficient, please run it up the chain of command. Now, onto our Awards ceremony."

To be honest, I could see the weight of the commander's words on everyone; there was some denial that we were just off the coast of Indonesia or some other place or got some different orders no one knew about.

He then switched to reading off those who got promoted. We were to walk towards the commander and accept the award/medal/rank with our left hand, then salute with the right. He went through many names, dodging mine for what felt like an eternity.

Commander "QM3 MacDermmott, please step forward."

I stepped forward with a crisp military walk and walked up to him. Saluted him, and he saluted me back.

Commander: "I am quite pleased to promote you to QM2. Remember your duties and responsibilities. Always remember Acta non verba."

Myself "Sir, it is an honor and a pleasure. I will do my best."

My left hand went out to take the award, my right hand to shake his hand, and a photo was taken. I saluted my commanding officer and went back to my spot information.

Commander: "With that crew, that is it for our morning formation; dismissed to your Divos. Please carry on the rest of the day with the normal routine."

With that, he lit up a cigar and walked up towards the bridge on the ladder wheels on the outside of his ship on the outside deep in thought.

With the old man's departure, we were released to our Department officers. Since I was attached to the Marines until further notice, I have reported to Gunny Hull.

Gunny Hull "You heard the skipper; what we got to do is keep this ship protected; we will be assisting the gunner's mates with mount watch and humping ammo around the ship (he meant to move it around) and some of you will be going back out there to see what we can get resource wise. I will leave the outside mission up to Sergeant Buford. The sergeant will choose to go out with his own Marines and Sailors. His group will be checking on Private Murray, and I want him to check in with the skipper to see if there is anything else he wants the Sergeant to look out for. Any questions?"

You could have heard a pin drop, and there was some crew waiting around from the other departments wishing to congratulate those who got promoted and others taking time before heading to watch or their other duties that needed to be accomplished.

Gunny Hull: "Dismissed, most of you carry on about your day."

Gunny looked at Sergeant Buford and myself and motioned for us to stay. The rest of the marines were horsing and joking around as they left.

Gunny Hull: "Look, this is a weird situation; I am going to have to rely on both of you to see this through. Sergeant, you are going to be the superior NCO, Petty Officer, you are going to work with him, make sure we get people back, we don't leave anyone behind."

With that, he paused and looked over at QM2 Moreli "Petty officer, is there a problem? I am trying to have a talk with the NCOs that report to me. "

QM2 Moreli: "Funny QM3 reports to me, not you; this is bull. He's not supposed to be the same rank as me."

Gunny Hull: "I really do not care what you think, the old man promoted him and said that he reports to me until further notice. Last I checked, Gunny is more than a bit higher of a rank than a Petty Officer Second class, and last I checked, You weren't allowed in the Chief's mess. Therefore I outrank you. You might have more time in service than McDermott, but I outrank you, and he reports to me. Is that clear? If I hear even a rumor of you bugging him, we will have a problem."

Gunny could quickly clean his clock with the wrong glance. He's easily number 2 on the people I never piss off list; maybe number 3; just don't tell Gunny. He quickly had a tempered look of murder in his eyes; this was an entirely new game. At that moment, I knew I was in the major leagues, even if I didn't want to be.

QM2 Moreli kind of deflated; his bravado snuffed out like a candle in a container. To be honest, I was pleased he would not bug me.

With that, Gunny put his attention back to us. "I am going to need both of you to resupply and get back out there. Take today, get your gear, and make sure everyone else's is in working order. "

With that, Gunny left up the stairs, heading back into the ship, near the berthing where my bunk would be.

With that, Sergeant Buford and I started making plans. It was him mostly talking and bouncing ideas off of me; I piped up when something did not sound right or looked like it might need some clarification.

With that, we headed to the Marines armory, which was one level above us toward the front of the ship. It was on the way toward the bosn's locker. The door to their armory is a small, watertight door that is about half the size of a normal one. There is a latch on the door. I heard from someone who was here on the last deployment that the Marines kept forgetting to latch the door. When that happened, they would yank on the door, causing the alarm to go off. Also, they forgot the sound-powered phone they could use to communicate with others outside and a combination lock (that was set by themselves before the deployment). Luckily for me and the rest of the ship, they knew about both items. A quick mental note regarding security do not mess with Marines. They horse and joke around about a lot of things, but security is not one of them.

Sergeant Buford went up to the door and proceeded to provide the guy at the Door of the armory with the checklist we came up with. The armory guy nodded, and the other guy in the small armory started going through their inventory to check things off. With everything checked off the list, we found everyone in the Marine Berthings.

We all gathered near the gangplank and headed down to the boat. BM2 Leblank was already on the boat. He looked at me wearing his Oakley shades, coveralls, a bulletproof vest, and that trademarked cigarette in his mouth.

BM2 LeBlanc: "Congrats, QM2, we're going to have to get some beers someday. Tell some stories over a few and just chill for a bit." His assistant (the cigarette) went up and down, appearing to nod in agreement with each syllable.

Myself "BM2, that sounds like a good idea. If we keep moving at our current pace, that could happen soon."

I should have honestly held my tongue at that moment, storming down. The gangplank with his LL bean backpack was the most annoying Junior officer I ever had the displeasure of interacting with. He looked like a combination of a nerd and a bully from any high school movie from the 1980's. He had that pasty white sunscreen on his nose as well. I mentally sighed; not Ensign Browne; he had attended Brown Ivy League College and rubbed it in everyone's faces. We initially thought he did not know his port from starboard. It was much worse; he did not know his left from right (the easiest way to remember the difference is that the port and left have the same amount of letters). The other problem with this officer was that he thought he was brilliant, yet the opposite seemed to be true most of the time. I was hoping if we had to have an officer assigned, it would have been LTJG Jorgenson.

Ensign: "This mission needs an officer; we cannot have enlisted traipsing all over the countryside and ruining our chance of being accepted in any polite society."

Sergeant Buford: "Well, if that is the case, sir, you will have to keep up with our pace. We have to scout as much as we can in the surrounding area. McDermott is keeping up with us just fine and not complaining. We need to check on one of our own and further around the coast and the city we already found and started communicating with. Sir, your uniform does not match ours, and I believe that khaki does not seem to blend in well with where we are."

Ensign Browne was still wearing his work uniform with the LL Bean rucksack. This situation was kind of sad, to be honest. He was like the little kid who wanted to be in every activity, even if it was something they couldn't do. To be honest, at times, what we were doing was even pushing me to my limits. Everything I am learning is on the job. It's been one heck of a crash course.

Myself: "Sir, with all due respect, you will be standing out like a sore thumb out there. I ended up getting the right uniform, and I went out there because of my familiarity with where we believed we were right now. We have already established a good reputation with some of the locals."

Ensign "QM3, I outrank you and, well, the Marines, I am a higher ranking officer."

Myself: "Sir, with all due respect, I just got promoted to QM2."

Ensign: "I really don't care. I… Out… Rank… You!" He pointed an index finger and jabbed it in my direction with each syllable.

Another figure was heading towards our location, and the drama unfolded on the Gangplank. It was none other than LTJG Jorgenson. He looked annoyed, and his nostrils flared.

LTJG: "Ensign Browne, what are you doing on the Captain's Gangplank?"

Ensign: "Sir, going ashore."

LTJG: "No, you are not; I have the list of those approved to transport those ashore and those authorized to go ashore. I checked it at the beginning of my watch; it's been the same for a week. I do not see an Ensign Browne,

I see a QM2 MacDermott, I see Sergeant Buford, a Corporal Harris (this is Causes Safety Briefs), HM3 Bosko (Sneak attack sasquatch), a PFC Williams, a Private Edwards, and Private Murray, sergeant I am very sorry about what happened to Private Murray. I do not see an Ensign Browne. The sergeant stated that you are not equipped to go out there, as did QM2. I tend to trust their judgment; QM2 was the quartermaster of the watch when we saved Fireman Moore. He was the only one on the bridge doing that watch. You know it takes at least 3 Quartermasters, and in all honesty, you need 5 (Five was our entire department. Our Chief and Divo were supposed to be on the bridge in the optimal situation)."

It was interesting to see LTJG Jorgenson stop Ensign Brown in his tracks, offer the sergeant, and offer the rest of us condolences. Also, commend us for our accomplishments. LTJG Jorgenson was what we called a Mustang. At one time, they were enlisted but went over to the officer's side. Most Mustangs are really good officers and really down-to-earth people.

We were then free to enter the boat. As I entered, BM2 bashed me in the left arm, where my rank would be, and said, "QM2, this is to help you keep your crow on" (the term for this is called tacking on the Crow. We referred to the eagle on our left arm as a crow. This goes back to the old tradition of those in the rank you were being promoted to get together, take your nicest shirt, and sew on your new rank without you knowing. The punching was a reminder that you could lose it and to help remember to keep it on)."

We sped off in silence until we got closer to shore. We observed the same exact horse on the beach the last time we were there. That same luxurious mane perfectly brushed white coat. I motioned to Sergeant Buford, and he pointed out the horse to the Gunnersmate at the 50 cal. They talked for a bit, and a wicked grin about a mile long appeared on the Gunnersmate's face; he opened fire on the horse, and it splattered, its false form shredded by the rounds of the 50 cal. GM3 was not messing around; I was told they had loaded armor-piercing rounds. It went through the pseudo-horse like a sledgehammer hitting tissue paper.

We made it to the shore, and in the same spot where we were picked up, we followed the way back to the city and made it back just before nightfall. Murray was in high spirits when he saw us. We still had to communicate by paper. Ronan was with him, and they were playing a game of sorts. The board itself was a square of beautifully carved wood with interlocking lines of art; in each of the corners, it had an oak leaf, a man, a heron, and an elk in the other. The stone orbs were meticulously polished in each of the round centers. This was Fidchell, a very tactical game, and we were both having a good time. Murray had a tankard and was sipping from it.

Ronan: "It is good to see you all again. Murray is doing well; I'm just teaching him the finer points of Fidchell. It is a favorite game of Kings, Druids, and Bards."

Bards were a step below druids; they would travel between towns and had as much knowledge as druids when it came to law. Think of a traveling storyteller and lawyer wrapped up into one.

Myself: "Ronan, we are doing quite well; we need to come back out here to check on Murray and still scout the lands around this fair city."

Ronan: "I can understand; the king's warriors reported a loud racket coming from offshore about two days ago, I take it that was your metal Currach?"

Currach were their boats; they were sort of low to the water, and the hull was what appeared to be a solid piece, with wooden slats along the bottom and a few parts of wood that would come up to provide places to sit and add structural integrity for the boat they could come in various different sizes. If the ship had sails, they would be square, not the triangle sails used on modern sailing ships.

Myself "Yes, we were attacked by a giant sea monster. The crew had fought it off. Yesterday, we had a celebration after fighting it off."

I proceeded to tell him about the Steel Beach picnic. The music, the food, and, well, the beer day.

Ronan: "That is rather odd, that you do not drink that much beer. How do you have clean water?"

I proceeded to tell him how we cleaned water and why adding alcohol to the water worked so well. It was a lengthy process of turning salt water into freshwater.

Ronan: "Fascinating, I might have to see one of these microscopes someday. I think we have a lot we can teach each other. You are all honored guests; please make yourselves at home. I will talk to the king for you. "

He departed from the room and gave Murray a look. Do not touch the board until I get back. I like to think Murray was just teasing him.

Ronan's room was very well organized, with a few books made of leather. The aroma was very welcoming and magical at the same time. You could pick out notes of sage, turf, and even a bit of wood.

Myself "Sergeant, this is their version of chess. It is a very serious game. The nobility love playing this game and love to have the most ornate boards possible."

Sergeant: "Understood. This is a game we'll have to learn, and Murray will have to teach us."

It was obvious that Murray was in good company and taken good care of, and Ronan's bedside manner was possibly some of the best I have ever seen. You could tell he was a man who cared about his life's work. He was a very learned man as well. This was not just some normal healer, political advisor, judge, or holy person (a druid was kind of all of those at once). Ronan's place was well furnished and clearly valued in this city by those who lived here and its king.

Ronan came back with the same servants, and they led us to what people would refer to as a hostel. We settled in for the night. The king's warriors had come back the day before we arrived, and the rooms we had used previously were for the king's warriors and guests. The Hostel was open and was typically used for any official visitor of the King.

A hostel is a lot better than what you would initially think. They are maintained by the king, and there is always food, typically beef, that has been boiled. The beef they could get was rather tough and had to be boiled for a long time. Boiling it also removes all flavor. It is then added to a perpetual stew. It is always on the fire, ingredients are always added to the cauldron, it stays around the same level and never goes bad.

The beds are not as nice as the ones from our last stay, but they are still wonderful and comfortable. The furs are still very clean, and the rooms are still just as safe. There was barely any woodwork on the couch beds; the pillows were still comfortable but not as well made or ornate as the ones at the king's estate.

Chapter 6

Frag Out

Our morning was pretty much about just waking up, getting something to eat, and waiting to approach the king for any sort of intel we could get our hands on before setting out again. We needed resources. We needed something to keep the ship going. My knowledge of history is pretty decent, and I do not remember anything in any of my readings or what I might be able to access in my brain. I do not remember anything about oil fields in the land we are in. We needed something; a ship without fuel would not work, and anchoring our ship permanently off the coast was a recipe for disaster.

Turf wouldn't work; it would if we were coal but using turf. Turf is an early form of coal, and we would need a lot of it if we were to use coal. I do not think converting the ship and everything else to burning turf would have been possible. Before going to sleep, we huddled around, basically spitballing what we would want to look for. It basically boiled down to money, food, and fuel. The cauldron could make a lot, according to MR2. However, we needed to schedule things, and getting caught up on ammunition after the squid fight was going to take time. I heard that the engineers were skeptical at best about whether the fuel made by it was going to work. There was a legend in engineering that one of the engineering chiefs used fuel for coffee creamer.

We all turned in for the night, the mission that was in front of us. It was a very open-ended mission, but still, people were counting on us. We had already made a good leeway into reputation. A mental and physical sigh of relief washed over us, knowing someone did not muck that up. Equally as relaxing was knowing Ensign Browne would not be coming with us for the time being. We had to really thank LTJG Jorgenson for that courtesy.

With that, I fell asleep, and I dreamed. However, it was the Vegas trip again, a bit more detailed and a bit clearer; the metal showed a very attractive blonde was chasing after me; she was all of the wrong kinds of trouble; I kept trying to push her away with politeness and even body language. She followed me back to my hotel room. I quickly used my keycard to get through and opened the door just wide enough for me to sneak inside. The door quickly closed and locked behind me. I wanted nothing to do with the wrong or right kind of trouble at that time. I was in no state to deal with it after having my heart ripped out.

The spiral that started was with my high school sweetheart. I purchased her a ring, not just any ring but an engagement. I had proposed to her and was elated. However, things went downhill from there. When I got to my first ship. It started when we were going through the ship's retirement process. She started to become more and more distant. The next day, the ship was to be retired, and after that, I was supposed to go home and get ready for the wedding. I received a dear John letter. A Dear John letter is a generic one that basically says I do not love you anymore. I have moved on, and tough luck, champ. Typically, it comes from the person breaking up and is received at the worst possible time. However, in my case, it was forwarded from my cousin and then sent to me. She did not even have the decency to send it to me directly or even call. I had to go through and cancel most of everything that had to do with the wedding. I felt bad about asking my mom for help; it was a mess. I couldn't come home, so I went to Las Vegas. I needed to get this out of my system before arriving at my new command; I needed to be as far away from home as I could be in an attempt to heal from this.

In times like this, I remember my grandfather's advice. He told me when you find the right one, you'll know. What I wouldn't give for some of his sage advice now. My Grandfather was a bear of a man, tough as nails. He was a man of the land; hard work was in his DNA. I helped him many times on his farm over the summers, helping pull in the harvest. My mom helped raise me on her own; my dad was long gone, and I never really got to know him. I would work on Grandpa's farm for some light spending money and after setting aside money to help my mom. Even after joining the military, I would put aside a little bit of money to help my mom. My grandpa could build just about anything, and it was built to last. At one time, he even put together his own truck. It was made up of parts from a *GMC, Chevy, and Ford*. He called it his GMChevord, and it still makes me smile when thinking about it.

There was another scratching in my dream; it was the blonde scratching at the door of the hotel room. I leaped out of my bed, fully armed (yet partly awake), and had my camouflage pants and boots on in one motion. Weapon drawn, my rifle was ready, and the rest of them were up, in various states of undress. They were equally armed, some wearing flip-flops instead of combat boots.

Causes Safety Briefs: "Ok, whoever woke me up is going to get an attitude adjustment." he laughed at the same time as yawing." He took point on the door. "Sergeant, it looks like those owls are back again."

Sergeant Buford: "Ok, bring the hate, keep an eye out."

PFC Edwards pulled out his shotgun and smiled, "Sergeant, I think I got some right here, I hope this is enough."

PFC Edwards was a very dark green southern man (the Marines refer to themselves as different shades of green). His ivory teeth were so bright they almost reflected back moonlight. As Causes Safety Briefs opened the door ever so slightly, keeping an eye on the owl. PFC Edwards slowly poked out the shotgun and pulled the trigger, and boom, the owl was shredded with buckshot, basically point-blank range. The door quickly shut in one fluid motion as Edwards pulled the shotgun back in.

Myself: "They come in pairs, so there should be another."

Right after I said that, Causes Safety Briefs violently opened the door, slamming into the owl, and without missing a beat, Edwards shot the other one.

Causes Safety Briefs opened the door and quickly smashed both glass jars, then grabbed some of the glass remains and a few feathers. He then politely shut the door. He opened his hands, showing his findings; upon closer examination, the feathers were pure snow white. The remains of the glass, even shattered, were smooth to the touch.

Sergeant: "Ok, we are going to have to do shifts switching out every 2 hours."

Myself "I'll stay on for the first two hours."

Truth be told, I did not want to go back to sleep with the dreams I had. I wanted those nightmares as far away from me as possible.

The rest of the first watch went off without any problems, even when I woke up in relief. Everyone else seemed to sleep well but me. I went back to sleep with my eyes open; I let my mind wander. I could see the maiden with the copper hair again; we were fighting something back and back. I was out of ammunition. We were spinning in circles, handing weapons back and forth. Before I could see her closer and see what we were fighting, the first rays of morning interrupted my reverie.

We observed the mayhem of last night; there were no feathers, just scratches on the door indentations where the owls would have died when they fell. We still had the feathers and pieces of glass in our possession.

Causes Safety Briefs "I am just going to say what everyone is thinking. That was nuts. We should talk to someone about this; what about that Ronan fella?

The sergeant just nodded as we continued about our morning routine, getting ready for breakfast and heading out. Breakfast, as all meals, were to be provided by the king, keeping in the traditions of hospitality.

We ate from the king's cauldron. It was much better than the galley food and a bit better than the best mre's. It will keep you going and fill you up. It's not going to win any cooking competitions. It was the same stew; however, each time, it tasted a bit different, and it was referred to as eternal stew; it contained a bit of this and a bit of that. The servants kept adding to it, ensuring it was almost always at the same level. A fire seemed to perpetually burn, never getting hotter or colder, just the right temperature to keep the hostel warm and the food from getting cold, spoiling, or burning.

I dipped into the coffee; thankfully, Sergeant Buford and I pulled a bit of rank and got us more coffee. We had enough for about two cups a day, no matter what MRE we had. I had snuck around at least an extra week for myself. The Navy runs off coffee. I am starting to get it down to a science with what we have here to make an acceptable cup. Fed and fully caffeinated, we went through the city towards the king's estate.

The guards looked at us and nodded; they motioned to let us through. The king was on his throne conducting business on trading, war, treaties, and the normal things any leader would be dealing with. The kingdom near him was pressuring him to declare war for something involving jealousy between rulers. Something of a lover's spat is what I could hear, and something about tracking down a bull to fight another one. With that, the messenger finished his business, gave us an odd glance, and left.

King: "If it isn't my favorite guests, I hope things are going well?"

Myself: "Yes, your majesty, things are going as well as they can. Do you know anything about these owls that attack at night? They seem to hold jars open and turn people into stone. We've killed a few owls already."

King: "Yes, we know a little; they have been a pain for quite some time. They have tormented us for a while now. They often seem to attack at night; the person they attack seems to be overwhelmed with grief, sadness, or unrelenting anger. "

Myself: "Interesting, do you know where they are coming from?"

King: "Sadly, no, it is hard to figure out where they come from. They are so silent. I have tried to keep my warriors watching all hours of the night, but nothing comes from it."

Myself: "Another question, we need to know a bit more about the areas around your kingdom if possible."

King: "I can tell you what I know, but Ronan also knows a lot. I would say if you have any more questions about the Owls, he would be your best source of information. Your Comrade Murray is a wonderful person; he is a wonderful company to Ronan. He's taking to fetchel rather nicely."

I translated this back to Sergeant Buford, and he nodded and asked if he knew anything about the possible plants or other ways people fueled their houses with heat.

I asked the king these questions, and he replied with a plant that Ronan might know a bit about and that they use for cooking oil and cleaning. I scratched my head at this revelation. Being a new E5 in a different branch but still an NCO, I wanted to ensure I was pulling my weight.

I relayed this back to Sergeant Buford; there might be a plant that could be used for fuel. I was hoping this would be enough to keep the ship moving. The nearest fueling ship is thousands of miles, years, or even who knows galaxies away.

With that, I politely bowed to the king, as did the other Marines, and we went to the room where Ronan lived. He was deep in thought, and Murray was near him, getting the books he was pointing at and bringing them to him. It was quite entertaining to see how they communicated. Murray still couldn't hear too well, yet they still managed with the language barrier.

Murray waved his hands and pointed at the door; his eyes lit up as if they were smiling. He still had that marine face on, that military discipline.

Ronan: "Oh glad to see you again. What brings you to my humble abode?"

Sergeant Buford took this one. He relayed to me what he wanted to say. I could tell it was eating at him to look out for the ship and for the people being impacted by this. If we look out for ourselves, it is too late to help them, then what? We exist running around this island without a single ally. The threat was not only going after them; they were also attacking us.

He nodded to Causes Safety Briefs to open up his ruck; the feather was immaculate, there were no bends, or any part of the feather was out of place. This was the first chance we had to notice that the feather was pure white. It was impossible; the owls where I grew up normally have shades of black and brown in them. The glass out of another pouch was clearly broken, but it was somehow perfectly smooth. When Ronan looked at the glass and the feather, a bit of color drained from his face.

Ronan: "Where did you get this feather and the piece of glass?"

I explained the story, even the event, with what we noticed in the village with Barra on how we killed the owls, and our first concern was to protect the people first. Ronan looked over the glass and the feather, very closely at both as if to examine it like it was an unknown material. He nodded along with the story as he was tapping in tune to a song at a concert.

Ronan: "This feather, I think you even noticed; no natural bird has this type of a feather. No natural animal would have this pigment; it's a divine being from the gods. This piece of glass you presented was not made by mortal hands; not even a master craftsman could come close to this level of perfection. Just who is behind this and why? I fear you brought more questions than answers to me. I shall have to pour over the books I have and reach out to my colleagues."

I nodded and relayed this back to the sergeant.

Ronan quickly shut his book and pointed at another one; he frantically flipped through the thick vellum pages. The books were made of animal skin and illuminated with wonderful colors, and one could get lost in the art itself. That moment of lightning struck him, and a sudden idea hit him. He lept off his bed and desk. The books sprawled all over the floor.

Ronan: "There is something you are missing from this story, MacDermott, I think you and I need to talk alone."

I relayed this to the sergeant. He rounded up Murray and the others, and they went back to the Hostel. It would be hard to get other information when your only translator is being questioned. Also, there doesn't seem to be an ancient Gaelic to English dictionary. With them leaving the room, Ronan went into Doctor mode.

Ronan: "There is something clearly bothering you, I can tell. You look like you haven't slept in a few weeks."

Myself: "That is true." I told him as much as I could. I could tell he was an honest man who wished no ill will on most people.

He nodded, "There is still something you are not telling me. I can tell it is a deep weight on your shoulders."

Myself: "Well, I had suffered a deep breakup before coming here."

What was interesting about the druids was that they firmly believed that mental health could impact physical health and vice versa. They were right.

Ronan: "So you have been burying it and crawling inside a bottle. Son, that is no way to live your life. These things are the worst pain; if you let it fester, it is a worse fate than death. I could tell you all the sorts of lies that people say like it gets easier. It only does if you start making the effort and that first step and beyond. I can only guide you towards the first step, but you gotta make it."

I nodded.

He continued. "Is she here?"

I replied, "No."

Ronan: "Then why are you letting her live rent-free and destroying your heart and mind?"

Myself: "She was the first one, the one I thought I'd spend my forever with."

Ronan: "It might have been the idea that her was your forever; you got to see the real her before it was too late."

Myself: "I explained the dear John letter to him."

Ronan nodded along and, when done, said, "I see sending a message to you while at war is one of the worst things one can do to the heart. Let me offer you some advice; if the only happy things she brings you are memories, it is over."

Myself: "I nodded; there was a weight that came off my shoulders."

Ronan: "If you want to continue to talk, please let me know. I can lend an ear and help."

Myself: "I would like that very much."

Ronan: "I would be happy to help you. I have seen your future, and I promise there are great things in it. Please send Murray back; he's going to be late to lose his daily game of Mitchell."

In the last part of that line, he laughed, and you could see the humor light up in his eyes. I made it back to the hostel in brighter spirits. I knocked on the hostel door, which was opened by Edwards. He beamed that it was nice to see you. That means we can plan and explore the city.

The sergeant called me aside, "So, how did the conversation with Ronan go."

I told him the entire conversation, leaving out nothing as I did before.

Sergeant concluded, "So I think I got whoever is behind this. They are going after people going through some sort of trauma. Dude, I am sorry you went through that."

Myself: "I am sorry I did not tell you about this earlier. I thought you would have thought less of me."

Sergeant: "Heck no, being a squid, you are doing pretty dang good. You're not a devil dog, but you are hanging with us. I was worried you would be as incompetent as that Ensign."

We both laughed at that; Ensign Browne would have been crying because he was set up in the hostel. No cell phone reception. It was a nice way to break the ice. After the laughter died down, we all huddled around a makeshift map that was the table. We started to draw with a grease pencil the outline of what we knew. One of the knives was designated as the Ashtabula. We had a cup in the city and a bit of cloth in the village.

Sergeant Buford: "We think we know what brings in the owls; they do not like sorrow, and they are people going through trauma."

Doc looked at us with a murderous stare, "I hope none of you are going through that right now. I'm not trained for that sort of stuff."

I think Doc could have scared the trauma out of people. He truly was a giant of a man.

Myself: "Doc, if anyone can do that, Ronan should be able to help with it."

Doc: "I am guessing the fish is how you know all this; honestly, I am not sure if that is a blessing or a curse?"

I smiply nodded and with that, we huddled around and decided to explore the city. There were many buildings, people bustling about, and farmers headed out to tend to their farms for the day. Just like the village, everyone had their own dog; most of these dogs were really tall, had wiry coats, and were very lanky-looking. These were clearly Irish wolfhounds. This breed goes back a long time. There are no longer wolves in Ireland. I would have to guess these gentle giants have something to do with it. They were mostly friendly and docile, making them perfect family dogs.

There were a bit more merchants in the city than in the village; there were people making weapons, candles, armor, furniture, clothing, and even a guy who would offer to make chariots. For that vendor, you were on your own for horses. There was a lot more than I had mentioned, but we were scouting out the city on our way out to explore the lands around the city. We were not going off the roads as much as we wanted to.

It was an obvious observation that having to stay on the roads was annoying my Marine Comrades. The signs were still very similar. However, we went the other direction, north, away from the city instead. This was a much darker of path. The trees seemed to get angrier as we went along. The woods started to get wetter, and the dry land areas started to have bridges growing between them. It also got a little bit foggy.

Along the way, we saw lights dance; the path along the King's Road was difficult to tell at points, with missing signs and bridges that would need some urgent repair in the next few days. The dancing lights would switch between blues and greens, flicking and dancing like someone was juggling them. In the distance, you could see a house.

The wind seemed to whisper, "Tayg, oh, how I have missed you."

That voice was very familiar; it was very feminine and very longing. It was my ex, no doubt about it. Somehow, she was here. I could see her in the distance. She had that very cute girl-next-door look; she wore the same clothes as always: baggy sweatshirts and jeans, which always hid those feminine features. She shot me a come-hither glance with those sharp green eyes. The lights seemed to spin and glow around her; I could see the stars in her eyes.

She cooed, "I am sorry for what I did. Can we give it another try?"

I realized that this was not possible; there was no way she could be here with us on this dangerous trail. In the middle of nowhere, in a hut. She always hated my last name and asked me to change it when we got married.

We started to get closer to her, and I yelled, "Hit the deck! Frag out!"

I lobbed the grenade, and it bounced right at her feet. My comrades, whipped to their senses, did hit the ground, and at that moment, she had curiously picked up the grenade to get a closer glimpse. I remember that when we went over grenades, the sergeant told me, "When the pin is pulled, Mr. Grenade is no one's friend."

The thing pretending to be my ex was taught her final lesson from Mr. Grenade. It rocked her world forever. There was nothing left of her. Just a crater. This seemed to get all of us snapped back to reality.

Sergeant Buford: "What in the Marine Corps was that? Everyone alright, check for holes?"

Everyone checked, and we were all right. We were just a little jarred and hopefully fully back to reality.

Myself: "Did you guys see what I saw? I think I saw my ex."

I described what my ex looked like. Each person disagreed, saying it was a woman who had either tried to seduce them or an ex had ripped out their heart. Well, on a positive note, it was not going to terrorize us or anyone else any longer. After we realized this, we saw a small mountain of bones on the shore where the hut was and could smell the decay of flesh. It was decided amongst us to burn down the hut and respectfully bury the remains.

We headed along the trail for a bit longer, the trail slowly transformed from a swamp to a forested clearing. This seemed to be a perfect place to set up camp for the evening. The clearing was void of any people. However, as we set up, others started to slowly get to the same campsite. They pulled up in a rather colorful wagon. They sat out a fire and started cooking, and music wafted over towards where we were sitting. They seemed to have that level of friendliness that was a little bit unsettling. There was something else a little off about them instantly offering food, drink, and just about anything else. I motioned to Sergeant Buford. I wanted to talk to him.

Myself: "Sergeant, I think there is something off about the guests near us. I would highly suggest not accepting anything from them, food or drink included."

They came over to our camp, offering food and drink. What I could see was a male and a female. They both had pointed ears and wore very bright colors that somehow blended in with the environment. Their hair was not natural colors; the males had mostly red, with light blue and purple swirling in. The female had purple hair swirled in green and orange colors.

Strange man: "It is a wonderful evening, fellow traveler, don't you think? It would be nice to share in some hospitality and company."

Myself: "Yes, the weather is rather nice here, it is rather calm. No, thank you for the hospitality. We have had a long day and wish to retire for the evening. We have to set out and travel a great distance in the morning.."

Strange man: "We do have a wagon and can offer to take you closer to where you need to go."

Myself: "No, thank you. We would appreciate walking and getting good air."

Strange man: "Suit yourself; if you change your mind, please let me know."

With that, they left our little camp. Our camp had no lights. We sat around joking and telling stories. We then did our nightly watch with the guests nearby. Nothing of note happened, just birds singing and their campfire and music playing on my watch. From what I could observe, there were a few people who joined their camp.

Chapter 7
Travelers

In the morning, we woke up to breakfast, MRE, coffee, and their wagon, which was missing. We took a closer look at where their camp was, and nothing was there. There were no remains of a fire; the only remains were of the people who visited. They looked like they had been dead for a long while. We quickly broke camp, respectfully buried the bodies, and moved on.

As we walked away, it dawned on me these were the fair folk, the fae, or as some might reference them, the fairies. Both my memories and the ones I got from the fish screamed dangerous getaway. Run far and run fast in the other direction.

It was morning twilight, one of those magical moments each day; the night was just about ready to give up its control of the world, and the sun was just waking up. The other time was twilight. At this moment, PFC

Williams pointed out that one of our lovely owl friends was flying away from the direction of the city. We followed the owl until it just seemed to vanish off the road. We stayed along the road until about the next nightfall, when it opened to a village. This village, at a distance, looked similar to the first village we saw. At a distance is the only way it looked similar to the other village.

The village itself was empty; there was nothing but statues, and you could smell the rotting food in each house. Every house and hut's doors were opened. It was like the statues lived in the town and just stopped moving. All of the people and the dogs were turned into statues. It was eerily quiet, with no birds, bugs, or other sounds. On the way in, PFC Williams pointed out a statue that looked like it was headed into town. This statue, like the others, was very detailed; it was Connal.

As we set up camp at the end of the village. Sergeant Buford started sketching out a rough design of the village. You could see that this was getting to all of us. We were the kind of people who rushed into danger, the ones who were supposed to bump in the night. After a bit of silence that seemed to drag on for an eternity. Sergeant Buford spoke up.

Sergeant: "This place is about the worst we've seen. We need to do an intel dump, and everyone needs to share what we know so far."

Myself: "The owls seem to be snow white; that threw off our druid friend Ronan. If what we showed him made him react that way, it must be something big."

Causes Safety Briefs chimed in, "We need to set a trap for one of these owls. See if we can figure anything else out on how to deal with this situation."

Williams: "Well, it seems they are attracted to sorrow and trauma."

Edwards: "This place is barren of anyone here at all; it seems some might have been caught in the crossfire." He pointed over towards Connal.

Connal seemed like such a happy-go-lucky person, very nice and polite. It seemed impossible he would have been caught up in this. It kind of made my heart sink a little to see him in that state. I think it angered the rest of us.

Edwards continued, "Sergeant, I noticed something interesting near Connal. We might want to check it out."

With that, we continued along the road. Edwards was not wrong; along the road, we found a chariot. Both of the horses were frozen in mid-run. The Charioteer was frozen trying to drive the chariot. The warrior was in the process of throwing his spear, still grasped in his hand. One of those jars was on the tip of the spear; it was tangled around the tip. The bottle, upon closer investigation, had a swirling sprinkling of smoke that would angrily swirl within the jar. Causes Safety Briefs reached out to grab the jar, threw it on the ground, and smashed it with a tomahawk. The swirls angrily swirled out of the jar, up towards the warrior's mouth and nose. With that, the stone slowly turned to cloth flesh and armor as the world's colors slowly crept into his form.

He roared, and the spear flew. "Take that, you dreaded beast."

He braced for impact and leaned heavily back, falling off the chariot. His body still believed he was moving forward as fast as the chariot could go. Doc and I ran over to him to check to see if he was alright. He clearly landed on his arm. Doc went to set the man's arm. He had the professional warrior mentality about him, was seasoned, and saw more than a few fights. He was athletically built. He had very bright black hair that was longer than our uniform regulations would allow. The lucky guy could also have a beard. The old man still hadn't relaxed the uniform regulations. That request looked hopeless since MR2 could quickly crank out surprisingly good razor blades with the cauldron.

I stopped about 2 yards from the warrior and calmly said, "Good warrior, we are only here to help. It looks like you had a bad fall. We are travelers from a far-off land. We brought one of our doctors with us; he can look at your injuries."

The warrior grunted and tried to push himself up with the injured hand. It seemed to be a little off. Doc moved up to him and got to setting the bone. He motioned for us to get the right sticks and branches to make a splint. Doc went to work setting the bone for the warrior, got it set into place, and to the warrior's credit, the pain yell was not earth-shattering. It went in with a snap. Doc told us it was not the worst break he's seen.

Doc: "QM2, tell him to keep it easy on the arm for a while."

Myself to the warrior, "Our healer said not to use your arm for a while, but we need to get you back to a place with better medical attention."

Warrior to me: "Thank you for your aid, I am not sure what happened, but I am famished. Do you have any food, and can one of you get my spear?"

Edwards and Williams started to look around for his spear. As they did that, I dug into my Ruck; I was able to dig out one of the MREs, and I dug out the one that would be considered the best, hands down, by many Chili mac.

Myself: "Good warrior, may I have your name? My name is Tayg McDermott,? I will work on food for you. The food is from our land. I promise it is not bad and will not kill you. It is very filling food."

He watched with eyes alight and curious as I went through activating the heat for the MRSs. To be honest, it still amazes me that this works. That we can get hot food without fire. I was amazed the cauldron could crank these out for us with little effort. I was told by MR2 that it could make just about anything. However, it had a one-track mind. You had to tell it what to make, and it could not be interrupted. As the chili mac was finished, I showed him how to eat it, and he went to town; he sat on the edge of his chariot and balanced the MRE bag on his thigh to eat. I made sure he had something to drink as well. You could tell he had a long day and traveled far. Sergeant Buford was near us. You could tell the warrior was sizing us up, as did the king. The more I looked at the warrior, the more familiar he looked. It looked like he was a very young Donegal. No flipping way. Sergeant Buford connected the same dots I did. It was pretty easy to do, like the kids' placemat at a diner.

After draining the beverage in one swig, he cleared his throat and licked the MRE bag clean. "I am Cormacc McDonngal, son of King Donngal McGreggor."

Myself: "We just came from the city where you live and were trying to scout up north. We are trying to find out what is causing this." I waved around at the village whose residents had been turned to stone.

He simply nodded and said, "We pointed at the charioteer and horses, who were tasked with checking out the village to the north after Connal did not come back. He normally goes up there to see if they need any goods from the city or his village. We all sort of trade back and forth, and Connal's father will arrange for goods from far off.

Myself: "Interesting, we think it might be best to go back, get you medical aid, head back to the city, compare notes, and we should head back to our people."

Cormac simply nodded. "Wise plan, I hate to leave my friend and my horses. But I do not think they will be going anywhere soon. It is nice to know that this process can be reversed."

Then we helped him gather his gear, organized our stuff, and offered to take some of his. It was clear we needed to get him medical attention. Doc set the bone, but we needed to get him to a doctor, and staying here was not a safe idea. It was roughly mid-day by the time we got done scouting the village. We moved at a decent pace, and doc kept an eagle eye on the warrior.

We made it to the camp we were at last night around the same time. Thankfully, the same people weren't there. The bodies were oddly gone, too. Still unsettling. We set up camp. Cormac thought it was weird; we kept quiet, light, no fires. We talked a bit, and then I told him we would take the night in shifts, making sure one person was awake. He offered to help, but Doc quickly shot it down. He reluctantly went to sleep. Doc offered to stand watch as well, but the sergeant did not have any of that either.

I offered to take the first watch again, but nothing happened on my watch. When I got comfortable, I fell asleep, and I dreamed again, or it could have been a dream. It thankfully was not the Vegas dream, not the dear John letter, the rage workout that followed. It was the redhead again. She could move. I could see her fighting alone in my dreams; she moved so gracefully, and the sword she used was like an extension of her beautiful arm. The slightest draw of that blade looked fatal. She danced a graceful dance of death; I could see those silver eyes shine with a vengeance,

I could hear her say, "Hold on, you can do this. My heart is yours. I will do this for you, and I know that you will do this for me. I know this because your heart is mine."

Chapter 8
Fight or Flight

I woke up to greet the day. We offered up another meal for Cormac. We ate our breakfast; it was funny watching him drink coffee for the first time. He was clearly caffeine-high after that first cup. I had to explain to him what coffee is as we made it back towards the city.

We made it back around nightfall, and we were greeted by the warriors, those who lived in the village. People were very happy to see Cormac. A lovely lady with chestnut brown hair and green eyes. She was very stunning and raced out to greet Cormac; she raced into his arms, and he caught her with his left arm. She gave him a very concerned look, and then they disappeared into the crowd. We made it back to the Kings Estate.

King McGreggor: "Thank you for bringing my son back. I am sorry about the village to the north, Connal, and his driver. I feel terrible for the horses, too."

Myself: "Your Majesty, this is what any good person would do. We have a few ideas on what is causing this and how it happens but not where it is coming from and who is doing this."

I went on to explain the owls, showing him the feather that we had from the remains. He was clearly deep in thought. I then went into the jars and saw how they looked perfectly. There was no seam on them. The smoke in the jar seemed to flow with anger; it swirled around with sparks. Ronan was with McGregor, also deep in thought. They were holding on to every word I was saying. I summed up what we went through over the past two days. How Doc had rendered medical aid to Cormac's arm and how he would need to see a doctor since our doc did not have access to the right equipment to make sure it was done right. Ronan promised he would look at the arm; after we compared notes, Ronan sighed and started to try to decipher this annoying mystery.

Ronan: "Ok, what I have so far is these owls are going after people who have gone through some serious grief, anger, or a combination of the two. The jar seems to take everything from them, and they are left as stone statues."

Myself: "Ronan, that sounds about right. The owls can be hurt, and if the Jar is shattered, the person does come back. We were able to do that with

Cormac and Barra. If the jar is shattered, the energy in the jar goes back into the person. When that happens, they will no longer be statues and will seem to have all of their memories."

Ronan: "That is truly fascinating. I shall have to look Cormac over to see if he is all right, medically and mentally. Our medical care might be a bit different from yours."

He was right. Our Doc was not trained in the mental health part, just the physical; that didn't mean that doc would not be above yelling at you to get your dome looked at.

Ronan looked at one of the Servers in McGreggors' employ, "Please go get Cormac. I wish to speak to him."

McGreggor had looked at us, "I cannot thank you enough for saving my son and continuing to try to fix this problem."

Myself: "Your Majesty, it is the least we can do; whatever is doing this can also go after us."

I explained how this happened to one of our sailors using what I knew.

McGreggor: "I see, this is truly something we must fight together then. I would be honored to have you stay at my estate. Please rest for the next few days."

Cormac had entered, and Ronan looked at his arm; he gently looked and was able to verify that Doc did set it right and perfectly. I had relayed this to Doc, and if you looked closely at Doc's eyes, he was ecstatic.

We were guided to our rooms, and the servants guided us to the same rooms as last time. We had baths drawn and clothes set out for us again. The servants had offered to clean our clothes. I nodded to avoid offending the king, ensuring we had everything we needed in our rooms. I stepped into the water; it was lined with lavender, sage, and other herbs. I drifted off, and I dreamed again of the lovely lady with the hair of burnished copper. I could hear music playing slowly. It was almost like that slow romantic synth wave from the 80's movies. Again, we were slowly driving the chariot to this music. I could almost smell the fields. I could almost hear the birds. It felt so real; my heart yearned for her. I could almost feel the warmth of her hand in mine. She reached up to touch my shoulder. I jolted back to reality with a hand on my shoulder.

One of the servants said, "My lord, your clothes are ready; we have already washed your clothes, and they will be drying in your room. "She left the room and closed the door behind her. I quickly dressed, already missing this lovely woman from my dreams. I headed out to the feasting area.

The king's table was something to behold. The king did not skimp out on any good food. It was similar to what we had before, but there were some changes. Some olives must have been imported with cheeses, wonderful bread, pork cooked in honey, and beer that was so soft that it could be cut with a spoon. A very light beer was flowing in each cup. This beer was honeyed with sage. It was refreshing; you could tell it would not get you inebriated. The warriors chatted, talked, and started swapping stories around the table. Food was passed around. The smells of oils, food, turf burning, and beer were all wonderful; it was something I did not want to stop. Ronan was there, too. He was enjoying the stories as well as telling more than a few of his own. He looked at me and offered to allow another warrior to take his place to be the next storyteller.

Ronan: "Tayg, something on your mind?"

Myself: "Yeah, would we be able to talk for a bit."

Ronan: "Sure, let's go outside for a bit."

Myself: "Sounds good. Would anyone be worried or offended?"

Ronan: "Of course not; you are among equals here. Besides, I am a doctor, if you forgot." He said that last part teasingly, in that kindly grandfather kind of way.

I followed him out. I told Sergeant Buford I was going to get some air and talk to Ronan for a bit. He nodded. The Marines started to pantomime some of their stories to the Warriors, and they went back and forth. There was a lot of laughter between them.

The crisp night air hit my nostrils; it was almost intoxicating. The only way it could have been better was at sea. At sea, you could see every star; the ocean stretched as far as your eyes could see. It was otherworldly. I mean, here it was, too, just in a different way. This was a different culture, a different place.

Ronan: "You have a different look about you. It's like that sadness eating you is gone, but there is something different now."

Myself: "Yeah, I don't think about it too much."

I tried to explain the entire situation. The Vegas situation, the love that treated me badly, how I took it out on the woman in Vegas, and I talked about my new dreams, the lovely redhead.

Ronan: "You are an interesting man, Tayg. There seems to never be a dull moment with you. I am glad you escaped being inside a bottle, and grief did not eat you alive, nor did your reputation be tarnished. Clearly, the woman who destroyed your heart was wrong; the blonde was not a good fit; she seemed to be the bad type of crazy. What you need is the good type of crazy."

Myself: "I think I follow. However, what about the redhead from my dreams?"

Ronan: "Oh, that's the good type of crazy; she's real. My boy, you have what's called lovesickness. You want her, you crave her, you need her. She's the right kind of crazy, and she's real. I can tell I can see it in your eyes. She doesn't seem like a dream or unrealistic."

Myself: "Do you know who she is?"

Ronan: "Yes, I believe so; however, we need to focus on the battle in front of us. You cannot go chasing after her in this state. Not with those blasted owls trying to turn us all into stone."

Myself: "You are right." My shoulders slumped. I was so close to figuring out who she was and how to find her.

Ronan: "I know it's not right; it's not fair. The things in life that are worth it seldom are easy, my boy."

Ronan, in his infinite Grandpa wisdom, was right. Pressing this issue was not going to make her appear in front of me. I thanked him; I had to set this aside. I had to do this for her. I had to do this for me. For if I were to fall, who was going to find her, who was going to cherish her, who was going to return those emotions? It might not feel right at the moment, but people were counting on us. The people in the city, the people in the villages around this kingdom. Not to mention our ship and our shipmates. I did not want to let them down. I wanted to prove I could do this; I did not want to let down and abandon Sergeant Buford, Causes Safety Briefs, Doc Mongo, PFC Edwards, Williams,, and Private Murray. Murray, who lost his hearing, I wanted to put the hurt on those who wished us harm on his behalf. That was the right thing to do, she would understand. She was clearly capable.

Ronan put his hand on my shoulder as a grandfather would. He needed to say nothing more and could already understand what was in my eyes. You could tell that he really wanted to help and tell me the name of the lady from my dreams. But he knew what events would unfold if he did. I did not hate him; it was clearly the right thing to do.

I went back to my room with the decorations. The incense was light, and I drifted off to sleep. I dreamt again of the lady who held my heart, the lovely maiden with red hair. We fought back and forth again, and we kept switching the same sword back and forth. The sword was light to the touch, struck with blinding speed, and looked like your normal sword but moved like a rapier. The carnage we inflicted. Those the sword bit were misshapen lumps of men. They looked hideous, like a drunk person tried to sculpt people from a dream eons ago. Each one was misshapen in a different way; some had bubbling lesions on their skin, just waiting to burst. Some had one bigger eye than the other, some had more or less digits than the others, and some of their fingers were oddly bent and shaped. However, they moved with a speed that misled their deformities. We could keep up; she had even tried to caress my hand while passing the blade. With that touch, I woke up greeted by the sunrise and the songs of the birds.

I greeted everyone in the common area; this was the same area where the king would hold feasts and business. My uniform was clean to the point of looking brand new. Our food was just as good as last night; it was plenty of dried meats, cheeses, breads, and an oatmeal-like dish. We had honey nearby, fruits, and plenty of honeyed water.

I made myself another cup of coffee as I dug into our breakfast. My fellow marines looked happy yet tired; you could tell they were up late last night. You could also tell there was a bit of drinking, too. They all composed themselves rather well. We sat around, actually talking and laughing at everything we went through.

Sergeant Buford: "We will have to head back to the ship; it is good to see Murray in good spirits."

Murray could hear us decently; it was nice to see that Ronan's medication was helping. It was nice to be able to meet with good and honorable people. Ronan seemed like a good person. I think we were getting a good rapport with the city and the king. Clearly, it was a good idea to check back in with the ship. We ended up staying one more day at the King's estate. I did not dream, I was able to actually get a full night's sleep uninterrupted. We chatted with the warriors at the king's estate. I translated their stories back to the Marines and their stories back to the warriors there. A fun time was had by all. Cormac was there, his hand still in the sling.

Our way back to the ship was unhampered by anything. No vicious horse monsters on the beach, no weird banshees, or anything else. We signaled the ship off in the stance, and later on, our normal boat came to pick us up. BM2 still had that cigarette in his mouth. It seemed to dance to the beat of the music playing on his radio.

We made it back to the seas next to calm; they were only about 1 to 3 feet tall. To tell, you have to watch the white caps and watch them go up and down. It helps to have a point of reference to see how tall the waves can get. It's one of those things that come in time, and your eyes have to have that experience of what to look for and how to look. The boat was moored to the gangplank, and we walked up. Requested to come aboard and saluted the flag, then the officer at the top of the gangplank.

It was LTJG Jorgenson at the top. He beamed, "Welcome back, I hope you have had some success out there."

Myself: "Yes, Sir, it was quite that and then some."

LTJG Jorgenson: "Well, I remember an old curse. May you live in interesting times."

Myself: "I would be inclined to agree with that saying, sir."

LTJG Jorgenson: "Carry on, QM2, Carry on, marines, the skipper is going to want to see you."

Myself: "Understood, sir; thank you again for earlier."

LTJG Jorgenson: "No problem, QM2."

With that, I ended up going past the medical hallway. They had four tiny rooms for all of the medical care. They had no x-ray machine, just really a few pieces of equipment, a medical-grade tiny dryer. I ended up making my way up past the mess decks; the same group was still playing that same game with the weird dice and books. I made it back up to the old man's estate. I looked scruffy by military standards, but I figured he would want to know our report as soon as we got back.

I made it back up to his room, knocked, and asked permission to enter.

Skipper: "Enter."

There were plenty of books and pages on his desk; some opened up on random pages, and many were hard-backed books, some notebooks. There was a cigar in his hand and a whiskey glass in the other hand. The dark amber liquid slowly and hypnotically swayed, appearing to dance with the rocking of the ship. This was clearly whiskey and possibly some of the stuff way above my pay grade. His cigar had earthly and mild tones to it. As the aroma gently wafted in the estate room. As before, I did not step on the ship's seal in the center of the room. I entered and stood at attention.

Skipper: "At ease, QM2."

Myself: "Permission to speak freely?"

Skipper: "Permission granted."

Myself: "Thank you, sir." With that, I stood at ease. I placed my feet shoulder-width apart with my hands behind my back.

Skipper: "Please relax, QM2, and have a seat. Did you want something to drink?"

Myself: "Sir, water would be fine."

Skipper: "Very well. Help yourself."

There was a pitcher with ice water near his desk. I got myself some water and ice. It was oddly refreshing to have just water without anything in it. I noticed there was another person in the room. It was one of the crypto techs. The people at that rate, called ICs for short, were the ones who decrypted and sent encrypted messages. Their office was very secretive. I was not cleared to be in their office, nor were they cleared to be in the chart house. In the military, you have security clearances for sensitive information, and this could be devastating or fatal if it were to fall into the right hands. There are different levels, and just because you have the right level does not mean you need to know the information. I tend to follow the philosophy the less I know, the better off I am when it comes to things like troop movement, upcoming plans, and anything similar.

IC guy: "QM2, nice to meet you, I have been reading your reports from both the chief's mess and the CO. I am a fan of what the Marines and you are doing so far. I have a ton of questions."

Skipper: "IC2 Reyes, just recording this will suffice for now."

Reyes: "Understood, sir, very sorry I got a bit carried away with excitement."

IC2 is clearly an inquisitive soul, one wanting to get to the center of every mystery. He's the type you could see in charge of a plethora of dusty tomes, knowledge gathered by others and cataloged by a system that only he could sort through. I started to relay the information to the skipper, and at times, IC2 would interrupt with around 20 questions per thing talked about. A brief example of this excruciating interview has been summarized below. If IC2 is reading this, I know your questions are from the best of intentions.

IC2: "QM2, how did you know that the lovely lady was a trap?"

Myself: "I am not sure it just seemed off. The person looked like someone I knew, and was in love with before this deployment. It felt odd that she was here. I did not bring her with me."

IC2: "So it was an instinct?"

Myself: "Yes, I think so. It just felt off to me something impossible."

IC2: "I see; what about the camp sergeant Buford stopped at? How did you know the people near you were not to be trusted?"

Myself: "The memories I got from the fish. I still do not understand that part."

IC2: "I want to know more about that fish. What else do you know about it?"

Skipper: "IC2, I know you have the best intentions, but please let QM2 finish; please let me ask the questions."

IC2: "Yes, sir, sorry, sir."

With that, IC2's shoulders slumped a little, and he eagerly got back to taking notes. I went back to talking about the campfire and the fey around the fire nearby. Why it was not wise to trust them, and that we ended up saving the king's son. However, elaborating on how just because it is the king's son does not mean he's in line for the throne. I advised the skipper on the hierarchy of their society, how colors are important, and how, when they are not fighting, they wear a decent amount of jewelry. I described their chariots, how they were very proud of their horses, and their pride in their horses equaled their care for them. The skipper nodded and took a puff of his cigar as I kept talking; he was deep in thought as he walked inside his estate room. His other hand contained the whiskey glass.

He always drank it with no ice. Something I could clearly respect. However, a little bit of ice can help accentuate the flavor and aroma. I reviewed the owls, the jars they held, and what we think causes people to turn to stone. We had killed more than a few of the owls, but we were no closer to figuring out who was sending them and why they were doing this.

Skipper: "Well done, QM2, I am glad you are out there with Sergeant Buford. Both of you are doing an outstanding job. I am glad both of you have done so well. It will be nice to eventually get more of the island mapped. We can possibly find a place to tie up to. Also, see if we can get some of the liberty we need. Everyone has clearly earned it. I agree with your initial assessments; we need to help the people out there first; we can manage with the caldron making us fuel; it's been interesting balancing bullets, equipment, and fuel. The old lady is doing rather well, and she's got a lot of fight in her, as does the crew."

With that, my chest swelled with pride; he was right. We found ourselves in a situation where there was no way to train us. This was not even in basic training; I can think about that, getting interviewed on this adventure just to have in battle stations (battle stations are the last test to see if you can make it in the navy; you are woken up randomly at night, have to get dressed and start running from station to station. All of the stations are based on historical events that happened in the Navy. One of the scenarios is trying to get injured people out of a ship that has started to sink). I smirked for just a second.

Skipper: "Something funny QM2?"

Myself: "Yes sir, I am thinking about what will happen if we need to prove this later on and if this training gets adapted."

I got an honest chuckle out of him; it was probably the first laugh I had ever witnessed coming from him.

Skipper: "Thank you, QM2, you got a point."

Myself: "Sir, you are welcome, I think that is all I have."

Skipper: "Very well dismissed; I think we are going to have to think about our next steps. We have some things going on on the ship. There was another attack on the ship. We think it was the same squid."

I could see where that could be a big problem; we normally had other ships with us. Having to be self-sufficient for everything has gotta make it rough. Every ship in the Navy is a bit different, and they all have different roles. We are supposed to only pick up marines, drop them off, and offer humanitarian aid, mail, or other supplies.

Myself: "Understood, thank you, sir."

With that, I left the Old Man's estate room. I went back down to the mess decks after talking to the old man. Evening chow was already over, and the mess decks were cleaned. At that moment, the TVs were getting ready to play the evening movies. Typically, we would get to see movies right after they left the theaters, but before one could purchase them to watch at home. If it wasn't a new movie, it was usually someone's favorite movie.

Now, others were playing games. The two that were usually played were poker and spades. There were the people who played Euchre. That was more my speed. It was a game more popular in Michigan and Ohio. Spades, I could never wrap my head around it, and poker kind of bored me. I liked the team effort of Euchre. I saw a few of the second classes playing cards.

BM2 Leblanc noticed me and nodded, "QM2, I need a Euchre partner. Are you available?"

I nodded, smirked, and walked over to the table where the other two were sitting. Now, I happen to be from Ohio (it felt like an unofficial sport in my home state), and I typically do not advertise it. I played a ton of euchre in high school, many times every day at lunch. On the other side of the table was both QM2 and QM3. I internally smirked; how ironic. Time to play the dummies and get them to eat some humble pie.

QM2 Moreli: "Looks like Leblanc found a partner; nice to see you show up. It's going to be Davidson and I as a team and Leblanc and you as a team."

Myself: "Seems fair; how many hands are we playing, and what game are we playing?" I said very naively.

Moreli: "We are playing Euchre, first one to 10 points." He proceeded to deal out the hand while terribly explaining the game. "Don't worry. I've got you covered the right way."

The game is played with a reduced deck, keeping the cards from 9 to ace. Each person would be dealt 6 cards. To the left, the dealer makes the first bid on how many hands the team believes they can wind for the round. It goes around the table until someone passes, or it goes around once. The winner chooses what cards will win. If high is chosen, Ace will be the high card. Now, if a suit is chosen, for example, hearts, the highest card will be called the right bar, the jack of hearts, and then the left bar jack of diamonds, then it will go from ace to 9 of hearts. A heart card, if the suit chosen (also called trump) will always win over any card from any other suit.

Now Moreli only told me about calling high or low, as he dealt. BM2 was to his left, so he bid 2, Davidson bid 3, I looked at my hand bidding 4, I had the jack of hearts, the queen of hearts, the nine of hearts, an ace of spades, and the king of hearts. I called hearts as trump. Moreli passed.

We played the hand, and between BM2 and I, we trounced them, getting four out of five hands. Thus getting us four points. We ended up winning the second round in a similar way, and in the last round, Moreli was going to bet us sodas. We had no alcohol, so sodas, smokes, or dip was usually used as a currency. I didn't smoke and still don't, so sodas it was.

I looked at BM2 and nodded. Myself: "Ok, whoever wins the most points next gets sodas from those who lose."

I heard Moreli laugh, and Davidson beamed a smile ear to ear. It was Leblanc's turn to deal; he dealt out the cards and looked at his hand.

Davidson: "3 diamonds."

I looked at my hand, Jack of Clubs, Jack of Spades, 9 of Spades, queen of Spades, and 10 of Spades. The odds of this are practically impossible. "5 Spades."

QM2: "Looks like you are playing alone."

Technically, he's wrong; you have to specify that you are going to shoot the moon and would be playing alone. I remember from my great-grandmother that the person calling points was supposed to do that. It's double points if you do, but you got to win all 5. But hey, I'll let it slide just to rub it in.

I played the right bar first; they played their highest club cards, then played the left bar, cleaned up the rest of their clubs, played the queen, they could not follow the club suit, played the 10, and lastly, the 9.

Myself: "Looks like we won, I'll take a cola."

BM2 smiled, "A cola sounds good, too; any kind of soda you didn't have to buy is a good soda."

It kind of felt good to trounce them so bad. I ended up taking my soda shaking BM2's hand, and he excused himself to go to the smoke deck (this was the authorized place to smoke). I excused myself and went over to see the people with the books and the dice. It was something fascinating. There didn't seem to be teams, and everyone had a few papers with them, the books, and the funny-looking dice. It was kind of an interactive story game. It seemed a little similar to what we were dealing with out there. There is no way we are in some silly book. I mentally pushed that away. They were in some sort of castle ruin, killing what they described as a filthy goblin that munched on pickled bugs and other nasty things. I drank the rest of the soda, put the can in the recycling, and went out to get some air. Those moments at sea, seeing all the stars, and being as quiet as possible are something. I remembered bioluminescence, and it always threw me off in the warmer waters. The effect happens when microscopic organisms are disturbed in the ship's wake. The phenomenon created a pink or orange glow at the wake of the ship, which always annoyed me. I know ships aren't known for being stealthy, but one can hope not to be seen.

I looked out over the water and let my mind just kind of relax. It was good to just let it wander, stretch, and think about nothing for a few minutes or so. Time just seemed to just not matter. There was Sergeant Buford. He let me be for a moment, then piped up.

Sergeant: "You might be onto something doing this? Not a bad way to just kind of let what's on your mind off for a moment, to reassess the situation."

Myself: "Yup, it's kind of nice, and it helps put things in perspective. What's important, what's not, and see the big picture. Besides, I like the salt air and seeing all the stars is a big bonus. I used to do this for a moment or two between recording positions on the bridge."

Funny, that felt like an eternity ago, not just 3 weeks ago. Clearly, that's not what I thought my life plan was; I mean, you don't plan trekking into a mythological land with marines, guns, and explosives.

Sergeant: "I can see what you mean by that. It wasn't on my list either. We got you a little something. It's not much, but you've done good for a squid."

He handed me a Velcro patch, and it said I drink caffeine and know things.

Myself: "I cannot thank you enough, I've had good teachers. I don't mind going back out there. We should have Murray back with us soon; we can get a bit closer to figuring out what's causing this problem."

With that, the ship got nudged in a different direction; it was like someone had wanted to play with it in the bathtub and push it in a direction it didn't want to go. The collision alarm went off.

Over the speaker, "All hands man your battle stations. Head up the port side and down the starboard side. Set condition Zebra."

This was the condition to secure (shut all watertight hatches). We were in a terrible situation; I had to race up to my bridge position. I nodded to the sergeant and raced to my position. I made it to my combat station and ensured the 60-caliber machine gun was locked, loaded, and ready to go. Out of the water, the longest limbs had reached out; this was a massive squid, and the arms easily reached almost a football field in length. They were trying to stretch around the ship, so I quickly put in my hearing protection and powered it on. The CWIS powered up and went to town; the device looked like a very angry robot from the *Star Wars* movies. When it went off, it sounded like gears grinding for longer than one should let them grind. I had a clear shot of one of the tentacles, and I went to town. I was working the 60 like a violin playing for a 50-piece orchestra, and this was my solo. This squid was getting hammered. The CWIS was designed to take down missiles, not really squids, but it did not care.

The CWIS turned and started to work its magic closer to the squid's bulbous head; it started to work toward the eyes, and one exploded with a rubbery pop. Goop rained on the deck. It smelled like a rotten dumpster fire at sea, and that fuel was nothing but burning dead fish. We all had focused on the head with everything we had, 50, 60 cal, CWIS towards its head. We had turned its head into Swiss cheese. This must have been the same squid; you could tell it had tons of scars.

I could see from the Deck Cause's safety briefs that he was running towards it with his ax and cutting through one of the tentacles. He was making pretty good progress. It was clear the wounds it had received were mortal. It kept trying to flail, trying to fight; however, messing with squids and marines was a bad decision. We just want to play cards, listen to our music, drink coffee, and dream of the next beer in peace. Mess with that, and you will not have a good day. The Marines are a different breed. They are like that angry dog you don't mess with. They worked the gun mounts with the precision of a master painter. Mayhem was their medium, and lead and explosives were their tools. There wasn't much left of the squid, just a bloody stump where the head would be a few tentacles and some warm barrels.

Over the 1MC, one could hear "Ceasefire, Ceasefire," followed by the trill of a bosun pipe and a very familiar voice.

"Crew, this is your Captain speaking; good job. I do not think we will be dealing with that squid again. Please stand down from General Quarters and clean up your stations. Tomorrow is going to be a holiday routine; you've all earned it."

You could have heard a pin drop after that, and then we tried to clean up the squid guts as best as we could. The CWIS went through it like it was chucked into a wood chipper. It was almost impossible to clean it off the ship without the fire hoses. Lucky for me, my station was covered, and most of the guts had already slid off after the fire crew had sprayed it off. I took a mental note of who was doing the fire duty, heck I was making a lot more as a second class. It was almost double to be honest. I went to buy everyone on the fire team a soda and a big bag of jerky. I started handing out the jerky and the sodas. Nods and a pat on the back from a slimy hand here or there, and an offer to clean off my uniform with the hose on a low setting. We got the ship cleaned up pretty quickly. There was some laughing and goofing off. We trudged into bed, watches were relieved without interruptions, and the crew cycled through the day getting some sleep.

Not even the XO wanted to fight the captain of the crew to get a break. Our XO was, at times, the bad guy. Usually, he was the one who was the anti-fun officer. There always had to be one, and sometimes both were that way. There had to be a balance to the force, as some of the more nerdy people on the crew say. I thought of moving my belongings to the Marines' berthings. I made sure all the marines had bottom racks, and we worked to ensure our spaces were well taken care of and maintained. I got in touch with the Damage Controllmen (DC for short, these were the guys who were our firefighters and helped out with keeping the ship in one piece if it got hit. They worked with the Hull technicians on everything but the plumbing) and trained them on using what we called fart bags. They came in these orange boxes about the size of a lunch box. They got the hang of them, and even more than a few of them even started training to help out the DCs with firefighting if needed. The crew was coming together rather solidly. We were shaping up to be a force not to be trifled with. Gunny had motioned to me that he wanted to talk, so we went to another space with a door that could be shut. He had one of the privates stand outside the door to make sure anyone but Sergeant Buford, him, or myself were permitted to enter.

Gunny: "So QM2, what happened out there."

I explained everything, with Sergeant Buford filling in, agreeing, and providing his side of the story."

Gunny: "I see, so Murray is almost back in action. I think I want to meet this Ronan guy and thank him. We try to set a trap for those owls. They seem to try to fly closer to the ship but then fly back. I don't think they can fly this far out. The ship is doing alright right now, MR2 Sutton is able to keep up. From what I have gathered, he's juggling between projects to keep the ship running."

Sergeant: "We got to figure out where those owls are coming from. If we can find that out and find out who is behind it, we can put a stop to this."

Gunny: "Isn't that the question everyone wants the answer to. That village, with everyone turned to stone, might be a good starting spot. That might be ground zero."

Myself: "I think you're onto something, Gunny. How do you trap one or figure out where it is coming from, though?"

Sergeant: "That's something I've been trying to think of."

There was a knock at the door, and the private tasked with guarding the door said, "Corporal Mcgee said that he's here to see you, Gunny. He said it's urgent."

Gunny: "Ok, send him in. I think we might need his craziness."

The door opened then closed, Causes Safety Briefs entered. He had a mad look in his eyes, a twinkle of mayhem.

Causes Safety Briefs: " Gunny, I think I know what we could do. It's similar to duck hunting, and we know what it wants. We just build a duck blind, make some decoys, and use crying sounds to lure them. We would need to see what direction they are coming from."

We nodded, it made sense, it was a good plan, if anyone could cook up something to sound like crying MR2 could, we just needed to make something look like it was alive to take the bait. It was a good plan, solid and simple. We proceeded to draw out the plan on paper with pencils, a very rough map of the village. Trying to see the angles the owls could come from, we had a mental picture of the landscape and got a good idea of what we could do. Over the next few hours we made plans, picked apart every detail, everything that could go wrong. The door never budged in the time we planned. We looked at the results and were satisfied.

With that we knocked on the door and the private opened the door we left and went to the mess decks. I told Gunny about the cards last night, he laughed and patted me on the back. He headed to the chief's mess

Gunny "Before you go you both need to head up to the chief's mess after evening chow. They want you there by 1800. The chiefs want to hear what else you have found out, I think running this plan by them might be a good idea."

Sergeant: "Sounds good, thanks Gunny."

Myself: "Gunny, can I have a word with you before you leave."

Gunny: "Sure thing, QM2."

Sergeant Buford left at that moment, off to get lunch and when the door shut.

Myself: "Gunny, thanks for standing up for me with my previous LPO."

Gunny: "I hate people like that QM2, I hate lazy bullies. He was going to mess with your gear and belongings so we moved your stuff and I figured you wouldn't mind. Trust me the chiefs are getting sick of him and the skipper isn't a fan. You're doing good and any officer or senior NCO would be an idiot to not have you in their direct command. Son, you are doing pretty good being thrown into something entirely new."

Myself: "Gunny, thanks I'll try to not let you down."

Gunny: "Just do your best. I'm off to get lunch before chow is over. "

With that, he opened the water tight door and went off to the chief's mess.

I secured the chairs, shut the lights off and closed the door.

Chow was nothing special, it seemed to be getting better than the terrible stuff we had before leaving our home port. I wasn't complaining, we seemed to have chili mac, there were carrots, peas and other veggies on the side. The crew seemed to be in better spirits and the stories were already getting crazier. I ended up sitting near a few of the other Second classes on the mess decks, we kind of made our own section at a few of the other tables.

Eating on a ship at sea is a different experience, the ship is rocking so you need to ensure your food stays on your plate and table. You have to have both of your arms up to the elbow on the sides of the plate; you only lift your arms up above that section. You hunch your back over a little bit. If you have a drink or soup you only fill it up ⅔ of the way nothing more.

You eat quickly since the entire crew needs to eat (our ship has 250 Navy and around 50 Marines so 300 people needed to eat most were lower enlisted then you had the officers and chiefs with their own mess), people start to give you dirty looks if you stay too long. There is light conversation on the mess decks until the chow hours are over.

We talked quickly about the previous night. Some of the second classes wanted to chat after evening chow, I told them I might be able to, I had to be at the chief's mess after evening chow. After lunch I was going to get some rack time and get caught up on sleep. After I was done eating, I went back to the berthing and climbed into the bottom rack. I was given the one in the back of the berthing, it was rather dark and perfect. I shaved in our head (head is the navy term for bathroom) and returned to my bunk. I got my music and fell asleep.

No crazy dreams, no redhead, just peaceful sleep. I oddly did not dream of anything that time, my alarm went off and woke me from my slumber. I felt a bit refreshed, so I went to the gym with plenty of time showered then went to evening chow. I sat with some of the other second classes again, sergeant Buford was with me too. We started light ribbing and talking about other things. I had a bit of time to kill so I went outside to get some air before heading to the chief's mess.

I always enjoyed nautical twilight, this is when the sun is somewhere between 6 degrees and 12 degrees below the horizon, it's that time between day and night. I like the nautical daylight but with a cup of coffee unless I get some rack time in. I looked at my watch and it was time to make it to the chief's mess. One never makes a chief wait.

I made it to the chief's mess. The door had the artwork of all three ranks of chief, just the anchor is a chief, an anchor with one star is a senior chief, and an anchor with two stars is a master chief. I knocked on the door.

Myself: "Permission to enter?"

A muffled voice from the other side of the door responded, "Permission granted."

I opened the door, some of the chiefs were finishing up their food, others some were sitting down playing cards and the rest were just chatting.

HMCS Puletua: "At ease QM2, please have a seat. get something to drink if you want."

Myself: "Thank you chief, I think water will be fine. It's weird out there they do not really have clean water."

HMCS Puletua: "Interesting, I would love to hear more about that."

Myself: "I would be happy to talk about that, and their medicine, it is quite fascinating considering they do not have microscopes, or an x-ray machine."

HMCS: "That is fascinating, we'll talk later, the rest of the chiefs will be arriving soon."

Myself: "I would love to Senior Chief."

With that I got a seat, the rest of the chiefs slowly came into their mess hall. To an outsider many would assume nothing happens here, however those in the know this is where things get done, this is where the navy is truly run. That's what the chief's say, and well they have a good point or twelve.

They had the same concerns on the limits of the cauldron, they used the old adage of robbing Peter to pay Paul to get things done, it kept cycling between projects of making ammo, guns, fuel, food and uniforms. Hearing this made me want to get back out there, help the city we found, and figure out how to fix this problem. From what MR2 said the cauldron could crank out items but it takes a while and does not like to get interrupted and it only seems to understand him. I also heard it was a bear to get to the room behind the gym on the mezzanine deck and get the stabilizers on it was a chore and a half. It is kind of ironic we ended up here an amphib (amphibious ship) rather than a carrier or even a destroyer. This ship is old by ship standards, to explain what I mean, take your car, remove the weather protection, weld the hood shut and park it near the ocean. Now get super mad if it starts to rust and that's a good idea on what it's like battling rust.

In came one of my favorite chiefs, he was there when I checked in and was always friendly and nice to me. He was on the soft spoken side, and taught me a lot about firefighting and damage control. Damage Controllman Cheif Beck, he had medium build.

DCC Beck " Contgratulations on getting promoted QM2. Well deserved, glad you are headed out there and I bet it's crazy out there."

Myself "Thank you and yes it is chief."

With that Master at arms Master chief (MAMC try saying either of those 10 times fast.) Master at arms were pretty much military police, they also were very meticulous about uniform regulations pretty much on par with Quartermasters (we are on the bridge so our uniforms need to look perfect).

MAMC Esteves: "Good to see you QM2, congratulations on the promotion."

Myself: "Thank you, Master Chief. It has been a pretty interesting few weeks."

MAMC: "That is one way to put it."

With that he nodded for me to continue, I caught them up on what I told the Commander, not leaving out any details. Keeping in how we saved the King's son. A brief information dump on their culture: what is rude and what is not. I went over the hut along the path, whatever the creature was that lived there, the camp with the fair folk. I added that you never call them fairies, they are obsessed with manners and use them to their advantage. How clean water was hard to come by, what they did to clean it, and how well they ate. The owls ,what they do, how much damage they are doing, what we know about them and how to counter them, but we do not know who is behind this and why.

The chiefs had started to look at each other, nodding along with what I was describing.

My Chief QMC: "Well this is not a good situation any way you slice it. We are going to have to figure out this owl situation. You said that there was a jar that was used to turn people into stone?

Myself: "Yes Chief, they seemed to be able to open it up and when full the jars seemed to have swirls of smoke and sparkling it was almost like an electrical fire in the bottles."

QMC: "Well that is interesting, we would need to find a way to track these owls. You mentioned a village where everyone was turned to stone?"

Myself: "Yes Chief, that is where we found the king's son. "I briefly described the town the direction we went along the road, but not sure how far we were from shore. The concerns Connal told us about departing from the king's road."

QMC: "We might need to get closer to that part of the island, yet far enough away from the owls."

MAMC Esteves: "Thank you for the information, get some rest QM2. The Marines and yourselves have done really well so far to help with getting some allies and helping them in this situation."

Myself: "Master Chief thank you, I shall. Please let me know if I can be of any further assistance."

With that I excused myself, got some air and hit my rack. That night, I did not have any dreams, the redhead did not show up, just the rocking of the ship to lull me into a deep sleep. My bed was already a million times better, this helped with getting proper sleep and allowing the crew to function better. The food was about give or take about the same, sometimes terrible and sometimes just shy of amazing. The TP was better, no more John Wayne TP, it was called that because it took crap from no one. What came out of the caldron was decent middle of the line stuff from any store. To you that might seem bland, but for us it was living the high life.

Chapter 9
The Promotion

The next morning was a day of relaxing, I helped the marines move ammo. At the same time we swapped out barrels quickly and efficiently. We got everything up and swapped out in a few hours. After that it was another steel beach picnic. It was nice to chat with people I hadn't seen in a while, I told them what I thought was alright to say. I told them how it was still more than dangerous on shore. I explained we were looking into it and helping to stop this from happening again. The skipper was right we needed this, it wasn't the same as being able to go ashore but the risks were too much, having a good chunk of the crew turned to stone would be catastrophic to keeping the ship moving. I was told in the trips around the island where we were that it was one of the easiest to anchor.

The other places they tried would just not hold the anchor as well. The sea bed matters, the problem we had was the chart we had was only the island zoomed out, it did tell the sea bed but things seemed a bit different. The problem we was we did not have any charts, MR2 said that he might be able to produce some new ones with the correct scale, but it was not considered a high priority. We had to resupply ammunition, firearm barrels, fuel and food. So for now the ship would be operating in the same area. We couldn't risk it, it was not worth trying to go around the Island and end up beaching without a way to get out. Running aground, or getting stuck on land is something everyone in my Rate fear, no captain wants it to happen either.

The steel beach picnic was just better than the others, I was told the chicken was soaked in BBQ sauce the night before, then cooked over coals. The sliders weren't dry hockey pucks like before. We had sodas, potato salad, and chips. The stuff that was cooked was pretty good. It was like we were having good food again. SH2 Wayne was there, he was chatting and laughing.

Myself: "How's it going SH2?"

SH2: "Well, congratulations and welcome to the E5 club. I just got off of watch, I just dealt with EW1 Dalton, he really screwed up."

EW was short for Electronics Warfare. They maintained and operated the defensive systems of the ship, He and well the other EW maintained and used our defensive countermeasures that weren't CWIS. EW1 was one of those booksmart types, no social skills, power went right to his head. He kind of walked funny too, he was pigeon toed, he would hold his left hand down and rub his wrist in weird counter-clockwise motions when thinking or stressed. He had no leadership skills to speak of, just knowledgeable about his system and that was it. He would always get angry at us if we were not listening to whatever dumb thing, he wanted us to do, it was usually nonsensical and a colossal waste of time (it was like the good idea fairy constantly whispered in his ear. The good idea fairy is used in sarcastic tones when a really dumb idea is suggested).

Myself: "What happened?"

SH2: "So we are having to stand a roving watch, I don't mind doing it, besides turning over with the Marines is not that bad. You missed a doozy on what had happened."

Myself: "Ok I am going to want to hear that too, but what did EW1 do?"

SH2: "Well I was getting ready to relieve EW1 on the rover watch, he had dropped his M14 (The riffle we currently using on the ship)."

Myself: "Well, that is terrible, did it go off?"

SH2: "Well no, it didn't and it gets worse than that, I am not joking he picked it up and started looking down the barrel. I told him nope I am not turning over with him. No way am I touching that fire arm. "

Myself: "I don't blame you, I wouldn't either."

SH2: "The marines picked up the weapon, cleared it, checked it and swapped it out for me. They even offered to stand the rest of the watch. Weaps found out about it and got pissed at the old EW1. He's not allowed near any of his weapons and not allowed to make any extra work for his Gunnersmates."

Weaps is short for weapons officer, he's the one who the Gunnersmates report to. Their department is incharge of making sure things like the 50 cals, 9 mils, M14's, the other weapon systems and my favorite the mossberg shotgun work. Ensign Everett is a mustang as well, he graduated from Michigan university but I won't hold that against him too much. He was generally really funny on the bridge, you knew it was going to be a good watch when it was LTJG Jorgenson, ENS Everett and pretty much almost anyone else. Both of those two were the good kind of officers.

A dang type whistle escaped my mouth.

SH2: "I know right, so onto the marines. You're going to want some popcorn and a chair for this one."

I grabbed one of the MWR chairs (Morale Welfare and Recreation, each ship had its own fund and it was to help us relax and have fun when things got too crazy, this could be activities in ports, to contests. Like I heard last deployment they had a grow a beard contest, best beard and worst. It had its own officer in charge of it, he was a decent guy and the guy making sure we all got paid).

I nodded, and SH2 continued. "Ensign Browne was moving through the ship in the morning, a security alert training drill was called."

A security alert is when all hands are supposed to stay where they are, and only the security force (usually underway it is only the Gunnersmates but the Marines not on gun mount watch are joining in on this. Both took even training very seriously.).

SH2: "ENS Browne was warned about this exact thing, he ended up getting zipped tied to the bulkhead (Wall), with guess how many ties?"

Myself: "Four?"

SH2: "They hit him with around 12 from what I heard. He was hog tied then zipped tied about 3 feet off the deck (floor)."

I had to fight back laughter in case anyone heard me, I had to keep some sense of respect for the rank. Both of us are at the rank where we are supposed to be setting the example. If you knew me well you knew I was laughing with my eyes, this was possibly one of the best pieces of news I heard in a while, I mean it was not the lady from my dreams, who I was assured was real. That was a woman, whew. So this must be the love sickness that Ronan was talking about. She was a whirlwind to me, I could move mountains just thinking about her. She was able to reach out to the depths of my soul, places where no one could sail before. Two things first, save the area we are in, save our ship then go find her. Clearly, she could fight on her own, but she would not turn away help.

I went and told him about what the landmass was like, some of the dangers out there. I told him about the food, how different the drink was, the music and how the language sounded. I then told him why they are only letting a small group go ashore. He seemed to understand why, it sucked and I wish we could get the situation taken care of. I went over the owls.

SH2: "You know getting something that could track an owl might help with figuring it out."

Myself: "Not a bad idea, I don't know if we can make something tracking, since GPS doesn't work here."

SH2: "Yeah that would make it difficult, there might be something easier."

Myself: "I think you're right, maybe just how far away and what direction it is away from the holder of the device."

SH2: "You might be onto something."

Myself: "Thanks SH2, I'll see if I can bring you back something from the next trip."

WIth that I finished my lunch, and excused myself. I threw out my trash and went to look for Sergeant Buford.

I found him in the berthing, he was waking up from some sleep.

Myself: "Sergeant when you have some time I think I have an idea I want to run past you."

Sergeant Buford: "Sure thing, you could use some sleep though, I know it's been a rough few weeks. I think we are going to try to head out in a few days, Private Murray's hearing should be back and well we should be resupplied by then and we would need to regear him too."

Myself: "I agree with both of those ideas, I was having a conversation up on the flight deck, and I got to thinking, couldn't we make a device that can track an owl to see where it flies?"

Sergeant Buford: "You said it yourself GPS isn't working."

Myself: "Yes that's true, so what we could do is have the device always be the center, just have whatever is placed on the owl track the distance and direction away from us. Sort of like relative and true bearing, this would always be relative to us."

Sergeant Buford: "That all seems plausible, however we would need to see if the MR2 could do it and get Gunny and the skipper to sign off on it. Sleep on it, we need to get the topographical maps updated as well. I still remember the Kings road."

When he said that the hairs on my arm and back of my neck stood up, I also thought of that creature with the dancing lights. Those situations were ones that would stay with me and were ones I did not want to be unprepared for or willing to go through.

A familiar trill followed by an unfamiliar voice came over the 1MC, "Gunnery Sergeant Hull, Sergeant Buford and QM3 I mean QM2 MacDermott report to the Captain's cabin."

I nodded at Sergeant Buford and said, "Well no rest for the moment? Better not keep the old man waiting."

I got a quick shave and made sure my uniform had no summer creases (some are here, some are there, hence summer creases). It is best to always look squared away especially when you are going to suggest something crazy to the old man. The old enlisted adage, "If you cannot amaze them with brilliance, baffle them with bull crap" would not work on him.

I made it first to the room, knocked and asked, "Permission to enter."

His voice always inspired courage "Enter QM2 and please have a seat."

Myself: "Thank you, sir. "

He did this for both Gunnery Sergeant Hill and Sergeant Buford. They entered and found a seat as well.

CO: "Please at ease all, also please speak freely and would you like anything to drink?"

We all just asked for water, I wasn't sure if I was going to get any rack time.

He continued "First of all, I want to thank you and ensure that Gunny knows your work is appreciated and crucial. I don't think I have to spell out that we are in a unique situation and how we are on our own here."

I shook my head "No, sir."

Skipper: "Outstanding, so the owls turning people into statues." You could tell that the words sounded odd strung together and to say them in any other situation might be probable cause to be relieved from command and the Navy.

Gunny: "I know it sounds odd, but I trust these two. The problem we've come up with is how do we track these targets, who is behind this and why?"

Skipper: "I agree, we cannot use GPS, it doesn't work. We aren't receiving any communication from any satellites. We've still found no ships in the area. The best source of aid is people who need our help. I would like to see if you can get someone to come on board. I would love to chat with them. I think Ronan might be the most likely one."

Myself: "Understood sir, I think so, I do not know if we would need to call in a favor."

Skipper: "I think I see what you are getting at, their society works off of status, calling in favors quickly might be seen as a bad thing."

Myself: "Yes sir, that is correct."

Sergeant Buford: "Sir, we can get back out there, Private Murray should be combat ready, Ronan was looking after him. We could talk to the king and Ronan and see if we can get them to talk with you. That and scouting around that village we found to the north, the one where everyone was turned to stone."

Gunny: "Sir, I think Sergeant Buford has a good idea. I do not think either of us are idle men, nor do I think the crew wants to be idle."

Skipper: "Gunny you are right, I think letting the men get on land for a bit would be a good idea, however the threat of the crew getting turned to stone would be catastrophic."

Myself: "Agreed, I think having a feast onboard the ship, and inviting the king might be a good idea?"

Skipper: "That is a wonderful Idea, See if you can convince the King."

Myself: "Yes sir, we'll ask him about that. When it comes to the device for the owls, I think a device that can just track distance and direction would work, I think eliminating the parts that aren't working would make it easier."

Skipper: "I like that idea of a device and We'll see what the officers and chiefs can come up with to help with fine-tuning it. I know we have some rather industrious people on our crew."

The old man was right, we had some rather creative people who could build about anything out of nothing. That's the benefit of having crew from all over the place, the asvab (Armed Services Vocational Aptitude Battery) test is one of the things done well. It tested multiple categories, mechanics, shapes, logic puzzles, assembly, science and more. I mentally chuckled when the old man said industrious people, he meant the engineers and MR2. There were some rather creative guys from the south in those departments they could get anything running and well their work around methods would make an engineer question reality if not at least their life choices. I was curious about what they were cooking up to be honest, for ship defenses. We didn't have much but the CWIS, 50 cal, 60 cal and small arms fire.

With that the skipper asked, "Anything, else?"

Gunny: "Sir we might want to start mapping out the island, both on the water and on land."

Skipper: "That is a wonderful idea, I think that would give us some time to get that device designed and produced. We should be able to squeeze that in the time before you head out again. Constantly having it cycle through bullets, food and fuel is a challenge from what Sutton told me. Anything else?"

All three of us shook our heads roughly in agreement simultaneously.

Skipper: "Dismissed, please get some sleep and resupplied you are going to need it. I think we need to get you both back out there, possibly build that relationship with the people out there."

Sergeant Buford: "Understood, sir."

With that we left him to enjoy his cigar.

I made the zombie walk down to my rack, crawled into the bottom bunk and shut the curtain. I drifted off to sleep with the rocking of the ship. We were on a chariot, the horses were taken down quickly. I grabbed her and held her in my arms as we jumped and fell out of the chariot. My shoulder took the blow and threw it out of the socket. I quickly popped it back into the joint. My weapons were nowhere near me, as a flood of angry misshapen warriors swarmed us. We only had her sword, they swarmed us and we quickly went back to back, passing the sword between each other. Her sword felt light, almost like nothing in my hands. We kept stepping to the right, and one of us would slash then pass the sword to the other person. I got hit and woke up in a cold sweat.

I got out of my rack, grabbed my shower shoes (flip flops) and went to the head (restroom). I threw some cold water on my face, went back to my bunk, and put on my camies and boots to get some air.

I made it outside, and standing out there was MR2 Sutton and he had that southern accent from Alabama. He was the only guy who could make parts and almost anything ship related. We never had a chance to really talk to each other, only kind of seeing each other in passing. He was packing a pipe and getting ready to smoke at the smoke deck.

MR2: "Mind if I smoke?"

Myself: "Nope, go ahead."

MR2: "I know it's kind of late but I like to get out, get some air, see the stars. Got to get some more parts out for the ship."

Myself: "Cannot blame you there, I couldn't sleep so I thought I'd clear my head."

He lit up the pipe, it was sweet and fragrant, he proceeded to blow smoke rings.

MR2: "How is it out there? I've been hearing nothing but the craziest rumors."

I told him pretty much what I've been telling the rest of the crew, what we needed to do out there.

MR2: "Dang that's got to suck for them, I feel bad for Firemen Morris. More than happy to help you guys get even out there."

Myself: "Thanks, we are trying to get something that can help us track the owls doing it."

MR2: "That should be something we could cook up, I got a few other ideas but we gotta get some breathing room." I kind of feel bad for MR2, dude was stressing out, he was thrown onto an old ship falling apart at the rusted seams with a bunch of squids.

He was right, the running gag was there was a fireman at the bottom (fireman is an undesignated person working in the engine room, meaning they do not have a rate, you had Airman for aviation and Seaman for anything surface. You had to strike a rate.) constantly rearranging rust flakes so we do not sink.

Myself: "Thanks, I feel bad for Morris, he seems like a good kid."

MR2: "Yeah from what I noticed, thanks for saving him. I heard you were one of the main ones behind saving him."

Myself: "No problem, I mean anyone should be doing that."

MR2: "Yeah, one would think, there are dirtbags in all of the rates."

He had a point, He alluded to Davidson and the people we wanted out of our way most of the time, this could be on fire fighting training. Everyone had to be trained. You were expected to train to the best of your ability. So an officer could be in charge of the communications and helping out with suiting people up, because they cannot get qualified. There were those who could, those who couldn't and the dirtbags. For those who were here and wanted to be, we did not like the latter two, the former we could work with.

Myself "Yeah, I see where you are coming from. Going to see if I can get us hooked up with some good food. I described the food we had at king McGreggors table, that they had drinks as well. They used alcohol to clean up the water, it was just a tiny bit usually they used an alcohol with honey to do so.

MR2: "Dang that sounds good, I'm drooling just thinking about it. I'm not envious, you guys are dealing with all sorts of scary crap out there."

Myself: "Yeah it's pretty wild out there. I am hoping we can figure out this owl thing, not sure what to do after that."

MR2: "Yeah I was supposed to be getting out after the last deployment, the Old man pulled some connections to keep me on the ship. He said that there weren't too many Machine Repair men like me."

Myself: "We kind of got the short end of the stick, but hey extended deployment, I guess we'd get hazard pay?"

MR2 snorted with that, smoke rings came out of his nose rather than his mouth.

MR2: "Warn me next time you tell a joke like that."

Myself: "I'll try but no promises" I gave him a sheepish grin. " I am going to try to get some more sleep, take it easy and it was nice chatting with you."

MR2: "You to QM2, congrats on your promotion."

Myself: "Thanks"

With that I went back down to the rack, I slept with no dreams.

Chapter 10
First Blood

I awoke to the announcement "**Reveille**! **Reveille**! **Reveille**! All hands heave out and trice up!"

I got out of my rack, made it to the head, brushed my teeth showered and shaved. Made it to the Mess decks for coffee and breakfast. I sat near BM2 Leblanc, Sergeant Buford and OS2. We were all talking while eating, I finished and got another cup of coffee to go. We went out to talk before morning formation. I finished my cup, rinsed and dried it out and put it back in my rack before heading to the mezzanine deck.

I fell into formation with the marines. I ignored QM2 Morelli and QM3 Davidson. I stood near the front of the department. Gunny looked at us and began.

Gunny: "Thank you all for the hard work so far, everyone on the ship you've been crushing it with the gun mounts, helping out the Gunnersmates, standing the gun mount watch. I know it's not ideal and I know that most of you would rather be out there giving them hate. Buford and McDermott, both of you have been doing an outstanding job in the field and those who are reporting to you. I know there has been a lot of pressure on all of us."

We all kind of took that in, for many of us getting this much praise meant something bad was around the corner. Things like this could take many different forms, surf and turf being served in the general mess might be the most infamous. The other is the ice cream social, some ships did one or the other. This was given to soften the blow usually in the enlisted mess saying deployment has been extended or something equally nefarious.

Gunny: "Sergeant I am going to need you, QM2 and the same people headed back out there, start chatting people up, go back to that village with all of the statues and figure out what's nearby. We figure it will take a few weeks possibly to cook up the device that both of you suggested to the Commander. Other than that, please keep up the good work. At ease and Dismissed."

Gunny walked up to us, he pointed at us "Not you two. We need to chat for a moment."

Myself: "Of course, Gunny."

Gunny: "So you two are going back out there, Murray should be good to go, It feels weird to have an outsider medically clear him. I want you then to head back out to that Village where you found the king's son. Scout

out there for a few days, make it back to the city and head back. If you can convince Ronnan to come back with you. "

Sergeant Buford: "Understood, I am sure we can complete all of that. Ronnan seems to be a rather curious sort."

Myself: "Gunny, Sergeant Buford is right he kind of reminds you of an inquisitive Grandpa. It would be easy to convince him, but the trick might be convincing the king. Ronan is kind of the main advisor to the King McGreggor."

Gunny: "Sounds like you have a few days to get resupplied, plan things out and head back out there."

Myself: "Understood."

With that Gunny disappeared leaving the rest of us to converse on the mezzanine deck. We went back to the same space, and another private was voluntold to stay outside to make sure we were not interrupted, the rest of the crew was invited in there and we started planning. Sergeant Buford had sketched out a map of the village. He put down the pen.

Sergeant: "Here is what we know about the village, not too much about the surrounding area."

There is an open area and it looked doubtful that the owls would be coming from that area. We need to see where an optimal place to set up an ambush would be. Causes Safety Briefs looked at the map, he pointed.

Causes Safety Briefs: "There right around where roads were, roughly where Cormac's chariot was."

On both sides there was a wall that would provide cover. It was clear what he planned we could easily hide from prying eyes, use it to our benefit to escape.

Sergeant: "That seems optimal, the drawbacks are we would have to split up."

Causes Safety Briefs: "Yeah, however that's the only optimal spot that could allow a proper escape route."

Williams: "Sergeant, it does provide full cover however we would really need to be careful not to hit anyone."

Sergeant Buford: "Of course, good looking out."

We went back to the map, many of the doors for the houses were destroyed or blocked. I could see what Causes Safety Briefs meant. This was an embrace the suck kind of situation. We had to make do with what we had and use the element of surprise. Cause safety Briefs was asking for claymores, light machine guns, and wanted to go out armed to an individual tooth. Sergeant Buford took it all in stride, he nodded and shook his head at parts.

Sergeant Buford: "I understand wanting to go out there ready to take on the world, however we are 6 people, having us hump all that out there would not be feasible. We are going to bring as much hurt as feasible."

Causes Safety Briefs reminded me of a character from that movie *Tremors*, if he got his way, I think he would out prepare that guy.

Myself: "Sergeant, do we know if the device has been built yet? I know people are working on designing it."

Sergeant Buford: "QM2, you are right but I want to start planning now, we need to get back out there and I do not want to be caught off guard again. I think we got a decent plan, now what about seeing if we can get someone on board the ship."

Myself: "From what I know, King McGreggor would visit at most, I think the most logical choice for a diplomat would be Ronan. That's kind of one of the hats he wears."

Speaking of hats, I think I am running out of hat boxes for all the ones I seem to be wearing and I would imagine it feels like I am juggling them while one is on my head and having to switch, it's still in this situation, being on intel, a linguist and being semi-permanent temporarily assigned to the Marine detachment was making my head spin at times. I wanted an interesting Naval career but this is a bit much. I would be curious how recruiters would spin this? Join the Navy let the terror begin? If that's so, then the Marines could be the few, the proud one who used C4 on a banshee. The second might have to be shopped by some PR firm but you get the gist. My eyes had lit up and I got a smirk on my face for a brief moment and sergeant noticed.

Sergeant Buford: "Something funny QM2?"

Myself: "Yes sergeant, I just thought about how the recruiting motto might have to change. I was thinking: Join the Navy, let the terror begin and the Marines could be "The few, the proud those who used C4 on a banshee."

This had drawn a bit of laughter and got the ice to break, these were guys who wanted to put the hurt on those who wished others harm. I remember a saying from my grandpa that laughter can be a good way to break up tension, break the ice and get everyone to rally back around the task at hand.

Sergeant: "That's pretty good, ok so we need to head back to the city, see if we can get an audience with the king, bring that up to him, leave the message here to expect us back in a week. Not sure how many people he would bring with him."

Myself: "I think that's a good idea, I would say somewhere between 10 to 20 people. I am thinking we plan to have it be a Sunday, for a couple of reasons. 1 the best food is usually at a steel beach, 2 it gives us a chance to put our best foot forward."

Sergeant Buford: "Honestly convincing them to visit is going to be easy, I think we should run this buy the old man and see how. It is his ship."

Myself: "Yeah I think so, I think we should talk to him before going out."

Sergeant Buford: "With that is there anything else?"

There were a lot of no sergeants from everyone.

Sergeant Buford: "Then start getting ready."

As they left, I looked at Sergeant Buford and said "sergeant, a few words before you head out."

Sergeant Buford: "Yes QM2?"

Myself: "I was talking to MR2 Sutton, he seemed like he wanted to build us some gear for the field, possibly working on something to catch and track one of those owls. He took it pretty personally, since he kind of liked Fireman Moore."

I explained that Firemen Moore was kind of their scruffy booter mascot of engineering. He had the nickname Buddah. It was based off of his Boston accent and how he couldn't say Booter. A booter is someone who just graduated boot camp and their school for their rate.

Sergeant Buford: "I understand and respect that, we'll get him fixed up then. Well, we need to talk to Gunny, then the skipper before we head out."

Myself: "Yeah makes sense, we got to be the ones wrangling these yahoos. I wouldn't have it any other way."

Sergeant Buford smiled then motioned to the door up the stairs past the caldron area. We went through the inside of the ship past the knee knockers (these were spots that you think there would be a door and there is a lip that goes up to about your ankle, if you miss it you knock your knees) that would be along the p-ways on the main deck (p-way is short for passageway, and the main deck is the first deck you step onto when getting on the ship).

We passed the mess decks, breakfast had finished right before morning formation. You could smell the bleach in the Cadillac (mop bucket with wheels, I guess the joke is it's a sailors first car without 30% interest). We went past the mess decks to the chief mess to see if Gunny was there. We knocked and entered and saw gunny enjoying a cup of coffee. We went over our plans with Gunny, he acknowledged the terrible terrain, and agreed with Causes Safety Brief's on the fence being the best place possible. We also went over getting the king and his advisors on the ship to meet the skipper and help improve relations.

Gunny agreed with our plan, and advised us to run both of these past the skipper. He also inquired about how Private Murray was holding up and recovering. It was baffling to hear from Ronan that Murray's hearing problem could be taken care of, we made sure we went to Sutton to get new hearing protection for Murray, get ours replaced while we were at it, ensured that everyone also had their kit looked at, ammoed up and resupplied then headed back up to the skippers estate. We made it to the door and sergeant Buford knocked.

Sergeant Buford, "Permission to enter."

The old man had a cigar going and its aroma danced through his estate. He puffed on the cigar looking over the reports. He looked up.

Commander Alvarez, "Permission granted."

Sergeant Buford, "Sir, we have talked to Gunny and we have a few plans we want to run by you."

Commander: "Please go ahead, at ease and permission to speak freely."

We both had a seat, explained the plan at the village where we found the king's son, with the possibility to figure out where the owls were coming from. The skipper was deep in thought and paying attention to every word. We then brought up bringing the king onboard the ship to help improve relations between his kingdom and our ship. We suggested that a steel beach picnic would be good.

Skipper: "You both have a good plan considering the area, and with getting the king on board."

The skipper said around 10 to 20 people would be the most allowed on the ship. He also mentioned that we would always need to be with them. The thought that they could read our language was low but not impossible.

Myself: "Sir, we could get them on the ship via the stern gate, that is if they have a boat."

Skipper: "QM2 that could work, we would need to be careful with that, since their boats will most likely be made out of wood and not metal."

Sergeant Buford: "That makes sense, I think it might be best for us to talk to the king then head to that village and scout a little bit more around it."

Skipper: "I think scouting around would not be a bad idea, getting off the trail would not be a good idea."

Myself: "Understood sir. I do not think we will go more than a mile from that village."

Skipper: "Good, and thank you both for everything you've done so far. Please let the others working under you thank you from me too."

Sergeant Buford: "Will do Sir."

Skipper: "Sergeant and QM2 dismissed."

Myself: "Thank you sir, we'll be back by Sunday."

With that we about faced, saluted and walked out of the estate room. We met up with the armory and made sure everyone resupplied. It was lunch so we went to the mess decks. We sat with the other E5's at our usual tables. Lunch was grilled cheese with tomato soup. The secret to having soup on the ship is to fill it no more than ⅔ of the way full. I ended up using the entire sandwich to eat the soup. The food was still better than what we had before. I am suspecting the cauldron is making our food and it's better quality than what we had before we got here. We chatted as quickly as we ate and got caught up with some of the other departments. We walked past the ship's store and SH2 was inside. I opened up the door.

Myself: "SH2 how is it going?"

SH2: "Not too bad QM2."

Myself: "Going to pick up a watch, and a ship's lighters."

SH2: "Are you guys going back out there?"

Myself: "Yeah for a bit, it's still a bit crazy out there."

Sergeant Buford picked up some Jerky and a lighter. We both paid and went out. We went back to the berthing. The marines were goofing off in the berthing, and someone had picked up the orange box that we called the fartbag (the fart bag is used to escape out of a room that's on fire).

Sergeant Buford: "What do you think you are doing Private?"

The private put the box back and looked at the sergeant, " Nothing sergeant."

Sergeant Buford: "Private, Bob Ross thinks you're a mistake. I want you to do push ups until I get tired."

WIth that the private started doing push ups. Thankfully, Sergeant took the safety briefing seriously and getting one of the fartbags replaced wouldn't be hard but it would be a pain to have MR2 stop a project to make a replacement.

We met up with the rest of our group, went over our plans again, talked about supplies and just relaxed until tomorrow. Dinner was alright, nothing special just meatloaf mashed potatoes and corn. After the mess was secured and cleaned, we went to play a bit of cards until evening. I went out to get some salt air, clear my mind and then hit my rack. No crazy dreams, sadly she was not there to greet me. I missed her already. It was odd and defied logic that I could miss a person I never met. That same logic told me a dream woman was not real, this was delusional and not to put energy in someone who was not real. I should talk to Ronan again when I have the chance.

The morning sunrise did greet us with its warm embrace. After breakfast we went out, thankfully not interrupted on our path towards the shore. We made it to the city by nightfall and the trek was getting rather familiar to us.

We made it to the king's place where he had set us up in the hostel, we were advised he had visitors again and the rooms in his estate were being used. He however made sure we were welcome to the banquet. The food we ate was fantastic as every time before. I translated stories between the warriors, Marines and even I told a few of my own experiences. The other diplomates looked at us with a curious yet suspicious eye. Their language was rather similar. I could piece it together with some work. A man of average build with sea green eyes and very dark blond hair with a decent beard length stood up and pointed at us.

Foreign warrior: "I am Ariogaisos son of Lecus the high king of Gauland. Who are these strange visitors at your table, they drink your wine, eat your food and sit closer to your table than we do."

Ronan: "Easy Ariogaisos, they are guests of the king, they have done much to help us in our time of need. They have even saved the life of Cormac. I would trust any of them with my life. Their ways are strange to me as they are to you, yet I enjoy their company and they are honorable men."

Ariogaisos: "I wish to see their actions with my own eyes. Ronan, you are a diplomat who hides from the world."

Ronan gave him a look, that annoyed grandfather's look that you had too much sugar and it's best to stop.

Ariogaisos: "Ronan, it is true, how do we know these are not some foreign soldiers to murder us in our sleep? It is up to them to prove themselves." He looked at Doc " Name your game and we'll play."

Doc looked at me with an evil grin.

Sneak attack Sasquatch: "QM2, tell him I'll fight him with swords to first blood."

Myself: "Doc, are you sure?"

Sneak attack: "Yes I am sure, I got this."

Now what happened next was something to behold. The tables were cleared of food and our drinks were refilled. A ring was drawn around the middle of the hall roughly a 12 by 12 foot square.

Doc was given a sword shaped like a leaf by one of McGreggor's warriors, he swung it a few times.

Doc looked at me, "This doesn't have the level of give I am used to but it will work."

A wicked smile slowly formed on Doc's face. Doc towered over Ariogaisos, it was kind of comical for a few reasons. Arigaisos was 2/3rds the size of doc, and the sword looked tiny in docs hands, it was almost like a twig in his giant hands. Doc stretched and did some weird foot maneuvers.

Ronan looked at Ariogaisos and looked at Doc.

Ronan: "I want a clean fight, no stabbing below the waist, unless it is the feet. No going for the lifeblood areas." I think what he meant was the major arteries and no groin shots. I relayed the translations to Doc. Doc nodded in agreement. When I drop my cloth you will begin.

At the moment the cloth hit the ground doc's left arm exploded the tiny twig went for Ariogaisos' arm, and in a blink of an eye a scratch appeared on Ariogaisos' arm. Ariogaisos moved in for a cut and doc blocked. In the same action, Ariogaisos was disarmed, as Doc grabbed and casually flipped his sword back to 1 fuming Ariogaisos.

Ronan: "That is the challenge, I believe the one they call Doc won."

Doc handed the sword back to one of McGreggor's warriors after cleaning the blade.

Doc: "It is a fine blade, a bit short for me but well crafted."

I translated to the warrior, he seemed rather impressed with Doc's actions and compliments.

With that Ariogaisos was a little annoyed with being so easily beaten. I looked at doc and whispered

Myself: "Where on earth did you learn to fight like that?"

Doc: "I got into a historical group that fights with medieval weapons. We used to go into the woods and hit each other over the head with sticks."

Myself: "Stick fighting?"

Doc: "Not really we used Rapier, the Spanish word for sword, fencing would be the modern part they would use now. We would fight in a similar sized area. I'll have to tell you more about it, possibly start teaching the others fighting this way if we need it."

Myself: "Yeah might be a good idea."

With that McGreggors warriors and a few that were with Ariogaisos were patting Doc on the back and raising their glasses in honor of Doc. We ended up chatting with me translating back and forth for what felt like a few hours. We had excused ourselves, back to the hostel.

Chapter 11
Lovesickness

We made it back and were the only ones inside. Morning came we ate from the king's cauldron and washed up. We made it to the king's court after his diplomatic guests had left.

McGreggor: "Well that was a bit of entertainment last night. I was worried it would have been boring. You will have to excuse Ariogaisos, he's not as level headed as his father. He's not seen too many winters and his blood still boils hot."

Myself: "We understand and thank you for your gracious hospitality. Our leader Commander Alvarez wanted to meet with you on our ship. Would you be willing to meet with him?"

McGreggor: "How soon, I would want to prepare and not be a terrible guest?"

Myself: "Commander Alvarez said seven sun rises is enough time for him to prepare. He said that you may bring up to 19 guests."

McGreggor: "I can work with that. Will your metal turtle eat us?"

Myself: "King McGreggor, no but do you have a ship you can pull along ours?"

McGreggor: "I do believe we can do that."

Myself: "Excellent, our group here would like to explore the village where we found your Son."

McGreggor: "Of course, Please go there, check it out and on the way back we will both head to your floating turtle. My Warriors can take you about half way there by chariot if you wish. None of them wish to be turned to stone. They believe the village is cursed and those who stay there do not come back."

Myself: "I understand and yes that would work for us."

McGreggor: "Very well, I think that is enough business time for pleasure." He sat up and left the main hall.

Ronan stood up and said "Tayg, it is good to see you all. Private is doing better."

 It was interesting Ronan must have been picking up English, however he seemed to think Private Murray's first name was Private. That meant that

Murray's hearing must be back to what it was before. Murray looked over at us and smiled.

Sergeant: "Careful Private, any more smiling at me and I'm going to give you a reason to frown."

Private Murray quickly stopped smiling, "Sergeant, sorry it is good to see you all."

Myself: "You too, private good to see that your hearing is back we brought your gear."

Murray: "Thanks QM2, Ronan was good company. I picked up a few words in their language and taught him a few of ours."

Sergeant: "Good job, Private."

Murray: "Thanks, Sergeant."

With that, we headed out to the main area towards where the warriors lived. The warriors were not happy to be heading to the village everyone was turned to stone in. They kept their word and promised to drop us off at the camp we met the fair folk at. They said that they would be back in three days, and wait until the sun set on the third day for us. We made sure our water was filled and we picked up our supplies. It was nice to have the chariots carry our gear, it was a tight fit but we made it work.

The chariots raced to the camp grounds. The drivers looking around like death was waiting to jump out from any tree along the road. The king's road stones glowed brightly, even in the day. We made it to camp roughly around noon easily saving half the day. The warriors broke out their games and the charioteers got the horses fed, water and joined in the games. We put on our rucks and headed to the village.

We made the village by late afternoon early evening, we scouted around for a few hours until the sun began to set. We set up our camp on the outskirts of the village with it at least a thousand yards away. We ensured no trees were near our camp to ensure no birds could not be near us.

I took the first watch, it was so calm, no sounds and no animals. To me it was unsettling, usually animals are quiet before something like rain, natural disasters or anything else. I kept alert, still as the night itself. My watch ended with not a sound. I drifted off to sleep my ruck as a pillow leaned against the stone fence. That fence if used right provided perfect cover as Causes Safety Briefs pointed out in our planning. I was tapped on my shoulder and spun up with my rifle. I quickly donned my helmet.

We were all up, I noticed a very white flying bird with a very long flapping motion, it was like the wings were trying to clap as it flew.

I whispered, "That's an owl, no mistake about it. It's white too. Tango sited over by the small shack, It was headed to the wooded clearing. Sergeant, should I open fire?"

Sergeant: "Let's just watch it, I do not want to give away our position on night one."

Myself: "Understood Sergeant."

I kept my eyes on the owl until it flew out of my vision, I remembered the landmarks and hoped I could make them out during the dawn. We kept an open eye for the rest of the evening, and went back to sleep except for the one on watch. That eerie feeling did not relent with the sunrise. It casted a semi-permanent gloom over the village. The village felt like a knockoff amusement park combined with a ghost town on a day where everyone is on vacation. We went to the well and Causes Safety Briefs pulled out a pouch, he motioned to Private Williams to pull up the bucket from the well. When the water was pulled up he opened up the back and poured some water in the vial along with some chemicals, he then gave the vial to Private Williams.

Causes Saftey Briefs: "Williams, you're gonna shake this until my arm's tired."

Williams took the vial and started shaking it with a puzzled look on his face. Williams paced around in circles while he shook the vial. I looked at the equipment puzzled for a brief moment. He somehow managed to get a water testing kit, that resourceful son of a…

Causes's Safety Briefs: "Williams give me the vial I think my hand's tired." he laughed, as he said that. "Sergeant the water here is drinkable, it's not poisoned or anything else wrong with it, no toxic metals or anything. I think this is why McGreggor wants this place back and farm land."

Sergeant: "I don't want to know where and how you got that kit but that's good to know. Everyone fill up your Canteens."

We ended up splitting up into groups of twos, each of us were no more than 10 feet away from another group except for the two in the front and back. We were told to keep your eyes open. I suggested we gravitate toward where I saw the owl last night. I saw a bit more of the golden thread and a few bird feathers as pure as fresh snow in winter.

I put a few of the feathers and the thread in my ruck where it could not be lost or bent. There were no other items near the owl, you could see in the grass where it swooped down to attack a mouse, you could still see the blood in the grass. I motioned to the sergeant to come over.

Myself: "Sergeant, take a look."

Sergeant: "I see a disturbed grass and blood."

Myself: "That is right, but this is one of those owls, meaning they have to eat. This is an imprint of when it hunted. I suspect this is a mouse." as I pointed to the blood stains.

Sergeant: "QM2, how do you know this?"

Myself: "Sergeant, I took a lot of classes on tracking, identifying animals. The ones here I do not know their names but some of the skills such as tracking still transfer well. It looks like after its meal it went that way." Pointed in the direction of the woods.

Sergeant Buford nodded.

I continued "Typically they would be in a tree but I do not know with the way this one is acting. We should find owl pellets typically near the base of a tree. Basically, think of cat hairballs with skulls and everything else the owl could not digest."

Sergeant Buford: "That makes sense but it would be difficult at best to see if it does live in a tree."

Myself: "My thought exactly, however knowing it does actually eat could be beneficial putting some sort of tracking mechanism on it. Whatever we use must also be light, so it can still fly. This is something to work with."

Sergeant nodded again and said, "We can look around this area and see if we find anything, set up camp again and see what happens."

With that we kept the same formation as before. I pointed out the area where the owl came down on the mouse. We walked a bit around the area and as I thought we found nothing of note. Owls typically can fly far from their homes and when they live in a forest it can be a pain to try to find where they would nest if they do.

The rest of the day was uneventful, as was the night I watched out with not a sound to be heard nor an animal to be seen the entire night. It was beyond creepy how quiet it was. I was woken up by the sun announcing a new day. We were greeted with the same unnerving silence. It felt like all the animals had left, nothing but the sun was there. We scouted the village more but only found the same rotting food, statues, and buildings in the same condition. It felt like we were to get nothing back from the village and decided it was best to head back to the meet up point.

We trudged back to the spot where we were dropped off at the same place we saw the fair folk. The campsite was deserted, no flames, and nothing remaining from the last time we were here. It was odd to me that nothing was at this campsite from the fair folk who were here the last time we were here. We all stayed alert and waited for the warriors to show up, we talked with them for a bit and headed back.

We crammed into their chariots with our gear and raced back to the city. The visitors had left. The king had a little bit of business before the evening meal.

King McGreggor: "Welcome back. Have you found out anything?"

Myself: "Yes King McGreggor, we were able to track the owls for a while and understand their behavior."

King McGreggor: "I see, now you are planning on heading back to the ship?"

Myself: "Yes, I hope that you will wish to join us?"

King McGreggor: "I would love to, and I would like to bring some of my finest warriors and most trusted advisor Ronan."

Myself: "Of course, your majesty. We can allow up to 20 people counting yourself."

King McGreggor: "I think 10 of us will do, we have a boat and when will we head out?"

Myself: "Your majesty we can signal the ship in the morning. I will ride on the boat with you to ensure there is a translator."

King McGreggor: "I take it you are the only one who can translate?"

He was good at picking that up, that could be an issue later on. Hopefully I could teach at least the Captain how to speak the language. I am not sure how long it would take, or if anyone else could pick up on the language.

Myself: "Partly yes the other part one of my other jobs is navigation. I am rather good with ships and how they move."

No need to lie to one of our potential allies and I stick with honest answers. I did not wish to tell answers quickly proven false.

I continued, "There will be food, it might be different than what you are expecting, I will do my best to answer questions you have about it and anything else I can say."

King McGreggor: "You can say?"

Myself: "Your majesty, we have war fighting secrets we want to try to keep that way."

King McGreggor: "I understand and would think less of you if you did not."

I am starting to develop a lot of respect for this king and his people.

The food this time was pork cooked in honey and other herbs, I do not think I could ever get sick of this. I think it would make a wonderful jerky. The drink was honey with a little bit of sage. Their cooks were masters of their craft. The last time I ate that well was camping. The stories went well after that, I was asked by the warriors to tell a story this time. So I told the story of saving Fireman Moore. They reacted appropriately by getting angry when Davidson left to go get food, they cheered when he was rescued and their faces fell when they heard he was told to stone. I told them we were going to do our best to save him and others who met the similar fate.

There were hugs and pats on the back, after the story another warrior went into a tale on how they took down a boar. They had a long spear with a crossbar in it to help brace the impact and to make sure the boar could not go up the spear to kill the person on the other side. After they killed that boar another one went to attack. The first boar had broken the spear and they scrambled to find the spare spears they had. They had to use their normal spears to kill both boars.

My colleague's and possibly my jaw dropped, we were thinking the pigs on a farm were not really what they were describing in its ferocity. It was a delicious rage monster that could easily tear someone limb from limb if they lacked awareness. We quickly filed this under serious advice. This would be in our briefing to the Commander when we got back and included in the going a shore briefing.

The going ashore briefing would happen anytime before a ship pulled into port or anchored off, allowing people to relax and spend time off the shore. Part of my job is to help with the plans on how we are pulling in, what are the tides, when does the sun set and the moon rise. Believe it or not, the tides are influenced by the moon and sun's pull on the earth. In this briefing we would be told what places to avoid, the food to not eat and why, and the customs. Sergeant Buford and I are going to have a lot of work to do on this. With that I think it might be best to brief McGreggor and Ronan. I made sure to tell Ronan I needed to talk to him before retiring for the evening as the stories started to die down.

Ronan motioned to me to head outside for a moment, at that moment the night air had that summer crispness to it. It was just enhanced on how heavy the food and drink was. The birds were getting settled and there was the chirping of insects.

Ronan: "You wanted to talk to me?"

Myself: "Yes, tomorrow with the ship, your majesty has a ship that can carry you all?"

Ronan: "Yes, it can go off sails or rowing."

Myself: "Wonderful how tall is it?"

Ronan: "Around 25 feet." he used a different measurement.

Thankfully it could easily fit in the well deck.

Myself: "That should work well, we will be guiding the boat to the back of our ship. It will make sense when you see it. Make sure everyone has sturdy shoes, the entire ship is made of metal."

Ronan's eyes widened with amazement; his jaw widened ever so slightly.

Myself: "Everyone must stay with Myself and the rest of the people you know. No one needs to bring anything other than themselves. We will provide food."

I proceeded to try to describe some of the food I thought we would have. It clearly did not translate too well. Things like BBQ aren't exactly in the Gaelic language.

Ronan furrowed his brow "I think I understand, we shall have to try your food then. You surely must have different types of food, I mean you dress differently, one would come to a logical conclusion that your food will be different. Thank you for warning me about the shoes. I think that my king will be bringing around 11 of us."

Myself: "Ok, do you have a list?"

Ronan listed King McGreggor, his son, himself and he listed off a few more warriors and their drivers. The list came to 11 people in total, the king was not going to let his charioteer stay. Mentally I sighed he was on the lower side of the range. I was worried for a brief moment the king would want to take 30 or most of the city, honestly.

He paused to take another drink from his cup after that he glanced out at the open fields and talked towards my direction with his eyes out there.

Ronan "You are such an interesting bunch, it really is a blessing for you to be here. I can tell you are clearly not from anywhere around here, no need to worry your secret's safe with me, there is no civilization near here with what you have."

I simply nodded and took a sip from a warmed honey drink. I could get rather used to these, they made hot cocoa trivial by comparison.

Ronan "You are a lot tougher than you realize, you will get closer to realizing that soon, maybe not today, maybe not next week, you will want to talk to me after all this is over. Do not forget about our last talk, the love sickness that must be resolved."

Myself: "What happens if it is not?"

Ronan: "Have you ever heard of a death by a heart attack?"

Myself: "You mean a bad heart?"

Ronan: "No, it is ignoring what the heart wants the soul wants. She found you and you need her as much as she needs you. The fates have spoken as well as the divine, there is nothing you can do."

He went into telling a story about a warrior who ignored love sickness, he slowly grew weaker, his relatives scoured all over the land under every rock, behind every tree and he died when his heart burst, they buried him under a tree an elm tree, there was another woman who died after tripping over the root of the elm tree.

They buried her near the tree. He said that it was an apple tree. Both trees had branches that grew together in an embrace. He told me to think about this story and sleep on it, he said that the lady who can reach out to a person through their dreams is such a powerful one and one that can wait is truly one sent from those above. With that he finished his cup, and went back in.

I let my mind wander for what seemed like an eternity, time seemed to slow. I let my mind stretch and just thought of nothing, it raced along the fields, through the forests, passed the owls, towards the seas. I was jolted back to reality with a hard slap on my back. It was Doc.

Doc: "You doin alright Seamus?"

Myself: "Doc, yeah just a lot to take in. This was nothing like how I'd picture my second deployment, really earning that brass star now (brass stars on our ribbons and medals signifies you have another one, a silver one says 5 and a gold is 10) serves me right for saying deployments are easy and fun."

Doc laughed, "This is my first deployment on a ship, you kind of ruined it for the rest of us. What was the previous deployment like?"

I described the diplomatic deployment we did working with other allied nations, we would do war games with them, work with them and train for a few days. After that we would pull into port and party. Sadly we did not get to spend more time with the other sailors from other nations. It was pretty much a glorified cruise ship tour. I remember getting back home with around 200 dollars more in my bank account, our longest time away from land was around 2 weeks.

Doc: "Yeah that sounds like a vacation compared to what we are going through, not to say this isn't crazy fun. I was supposed to get out after this."

Myself: "I know what you mean, many people were in that situation, not sure how that's going to work with enlistment, there really isn't a big navy anymore. Everyone's alliances are just towards the old man."

Doc: "Yeah, there could be worse chains of command."

Myself: "You got a point there, not too many bad looking locals either."

Doc nodded while laughing, "It's not helping, we cannot understand them."

He had me there, with that we parted ways. He went back to his room. Another person approached me. The figure in the shadows was very feminine and shapley. Her white almost alabaster skin seemed to glow in the night sky, she pursed her ruby red lips, her raven-colored curls seductively bounced as she walked.

She purred, "Such a strong hand handsome warrior, care for some company?"

Myself: "I do not mind talking nothing more, I already have someone."

It was clear she must have had some relation to the blonde from Vegas, sheesh there is the right kind of trouble and clearly the wrong. She's like a car that's too fast at the off-base car dealership. That's got too much horsepower and at way too high of an interest rate. Besides I wanted the lady from my dreams.

She sauntered over whispering in my ear, "She's not here, it would just be us two."

Myself: "I would know and she would know."

She said, "Well if you ever change your mind, let me know."

Myself: "Doubtful that I got bit by the love sickness."

She playfully pouted, "You believe in that, you must have heard too many stories from Ronan and must have eaten bad food."

 She left after that, I walked to my room, inspected it to see if she was there. I did my best to put the table by setting my couch against the door. I heard it bang once, then steps walking away from the door. The morning had greeted us, roosters crow waking myself up. I moved the couch, getting ready for the morning.

I went to make the normal breakfast, grains similar to oatmeal with honey and put in fruit. I got the extra coffee packs from my ruck and bribed Cormac with another cup of coffee.

Cormac: "I see you slept rather nicely, rumor has it you rejected a beauty last night."

Myself: "Yeah, I told her I am spoken for." I explained the dreams and what Ronan had said.

Cormac: "Wise you say that, especially the story he usually tells when it comes to love sickness, you gotta have it to turn down Róis. Many men would kill to have her, and she's never been told no before."

I thought oh wonderful, I've never been the center of attention for any woman, I'm used to being told I was a wallflower from the discount bin. It was odd that I was considered attractive. I had two women, both very beautiful looking. The lady from my dreams was clearly the woman that was better for me. I think the dreams were hopefully just alluding to us being a team and looking out for each other.

Chapter 12

Roll the Dice

We ate breakfast with the banter in the morning, Cormac watched me make the coffee and he followed along. To an outsider this must have been a ritual to how I made coffee. I had to adapt it by putting in the freeze-dried grounds, then half the hot water put in the creamer.

Cormac: "Why do you do it that way?"

Myself: "Cormac, it's to make it easier. If you did not you would have to stir the creamer, the creamer sweetens the coffee and does not make it taste as bitter and acidic. Try some of the coffee without the creamer and you will see what I mean."

He drank it without the creamer, he spat it out. "This is vile. Why do you drink this?"

Myself: "It is something that reminds me of where I am from, it brings back many memories of being out at sea, land nowhere, making sure the ship is moving to where it needs to be, the hums of the ship, and well wake up. We would have a table with a picture of the area we were in, it would be surrounded with thick cloth that one could not see through. I would have to record where we were to make sure we could figure out where we were going and where we were so we did not crash the ship."

Cormac: "That is wonderful, we had to get to know the waters in the places we sailed. We always knew the home waters but had trouble anywhere else we went. Traders would keep their routes and sailing methods secret."

Myself: "I could see that, they got to make money and stay in business, however where I am from we do not wish anyone to get hurt. We typically also will rescue people if we are the closest ship. It is pretty much a rule of many of the lands nearby."

Cormac: "Would you even rescue your enemies?"

I nodded, "Yes, they would be treated honorably and released at the end of the fighting."

Cormac: "You come from a rather strange land my friend."

Myself: "I think we could say the same about you and others."

Cormact nodded, "Of course, so I was told we needed good shoes for today?"

I nodded in agreement. I tried to describe that the ship was made out of metal, there were heavy metal doors, and the walkways were narrow with steep stairs and places on the ship that the floor went up rather high.

We met up with the king's boat in all of its glory, it was hewn out of the finest woods, the hull was made out of ash sturdy and strongly filled in with tar and clothing to keep water from coming in. The sails were spun out of the best linens. She gracefully danced along the winds. She was clearly built to gracefully dance through the waters. She was a graceful warrior queen too. The warriors treated her as their regal queen, listened to her every need and desire. In turn she guided them along the ocean.

As we sailed closer off we signaled the ship with the normal dots and dashes, I saw a few more and was told they were asking how many souls. We flashed back with our normal number and 1 king and 10 advisors. I told the captain we are getting closer and we will want to drop sails. The stern gate was down and the ship was tipped back. This is why we get punched through the water.

The ship sinks back to allow water to go into the well deck, we have ballast tanks that take on or remove water. This allows us to take on craft or disperse them, of course the gate must be down. The gate was down, and the ship tipped up. The warriors rowed as the ship gracefully sauntered towards the Ashtabula. I kept calling out directions to the captain who relayed them to the rowing crew, the ship slowed as it went in the stern gate.

I was greeted with a BM2 Leblanc wearing his red flight vest and helmet with sunglasses. They were wearing the same gear when we had helios. His trademarked cigarette danced in his mouth as he ordered people to chalk and chain as carefully as possible.

He whistled at the boat, "Dang QM2, we should have rolled out the red carpet huh?"

I smirked nodded towards the king "He's a lot like the old man."

That got a nod out of him. He and the others helped the warriors out of the boat. They were taken aback by the strong grips.

The warriors, Cromac and King tried to take it all in, the smells, the sights, the sounds. It was a lot at once, I remember seeing my first ship. It must have been like that just magnified under an electron microscope. My first ship was a destroyer, she handled a lot better, being part of the tin can navy was a lot different than the Gator. The Gator navy was all of the amphibious ships. It was joked we were the forgotten part of the US navy. The ones forgotten for the recognition, the medals, the awards. She was still an impressive gal, not the youngest by far but she could still turn heads and she could still put up a fight.

The skipper met us down at the mezzanine deck. I told King McGreggor about what a salute meant and how to do a crisp one as we walked up the 25 degree incline up the ramp. The old man had offered the salute first as a show of respect. It was hard to see who out ranked whom.

King Macormact offered the salute back with the same determination and honor that Commander Alvarez had offered it. The king walked forward with his hand coming right out and gave a very firm handshake. The commander had returned it back.

Commander Alvarez: "It is good to put a face with a name, you must be King McGreggor, I am Commander Alvarez."

King McGreggor: "It is a pleasure to meet you Commander. Is your first name commander?"

Commander: "No it is John, Commander is a rank, we have a lot to learn from each other. Please follow me, you are in luck we are having what is a called a steel beach picnic."

I had to translate the steel beach picnic into a feast.

King McGreggor: "You feast there was a battle, I see many warriors here, few women."

Commander: "Yes we are all warriors, our ship was built this way."

King McGreggor and the others were sizing up the Commander as fellow warriors seem to do. I think Cormac could see why I would follow the Commander into battle and possibly never return.

Their sturdy shoes were made of many pieces of leather in two or three parts, with long leather strings more like leather shoe laces they would lace all the way up along a back part that went up just below the calf for some or around the middle of their calf for others. They were remarkably sturdy shoes, not going to protect their toes but they would work. Up on the mezzanine deck the grills were going, there was plenty of sodas and even a few beers, this was to be a party and killing a squid I guess qualified as a beer day. Either that or entertaining a foreign diplomat about as foreign as you can get I guess tips it in our favor.

I had made sure we took them through the line, I tried to explain the food, but it was not translating well as it did in our briefing, I made sure we got one of the marines to get the BBQ chicken and another to get the burger we showed them how to eat them along with the other types of the food. Ronan had got the chicken and ate it with abandon, it was watching a bearded toddler discover BBQ for the first time. I think more of the sauce got in his beard than into his mouth. They did not like the sodas or the beers. I can understand why. It was because they used so many flavors for their beers which were all made by hand and given proper time to ferment.

However they were amazed by the water with no flavoring, it was like easter candy to them. They grabbed around 2 to 6 bottles a piece. I made sure that we had a chance to use the bathroom and had to show them how to use it. They were amazed to not have to worry about wastes and to see water flowing from a faucet. I warned them this water is not for drinking, it has salt in it. We passed by a scuttle butt (drinking fountain, also synonyms for rumor mill, yes this is probably where the water cooler talks started). They were amazed by the magic of this and equally puzzled with the clean water. Everyone had to have a turn and several asked for another turn. I told them we have a meeting with Commander Alvarez.

They had no trouble with walking like sailors do, swaying with the pitch and roll of the ship (the rocking both fore and aft and port and starboard respectively) They were amazed by looking at all of the metal. The stairs were curious to them as well considering how steep they were. They saw the dice, card games and people joking in the general mess. I had to guide them almost forcefully up the stairs to the stuffy officers' mess. I know each of them even King McGreggor would rather be joking, playing table games and just having fun. I finally got them up to the officer's mess.

Inside the mess were tables, a few TV screens and a projector. I could see the bane of many enlisted personnel's existence, powerpoint. I muttered several curses under my breath and half prayers to whoever would be listening please do not be a brief of 800+ nonsense slides.

I got a weird look from Ensign Browne. As I sat near the King and his entourage. To me it was rather dumb, this was a place I was normally at when we gave navigation briefings. This was normally my job on saying what we would do, the tides, how we would pull in or even the weather. We divided up those categories, chief thought (and he was right) we all needed experience with planning and being confident to officers, so they would take us seriously when we make recommendations.

Myself to the king: "Your majesty this is how we do planning, sometimes our plans can be very thorough." I tried to warn him about what we called death by PowerPoint. If it was really bad we called it death and reincarnation by PowerPoint.

The slides started with the history of the ship, what our current deployment was, it was putting our guests to sleep. I was trying to translate what I could for them, most of it was not translating well. I had to make a mental note, our briefings if the king was going to see them needed to go through someone who could understand their language.

The presentation dragged on for about an eternity, to be honest I was even having trouble with staying awake.

With that I started to shake in my chair.

Ensign Browne: "With that we introduce our next guest King McGreggor."

I had to wake one of the guards to wake the king, they slowly woke up. The king stood up, looked at me and I nodded at him.

King: "It is wonderful to meet you in this metal ship. Your ways are very interesting and foreign to us. I hope that in the future we can become solid friends."

The commander nodded. "I hope for that too, how is the ship so far?"

King: "The ship is wonderful so far. I think getting some air would be a good idea. We normally do business over food."

The Commander laughed as he looked at Ensign Browne, "You hear him, it is time for the food and drink."

It was light food and some drinks, they had put out lemonade, it was tried and they asked for water.

The commander looked at me funny, "QM2 they just want water?"

Myself: "Yes sir, clean water is something rare to them. They normally have to flavor it with honey and alcohol to get it drinkable. You would have to drink a gallon of that drink to equal 1 beer."

Commander: "That makes sense."

Out came the pretzels, the cookies and pastries, they really liked the pastries and the pretzels, they mainly liked the pastries with the fruit.

I took mental notes of what they avoided and what they liked. I was going to have notes for the skipper after this, on the food, and I was going to have to tell him the death by PowerPoint was not going to be helpful for them. The easiest way to see their perspective is to get the commander or possibly another officer to check out how the king does business.

After that we were dismissed, the king wanted to go out and listen to the music or play what he called table games. The old man agreed and I was to take them to both. He went out and ET2 was still playing. They were amazed at how loud the instruments were and that some had cords and others did not.

We then went to the mess decks and there were many card games going, they did not like poker too well. They seemed to like Euchre and hearts. I had to bounce between tables and tell them what their cards were and how to play Euchre, I had someone helping me with hearts. It was crazy and fun bouncing back towards both tables. Towards the end of the evening, we had tea, they liked tea and going outside to get the salt air.

Ronan: "Tayg, thank you. Your people are a bit strange. I think the king would never want to experience that type of meeting again."

Myself: "I understand, I will be talking with my leaders on this. I noticed it as well. I was having problems staying awake too."

With that I had guided them to the berthing set aside for them. They were placed far away from the engineering areas. I ensured they all had the bottom racks and middle if possible. I ensured they knew where the head was and the closest drinking fountain. I ensured each of the marines knew they were to be respectfully guided back to our berthing if they woke up.

I went to get some night air, and Ronan followed me.

Ronan: "Tayg, anyway we could get some more of that hot drink?"

Myself: "Ronan, that shouldn't be a problem midrats should be now."

Ronan: "What is midrats?"

Myself: "Midrats is a late meal of leftovers. I do not think they would turn you away for hot water and tea."

We went up to the general mess, there were re-hydrated pancakes, burned rice with flakes of what possibly was eggs. I normally avoided midrats due to food descriptions of that nature. Ronan made a weird face looking at the food but quickly gained composure.

Myself: "My friend would like some hot water and tea."

MS2 Rigatti: "And?"

Myself: "He's a guest of the Old man"

MS2 Rigatti: "So?"

Myself: "You want to tell the Skipper, that one of his guests was told he could not have some hot water and fruit flavored tea?"

MS2 Rigatti: "Fine, I'll get you some hot water and tea for him."

MS2 looked at the person who was cranking at the time. Cranking in the mess is doing the cleaning and other work in the galley. You would get assigned that or work in ER09 doing maintenance for engineering if you were lower enlisted. This would be for a few months in either location, unless your department did not like you, some people were permanently assigned, every department had to send someone to either place.

MS2 looked at the person cranking, "Go into the officer's mess and get the tea and the tea pot."

The guy nodded and disappeared out of the mess, he came back 15 mins later. Explaining he had trouble finding all the parts.

MS2: "I'll set it up."

Another 3 minutes, and the water was ready.

MS2: "Here, is your tea anything else?"

For me, the answer would be no, as a rule I refused to eat two hours before bed. I wish to have food properly digested first. There are times where I have gone to sleep with nothing in my stomach and I will not be hungry before falling asleep.

Ronan shook his head as well. We both drank the tea in relative peace. Not that anyone could understand him, he got a few weird looks but that's about as far as it went. We talked.

Ronan: "You know you are going to have to track down that lady after all of this is over."

Myself: "Yeah I know, however it's going to be a problem."

Ronan: "How so?"

Myself: "I'm pretty much the only one who speaks, understands and can translate the language between the people here and, well, your people." I kind of laughed.

Ronan: "Well I plan on working on that."

Myself: "I don't follow."

Ronan: "I plan on learning your language."

Myself: "I would start with speaking. It's hard enough as it is, the writing is arguably worse."

Ronan chortled.

Myself: "I know lucky for me there isn't really a writing language and I'm not a druid or bard so I won't be taught that language."

They had an entirely different language called tree speak, it was written with symbols that stood for a different tree. It was used for record keeping, court cases, and medicinal records. That's all I knew about it.

Ronan: "I am not sure where to start, do you have anything?"

Myself: "I am not sure what we could do, I possibly could see if we can get you music to bring with you or maybe someone reading you books."

Ronan focused. I could see like he was speaking something but I could not quite make it out.

Ronan said in the English language melodic accent,: "How is this?"

I gasped, and thought to myself not too bad, others looked towards where we were sitting. It would be wise to not underestimate that one.

Ronan slipped back into is native language "A little bit of magic, bad thing is I have to concentrate to keep it up. I think if I continue to do this and work at learning your language this would help."

Myself: "I see, however you would need to go back with King McGreggor tomorrow."

Ronan looked at me with that dad look. "You do not know, King McGreggor is being assigned another druid, he wants me as well as I do to stay here as a diplomat. We are going to talk to the Commander."

Myself: "Commander isn't his name it's a title, it's kind of like King McGreggor, king isn't his first name it's his title."

Ronan: "So what is his first name?"

Myself: "Commander, since he outranks me."

Ronan pinched the bridge of his nose and shook his head. "You come from a strange group of people, Tayg. A very strange group of people."

With that we finished our tea and brought back in the cups, got a dirty look from MS2 Rigatti. We sat the cups near where the dishes were staked. Inside the people who cranked would have to wash the dishes. It was crazy condensed there. They had conveyor belts that were on rollers that you could roll in the plastic containers that had holes in them. The cleaner was affectionately named the dragon. The reason why is it would get so hot inside it would open and steam would come out almost like a dragon breathing fire.

Ronan pointed out the Dragon, "This is marvelous, is this how you clean your eating utensils?"

Myself: "Yes, we have a lot of people to eat and not enough space for all of them to have personal utensils. It also helps keep the ship clean in some ways."

Ronan: "Truly remarkable, there are some things that are wonderful as well as questionable, your taste in beer is one and that sickly sweet drink made with sour yellow fruit. It seems that Cormac has taken to that rich brown energy water."

Myself: "Yes coffee."

Ronan: "Yes he seems to think it must be ritually made, I suppose we have you to thank for that?"

I laughed. "That is just how I prepare it. There is a saying of working smarter not harder. It is made with hot water and usually drunk hot."

Ronan: "Ah, that makes sense especially since I have seen people get angry when they cannot find anything to stir it with. Burning your digits hardly seems efficient or smart."

Myself: "Yes."

Ronan: "Just be careful drinking hot liquids can cause your digestion to act weird. If you burn your insides too much."

I had to think about what he said, I suppose it made sense, after trying to translate it to English. I seemed to forget he was a doctor. I just felt comfortable with him, I guess it was the grandfather vibe he put on.

We made it back into the berthing area and I hit the rack and fell asleep. No dreams came to greet me. I slept rather well. The waves were rocking the ship just right. The beds were a lot better than what we first had.

The morning came to meet us, we stood with the morning formation. The king stood next to us. We stood at attention the entire time. They kind of looked and leaned up against the bulkhead (wall). They were disciplined just in a different way. Gunny stood at parade rest with the rest of us at attention.

Gunny: "Listen up, All of you are doing an outstanding job. It's good we are bringing the hurt to those who have not felt it in a long time. I know being here is not what any of you signed up for, but you are doing our beloved Corps proud. We are going to have to get used to where we are now, this is probably where we are going to live for a while now. With that sergeant, you are going back out there. We need more intel on what's going on out there and how we can stop it. QM2, you are going to go with the king and is party help them off the ship and get back home, then come back. With that Dismissed."

There was a filling out of the marines, a bit of goofing off from the lower enlisted with some stern looks from the higher ranking enlisted.

Gunny looked at us "I am going to have you go back out there. I want to talk to you about what you found out first."

We explained the owls, how they flew, noticed that they actually eat food and how they flew into the trees. We brought a feather back for Gunny to look at. It was the most pure white feather, it seemed unworldly. I mentioned the unsettling feeling I got, it felt like the saying someone just walked over your grave. That is the worst unsettling feeling I've ever experienced. I mentioned that there were no bug sounds, no birds or anything.

We reported that the water there is drinkable. There were no really defendable areas other than the waist high stone fence along the main road. We then explained the camp nearby and how the warriors would only take us that far in their chariots. Gunny nodded. I think you both should stay here for a few days after you help the king's ship ashore. I think reporting in with the engineers and Sutton they should be able to cook up something for you.

We nodded - it would be nice to get a break from going out into the field. We were dismissed. I went to the kings boat, the deck department untied the ship from the cleats and chocks. The well deck floaded and off we went, the king's boat gracefully danced towards shore, escorted by the captain's gig. We dropepd them off at the pier where she rested, hopped back into the captain's gig being piloted by BM2, the Gunnersmate and Corpsman.

I talked to Sergeant Buford on the way back. We talked about our plan with the information we found out. Possibly the best idea was to get the bird to eat the tracker. I went over the rough dimensions of an American field mouse, it should be similar to the ones here and easily digestible. We made it back without any interfearence.

A quick inventory discocovered that we really did not expend any ammo, and went through cleaning our rifles. We were just short on MRE's. It gave us the time to talk, relax and reorient ourselves. I never really thought about the Ashtabula in all of her majesty. I just thought of her as a hunk of floating metal we kept afloat. I thought of it just as a place to sleep, not really a home, nor a community. It was odd most nights the music would come out, you would hear pop, rock, country, jazz and more. Sleeping on those thoughts gave me a recharge, a deep respect, a sense of pride, she truly was a majestic old lady.

Being on the ship again, I helped move ammo to storage from the gym by the cauldron and ensure there was enough ammo near each gun mount. Also it was important to ensure there was proper maintenance of each gun. We had to swap out one of the gun barrels. The barrels do not weigh much, but the guns hang off the ship's side. What we learned to do rather quickly since the ship was moving, was to at least make this a four person job. One person sits upside down, two people hold on to that person's legs so they do not fall off. The last person was to hold the barrel from the top. We would remove the old barrel first then switch it out for the new one. We used to not worry about having a spare nearby but with the squid attack our SOP (Standard Operating Procedure) had to change. Another addition was to make sure there were enough rounds.

The Engineers were also looking into ways to see what was under the ship and ways to remind things to leave us alone. The hull technicians and DCC Beck did not want to clean up in the aftermath of that. It took them days to get most of the hull back into the shape it should be. They made sure we did not sink, it was rather clever of swapping around the ballast tanks which ones were full and how full they were to keep us afloat until she was repaired.

After that work, we were supposed to meet up with MR2 and a few other engineers to talk about our plans.

MR2: "Well we got a few ideas but we need more information to go forth. You said owls, how big are they?"

Myself: "Around your normal great horned owl to barn owl size."

MR2: "Ok, so we know what we are working with, we can get something to track, now GPS is not going to be possible. We can do both distance and direction from the reader. How do you plan on getting it on the owl."

So either there were no satellites or we were unable to pick up any of them. The reason didn't matter; the end result was exactly the same. I was also suspecting if that was the case we did not have any allies or enemy ships we could either count on or antagonize us.

Myself: "That is something we can work with. I did notice an imprint of one of the owls. I know it was one since it dropped a feather." I handed MR2 the feather.

MR2: "I have never seen a feather this shade of white without any flecks of brown or black."

Myself: "I am still amazed every time I see it, the eyes are also red too. Check this out."

I handed him the thread. He whistled.

MR2: "Dang not sure how they did this but that's not thread that's gold woven like thread, it's the closest to pure I have ever seen but you cannot make any dents in it."

Myself: "I did not know it was gold, I was thinking it was thread, this was also super weird that thread was attached to a jar that has no seams. It was like it was one piece."

MR2: "We are tangling with something that has tech I have never seen before, something we cannot do."

Myself: "Yeah I know right."

Part of me wanted to get him one of the jars, the other part of me wanted them to never exist again. To take away a person like that seems to be something worse than death.

Myself: "The jars that the golden thread is attached to takes is what turns the person to stone."

MR2: "I don't want one of those jars, heck I don't want to know how they work. I want them gone. Anyone going through that, the level of anguish to attract that I do not wish on anyone."

Myself: "Agreed."

MR2: "Care for a smoke?"

Myself: "Not really, but I wouldn't mind some fresh air."

We left the area, Sergeant Buford went to do whatever a Sergeant does. I joined MR2 out on the smoke deck. My work was done for the day, my rifle and handgun were cleaned and stowed. We made sure our equipment was easily accessible, considering I was now on the team who would deal with threats coming on the ship. We would rigorously train on security on getting very familiar with the ship, sneaky ways to get around the ship understanding the ways to use it's feature to our advantage and limiting the disadvantages. I think it's not wise to go into our little secrets. Who knows if this log finds itself in the wrong hands. I am pretty sure this is classified beyond my access if we weren't here.

I made it out to the smoke deck, as the sun was starting to set. People were standing near the butt can (where the parts of cigarettes were disposed of). It was always a rather clean area, those who used it knew if they did not clean up after themselves it would be taken away. Most people down here smoked cigarettes, some pipes, and a few cigarellos and swisher sweets (mini cigars, the skipper is really the only one who smoked cigars. I heard they are a time investment, and one must savor them). It's a habit I never picked up, I told myself just one bad habit and that would be alcohol. I know it's funny since we are not allowed alcohol on the ship.

There were a few people at the smoke pit. OS2 and BM2 were there. Seeing familiar faces I hadn't seen for a while was nice.

BM2: "Nice to see you QM2."

Myself: "Nice to see both of you."

OS2: "How is it going out there."

I explained how the owls turn people into stone, how they eat food, but we still do not know who was doing it. How our relations with the king were. That we wanted to fix the owl problem first before going out there. I explained the village where everyone was turned to stone.

MR2: "Dang, so what happened to Moore happened to others out there?"

Myself: "Yeah, it's messed with a lot of people."

BM2: "Just going to say this, that's not acceptable. Not where I am from, and a lot of the crew would think the same way. I know we aren't going out there but I am happy to drive your dead weight around. I'll also raise some hell on the coast too."

He smirked when he got the deadweight part, that Marlboro red still bouncing with each syllable in his mouth.

MR2 puffed on his pipe and blew a few smoke rings. "If I can help design anything that can cause some chaos I'd be happy to make it. I find it odd that the cauldron is only listening to me. It has been interesting moving it down to the room by the well deck."

Myself: "I think something to help us get around easier, they have chariots out there." I described how they would have the turning point around the back of the horse allowing it better mobility.

MR2: "So that's where that hitch came from, interesting. I think I can work with that. I got an idea already. It will be a surprise but it is going to take a while. Trust me you guys are going to love it."

With that he left while whistling a melodic tune, I think it was *The devil Went Down to Georgia*. I mentally shuddered at being on the business end of whatever he could cook up especially if he were to work with Causes Safety Briefs. Whatever they came up with would be fast, dangerous and loud. I counted my blessings knowing both of those two were on our side.

I kind of went away from the smoke deck to see the sun set. I always liked watching the sun rise and set at sea. I was hoping to see the phenomenon of a green flash. This happens as the sun is setting. Some might see it, others might not. It happens when the human eye is overloaded with colors as the sun sets. It can focus on green hence the green flash. I had been on two different ships. This was the first time I had seen it. I stayed out long enough to watch the stars appear. One of the more important ones that is the first one out and the brightest is the North star. It's a nice survival technique. Even though it's mostly north it will get the job done.

With that I went back to the berthing and went into my rack. I slept soundly and the rocking of the ship with the sea waves helped. The next day was a quick check on the gun mounts, no barrel changes. We started to plan the next mission with Gunny and Sergeant Buford. I explained talking to MR2 about getting the tracking item to match the dimensions and sounds of a field mouse. I roughly went over the dimensions, which were about the same size as whatever the owl ate the night we caught it.

Gunny: "This has to be convincing, we got probably one shot at best."

Myself: "Gunny you got a point, I mean the only thing we can do is see if they can get it to make noise."

Sergeant Buford: "We would need to tell MR2, then. I am unsure if he has anything set in stone, or that could work."

Gunny: "Best tell them now, instead of finding out they could have and well you missed that window."

Myself: "Gunny will do. I am going to talk to him right after this."

Gunny: "Good, now that plan. If you get exactly what you want, what do you plan on doing?"

I laid out the plan with the cover we picked from the last time, and used that same location to help hide us. If we could place the mouse roughly in the same spot or watch where the mice live we might be able to get one of the owls to take the bait. After that we would need to track it, not sure what the max range on the tracker is going to be. Hopefully that brings us back to the front door of whatever sicko is behind this. We find out who it is, dig up some intel and do something about it.

Gunny: "In a perfect world you might get that, you might only get one shot at whatever this is."

Myself: "Gunny, if that is the case those owls seem to take those jars away with them."

Sergeant Buford: "The jars are breakable, if they hit the ground and are struck they will shatter, when they shatter the person is returned."

Gunny: "What?"

Myself: "So I think it takes out the entire essence of a person and turns them into a statue."

Gunny: "You might want something non lethal then."

Sergeant Buford: "Flashbangs?"

Gunny: "Yeah might work and cause enough force to break those jars. Sergeant, make sure everyone has enough flashbangs."

Sergeant Buford: "Understood, I think we have a rough plan."

I learned in my time in the military about a wise ancient man he said, No plan survives contact with the enemy. I like to think no plan survives implementation, and to have no plan is to plan to fail. The other adage I really like is *If it's stupid but it works it's no longer stupid.* We went back to drawing out a crude map of the surrounding area including the trees finding a good spot to plant the tracker. I suggested planting it in the day considering all of the owls I have seen have all been nocturnal.

Gunny: "It looks like the two of you have a framework. I'd suggest talking to Corporal Harris. See what he thinks of this situation and plan."

In reality, Gunny's advice was very sound, run by the person who can cause the most amount of mayhem, one of the most resourceful. He brought a water testing kit, I was still flabbergasted how he got one. Very glad that I am not on the business side of the mayhem he could cause and thrilled to have a vip seat to the show. The problem is finding him, typically one needed to schedule an appointment with someone of that caliber.

We looked through the ship trying to find him, not in the berthing, the mess decks, or anywhere else we looked. We did not find him until he approached us at evening chow. Not sure if you would consider that dinner or supper. Not really sure, I was raised calling it supper. We were over at the E5 corner of the general mess.

Causes Safety Brief joked, "Permission to enter the E5 mess?"

Myself replying back with perfect deadpan, "Permission granted."

Causes Safety Brief: "I feel honored, Gunny said that you called for me?"

Sergeant Buford: "Yes, we have a plan for when we go back out there."

We started to fill him in on the plan, until we got a few dirty looks from MS1 Miller. MS1's job was to ensure people were eating and had time to get through the mess. The mess decks were not too big, we had around 12 tables for the entire crew. There was a certain amount of time to get the entire crew to have chow.

Myself: "We need to find another place to plan this." I pointed over to MS1.

With that we finished our food, headed out to an unsecured space. It was an engineering room near our berthing. We got a Private who did not go out into the field to guard the door.

Causes Safety Brief: "So, you think that we can get a tracker with the owl, that's rather impressive to dress up the tracker as bait. Gunny said flashbangs, I always wanted to use one, I am curious what they would do to those jars. "

Myself: "Agreed, I am rather curious as well."

Causes Safety brief: "I wish we had more time, I would love to see a round set up for our riffles or even the M79."

The M79 was also called the blooper. It wasn't normally used by other branches except for the navy. We used to joke that the navy is fighting today's war with your grandpa's technology. Not to say what we were using was bad or terrible, but our armaments weren't as new and flashy as others. The blooper was basically idiot proof. It is a one shot shotgun style grenade launcher, it is rather light all things considering how heavy some things were. Causes Safety Briefs was right, it was our first idea or nothing. The time to prototype a new round and get it designed and tested was not plausible or even possible.

I simply nodded.

Sergeant Buford: "So we get the bait we need to set it up in a convincing spot. I can see this being an issue if done at night. QM2 suggested during the day."

Causes Safety Briefs: "Well that puts another wrinkle in the plan, the prey of owls are also nocturnal. However we could easily find out where they ate or lived during the day."

Again he had a point, I can see why Gunny said run it by him, to fine tune it. He was finding holes in the original plan offering advice to make it better and we were making sure he knew what was going on and what to bring. We needed to make the best plan possible, and be alright with it being abandoned out in the field. Out there timeouts did not exist, you couldn't stop the clock. We had one chance at this, one chance to stop something causing so much strife, so much grief.

Many of us joined for reasons like this. We were the type who rushed into the fire, not for ourselves, not for the glory, but if we didn't who would. It takes a special kind of person to do that. It's got to be part of you, it's not trained. It can only be honed and brought to the surface. That's part of why I joined, my first ship I was the first down to the repair locker for our fire drills. I got scoffed at, saying it's just a drill, to me if you don't treat the training right how are you going to succeed when the real deal happens?

Myself: "Myself agreed, so we would need flashbangs, the bait and tracking equipment. I am not sure what else we would need?"

Causes Safety Briefs: "Just leave that to me, I'll get us the best equipment possible. Just don't ask any questions."

Sergeant Buford just nodded, he knew the rules plausible deniability, and redirection were the golden rules. The less both of us knew the better off we were. Both of us were in leadership roles. I was technically second in command, if things went pear shaped. I had to come to a realization that could be a possibility.

Causes Safety Briefs: "Anything else?"

Sergeant Buford: "No, thank you for your insight corporal."

With that he exited the room, we left later after folding up the map, and I put away my notes in my little government green notebook. This little guy along with the one government pen that worked out of the entire box. I guarded that pen like it was my rifle. The running joke is, 1 was reliable at all times, another would only write if upside down or at some other weird angles, and the last one would work on either even or odd days of the month. The rest of the box only worked on a day that did not end with a y.

With that we headed towards the gym area, MR2 was reaching in and pulling stuff out. You could see the food coming up in boxes come out of the cauldron. He had to be careful on how items were stacked. He was the only one the cauldron reacted to and knew how to use it. He technically reported to just the skipper but he worked with and liked DCC.

MR2: "What can I help you with?"

To be honest, he looked a little tired and a little annoyed.

Myself: "Do you know what the progress is on the project we would need before going out into the field."

MR2: "Yeah, it's coming up there are a few things being dialed in on it, it's going to be finalized in the next few days and I should be able to get to it by the end of the week I think."

Myself: "Do you think it would be possible to have it make sounds, specifically mice sounds?"

MR2 Sutton: "Yeah I think so, they were trying to figure out battery and power. I think that could work for it, and a little solar charger it would hook up to. Ironically I was able to remember the sounds of the mice where I gew up and the cauldron kind of went with it. You would be amazed at how it works with what I know. I got people from all over the ship trying to get things like cd players, mp3 players, laptops and even video game consoles."

I could only shake my head on that.

Myself: "Would you be able to print out some charts of the surrounding areas?"

Sutton: "Yeah ironically that's up next. I had talked to one of the chiefs about that. He's wanting back ups for that region and others. The problem from what he's saying is it's a bit different than what's in the caldron but something is better than nothing."

The chart when we were first there must have been ripped to shreds at this moment, we would constantly mark and remove our location from the chart every few hours or days depending on how far we were going.

Sergeant Buford: "What about land maps?"

Sutton: "I can get to those after we get your mice printed. The Commander asked to have a few printed before you headed out. Other than that, anything else?"

Myself: "Yes we would need some flashbang grenades made if possible."

Sutton: "I think I can get you 24 at the most."

Myself: "Thank you, and thank you for doing all of this."

I could tell that he had hardly been thanked for basically working around the clock during and a few days after the squid attack. With that we left, it was movie night on the ship again. I wasn't sure what weird movies they were playing that never matched up with what was being advertised on the one tv channel we still got the ships channel. One was some silent black and white monster movie. I tuned it out on the mess decks. I was still rather curious about the people with the books and dice.

They were at it on the mess decks, they had their books that looked like they were printed out instead of the books they had previously. They were still just as excited.

I asked a person who was not directly interacting with the group. "What game is this?"

One of the younger guys replied, "Petty officer, that's the weird game with the paper, dice and pencils."

Myself: "Thanks, Seaman Richards."

With that he left. One of them looked at me and said "Well you're part of the reason we have the printed out books. The IC's found out that the books closely resemble what they think is going on."

Myself: "Sorry about that. They were a bit too curious and intrusive when they interviewed me."

Another Petty Officer, third class (E4), looked at me, "Still though, but they allowed us to make copies of it and still play on the mess decks."

To be honest, I am not sure why they left them with the digital copy. Having a copy in a binder would be just as good and easily flip through. I would love to learn how to play but being there and being friendly was something I just couldn't do. It could be considered fraternization.

E4: "If you join or stay longer the others in the group would have to leave."

With that I left, It was back to the Euchre table for me, however no one was really playing any card games. I decided to go to the ship's library for a bit. There were some random books in there, Some romance (not sure how they got in there.) some detective, some science fiction, fantasy (well that genre got ruined and one might need to forget about it.) a few westerns, some historical and a few mysteries. I kind of looked through the books considering I had read a few of the others and was not looking to read my last series at the moment. I did not find anything, nor did I have a book willing to swap out for the moment. As was the custom for the library.

I went out to get some air at the forecastle (you would call it the front of the ship, pronounced Folksal. I think it comes from the old sailing ships, thinking it was the front of a castle the most defended part). The front of the ship is where the anchor chain would home from the bosin locker, then off the port and starboard sides of the ship (left and right.) Many preferred to get a good look at the ocean from the aft (back of the ship) of the ship. To me, I just wanted a bit of quiet, it was late and no one should be out here. I was mistaken, there was a cherry glow of a cigar.

I saluted, and responded "Evening Captain."

Captain: "Evening, QM2!" returned the salute. "At Ease."

Myself: "Thank you, sir. I like to just take in the salt air before going to sleep, it helps clear my mind."

Captain: "Understandable, it is nice to see the waves for as far as the eye can see."

Myself: " Yes sir, we are still waiting on the tracker to be made, made a few suggestions to it."

Captain: "Good to hear. I am glad you were recommended, as well as Sergeant Buford."

Myself: "Sir if I may speak freely."

Captain: "Permission granted, QM2."

Myself: "I wanted to talk to you about when we had the king on board. What did you think of King McGreggor."

Captain: "I would like to talk to him again."

Myself: "I think he is under the same impression, he and his warriors were not impressed with how we do briefings."

Captain: "I understand that, it seems they enjoyed themselves at the steel beach picnic."

Myself: "They did sir, they really enjoyed the music and the bbq chicken. They did not care too much for our sodas, our beer, but the only thing they did not really like was lemonade."

Captain: "Good to know, I think the next time we might have to have some of our officers go ashore. I would like to work with you to get a packet together like we have prior to pulling into port."

Myself: "I would be happy to help with that, I think after we deal with this owl issue it would be a good idea."

Captain: "Good to hear, I think you gentlemen have a handle on that.":

Myself: "Thank you sir, one of King McGreggor's was inquiring about being on the ship long term as an advisement role."

Captain: "Interesting, I would like to know more about him."

Myself: "I think they think in a similar way, and they tend to respect us keeping secrets on how we fight and equipment to ourselves. He's kind of a judge, historian, doctor, priest all rolled up into one."

Captain: "Fascinating, those are all different positions not really related to one another."

Myself: "I understand sir, it is fascinating what he knows, and is willing to share. An aside though MR2 was able to help with figuring things out with the owls"

I explained what he brought up about the cording as I showed him, it was in the dark but there was no denial on how expertly crafted the threading was and how it was made out of almost solid gold and you could not dent it with your fingers. I then pulled out a feather from the owl.

Captain: "Is that a feather from one of the owls?"

Myself: "Yes sir, not a spec of black or brown in it. Albino's of any animal would be really rare; the only types of owls we have seen were like this. "

He simply nodded, this makes sense with all of the craziness going on out there that you talked about previously with the IC's. It was becoming clear to many of us this place was not where we were before, it really didn't matter if it was still earth, in the future or past. It seems that we were the only ones here.

Captain: "If you'll excuse me, I know at least I have a long day tomorrow."

Myself: "Understood sir, I think I might to, thank you for the talk."

Captain: "Yes, it's one thing I've always appreciated about being underway."

With that he excused himself, I saluted, he returned it and went back into the ship. I could see a few fires burning in the countryside, a few lights but you could see all of the stars like we were out at sea. There was no light pollution here.

Chapter 13

Village of Stone

I then left the front of the ship, I sleepily stumbled back to my rack, crawled into the bottom one, and as soon as my head hit the pillow I crashed hard. I dreamed of a chariot racing around the countryside. No creepy horse good sign, but bad, no redhead, good it was sunny, it was a nice trip, I had no charioteer and had to do everything myself. It was crazy trying to look around for threats and steer the chariot along the way. I was racing the chariot, and heard that gnarly trill again, in my dream I had ran over a bird with the chariot.

However, that was not the case, I heard the bosun's pipe with the 1MC (1 Main Circuit, announcing system) saying "all hands heave out and trice up." We never had to stow the bottom bunks anymore; they were all built in together. The bunks themselves would stand up 6 feet in height. I went through my morning routine, getting to the general mess and getting my two cups of coffee.

The morning formation was pretty much the same Gunny wanted us to make sure maintenance was kept up on the gun mounts, helping the gunner's mates with keeping up the weapons on the ship too. Sergeant Buford and I swung by the culdron to see if our tracking device was done, he was just starting on the tracker, and the mice were designed. He had set us up with plenty of flash bangs, enough ammo to choke a horse or 12. Enough MRE's for a week and a half. We were kitted out to bring the hurt, he even got us some C4 in case we needed to make a door where one wasn't. However, it could also be used to make someone's day miserable for what was left in their life.

We had to catch everyone up on the plan and ensure all our gear was good to go. We made sure we had extra hearing protection. We did not want another issue that happened with the banshee again. It kind of sucked being the intel and recon at the same time, we had no one else to rely on. We were kind of going out there trying to invent the wheel with nothing to rely on. Complaining wasn't going to produce the intel we needed, it was time to "Embrace the suck." Just dig our heels in and get it over with. I tried to keep my eye on Causes Safety Brief's, it was near impossible, I could not figure out where he got his supplies from.

The rest of the day was relaxing and we were headed out tomorrow. Sutton showed us the digital mice, they looked almost real. He showed us how they worked along with the sounds. They had tiny solar panels on their backs to help keep the battery charged. The sounds are about spot on for the mice, they couldn't move due to the battery. He turned on the tracker, it was military simple, we could see direction and distance. It was a simple display but effective. Very military proof to be honest.

With that in hand, I would be the one using it. It seemed simple enough to use and follow. The tracker reminded me of our military gps unit on the ship.

I didn't mind the benging voluntold to use the tracker, Sergeant Buford would want to keep every solid shot ready. Besides I imagined it would be similar to recording the positions and calling them out when we went into port. When in port we would have to call out our position every minute, the reason is when you get between land and water charts and maps for that matter get kind of weird. The earth is not perfectly round, we have to pretend it is, then cut it into squares, so each chart or map is distorted twice.

With that being said, we headed out the next morning. BM2 was with his trademark cigarette, at same time he was drinking coffee driving the boat. Absent was the boombox, everyone's head was in the game eyes on target and murder was in the eyes of everyone. We got dropped off on the same beach. It was eerily quiet like everyone knew what was going to go down, destiny had told them before our arrival.

There was no one on the beach, nothing but the wind and tide to greet us. We made it into the village without interruptions. All of the houses were closed up, none of the dogs were even out, it was a ghost town. We ended up making it to the city by nightfall. There were a few there to greet us. The king was busy and unavailable, same with the warriors. We were set up in the hostel for the night. There we were trying to get pre-show jitters out of our system. Everyone seemed to have their own methods.

Private Murray was doing pushups, Sergeant Buford was cleaning his shoes. Cause's safety briefs was pestering doc with jokes, his favorites were hey doc hold my beer and the marine equivalent of mommie look what I can do. Doc was slack jawed, annoyed and laughing at Causes safety brief's. Williams was taking apart this rifle while singing gospel music. I was listening to heavenly celtic harp music. I was lucky enough to have an mp3 player loaded with my favorite music. The singer sounded like an angel, I could understand a few words, I think it was a modern version of the language I had uploaded in my brain. From what I could gather it was an old lullaby, the song was beautiful at the end it was just the beginning of the song played in reverse with lighting.

The fireplace crackled and popped as the flames slowly stopped dancing. It was still warm in the building. I slowly drifted off to sleep. I was dreaming I was on a chariot again, trying to keep up with an owl. The trees seemed to grow up and closer as I raced to try to keep up with the owl, the horses were doing everything they could to keep up and not get launched. However it was getting tricky, I was launched and started falling towards the ground. I woke up on the ground.

Doc shot up, "What the… are we under attack?"

Myself: "No, I had a dream, it was a weird one."

Doc: "Ok, go back to sleep, try not to conjure up anything loud."

I crawled back into the couch bed and fell asleep. No dreams, just sleep. There were thankfully birds to greet us with the morning, jokes were being told around the morning meal along with a nice warm fire. The smell of turf burning with the scent of coffee was uplifting and energetic. To me it was a good omen, I could get used to this. Maybe once I retire, I will just import coffee, have a nice little house. Also complain about how the fish are not cooperating for dinner. Not sure how retirement would work with the old man.

Sergeant Buford: "We head out in 30 mins."

I just finished my second cup of coffee, cleaned up and packed up my gear. We had a long march to the camping spot where we met the fair folk then to the village of stone as I have heard some call it. Others called it the village of sorrows and that sounded too depressing. Camping at the spot outside the village would be the best spot or so we planned. Setting up stuff during the day we were hoping would give us an advantage.

As we left one of the king's warriors walked by us. I wanted to find out why the city and the village were so quiet. Something seemed so strange. Everyone seemed in such a hurry, and on a mission. I tried to get the attention of any of the warriors, they all were racing off getting their chariots up and running. There were lots of hugs, kisses. It reminded me of going on a deployment. Many of the other guys had this happen. It was usually when coming back but it still kind of hit home. It was nice to have someone in your corner who had your back.

With that some of the warriors had left, I was finally able to flag one down.

Myself "Warrior, what is going on?"

Warrior "Have you not heard we are going to war?"

Myself "With who?"

Warrior "The misshapen ones, have you not heard of them? They wish to destroy everyone who is not like them.They envy life, happiness and love."

Myself "They sound terrible, like violence and hate are the only things they understand."

Warrior: "Foreigner, sadly you are right. For generations they have left us no other options, we fight them and they fight us. This has gone on for generations."

Myself: "What made them want to attack now?"

Warrior: "If I had to guess it was that the village to our north was turned to stone, they think with our reduced numbers we would not be able to repel their attack."

Myself: "I understand, I wish you all the best."

Warrior: "Likewise, what you are doing is probably crazier, chasing after something that doesn't exist. It's like unraveling a tunic to find a missing thread."

I left giving him a firm handshake and a pat on the back with the other hand. I get what he meant, the foe we can see is no less dangerous than the one we cannot identify. At times it takes a while to find the hidden foe. I went back with that interaction to the hostel. I filled in our group with the intel.

Causes Safety Briefs: "So we might be coming back to a dumpster fire?"

Myself: "It seems that way, one of the warriors said they've been attacked by what he called the misshapen ones for generations."

Sergeant Buford: "What do they mean by misshapen ones?"

Myself: "I am honestly not sure. I gathered from him that they seem to only understand hate and vengeance. They are guessing that since the village to the north has been turned to stone, now is a perfect time to attack."

Sergeant Buford: "I can see why they would do that, we need to keep an eye out for them too I guess."

Myself: "The only things I can think of are two misshapen people or animals."

The name did not ring a bell. I really wish it did. I needed to chat with Ronan on this to see if I could figure out how to recall the memories uploaded to my brain. This not knowing stuff was getting to be annoying. It would have been helpful in the fight against the banshee. Worrying about the past wouldn't work long term. I couldn't let it eat at me. I had to focus on the mission at hand, I was hoping we wouldn't run into the misshapen ones.

We headed out, and on the road going north. Our speed was dependent on getting there quickly, so we made it to the camp just before nightfall. The camp was almost abandoned except for a group of 10 people near where we were. They were all cloaked and huddled around the fire. I could hear them talking as loud as possible.

Black robe: "You see the weird ones over there?"

Green robe: "Yeah kind of obvious, they look kind of puny."

Black robe: "Yeah, but they smell good, it's been a bit since we had a sup on something good."

Green robe: "Do it and he'll be angry."

Black robe: "If there isn't anything left no one will be wiser."

Green robe: "I guess, I could eat."

I signaled to the others; these were tangos (hostile targets).

Sergeant Buford simply nodded at Causes Safety Briefs and I swear that I could see that wicked grin from *The Grinch* movie form on his face. You know the animated one. He pulled out a black box and an RC car. What the heck was he doing with an RC car. He sat the car down and we watched him control it and roll it closer to the two guys. The car whined along closer to them. It raced to their feet as they threw back their robes to see better.

At that moment I could see the misshapen lumps that were their domes. These guys were so ugly they made the orcs from that big budget fantasy movie with the elves, orcs and dwarves look like underwear models. One had a red eye and a normal eye, the same one had one foot strangely longer than the other, it was very noticeable. The other had one giant bodybuilding arm and a tiny one that was so long it was dragging against the ground. The legs were tiny almost to the point they were too small to support it's weight and one of the legs worked backwards.Their skin was stretched and loose in others. These must have been the misshapen the warrior was talking about.

The car exploded, in a shrapnell of metal balls sparks and a loud bang. This car was possibly illegal in 12 different states and Geneva wouldn't be happy either. I had to appreciate his dedication to mayhem. With that, we opened up on them and the others, taking out 10 of these misshapen creetens. The bullets ripped through them, like knives through tissue paper. The smell that came off their corpses was beyond rank, it smelled like a veggie omelet MRE preserved in discount formaldehyde. Their skin was loaded with pustules and boils, some popped and others reforming. Their skin was so terrible it would give a dermatologist an existential crisis on where to start.

Myself: "Well, that happened."

Causes Safety Briefs: "I was not expecting it to go that well."

Sergeant Buford: "How many more of those do you have left?"

Causes Safety Briefs: "One more, it was only to test it out."

PFC Williams: "Dang, that was hilarious."

Sergeant Buford: "Ok focus, on point. We need to head out now."

It was dark, and we just brought bright lights and the loudest sound these guys ever heard of. Possibly we could have impeded their raid force even a little bit. These had to be the misshapen, it clicked these were the ancient enemies of these people. Their leader dove too deep into the dark arts.

Myself: "Sergeant these are the misshapen ones. Their leader had cursed them by focusing too much into dark magic."

Sergeant: "Good to know, if anything else jogs your memory let me know."

Causes Safety Briefs: "I was getting bored. Good thing we can take out these clowns too."

This caused everyone to get that smirk. This was the special smirk, you were in our territory. I've heard it referred to as the wolf smirk. These were professionals who just found something they can push to their advantage, they get to go bump in the night. Their only lament is there were no survivors to warn people about the angry marines hiding under their beds. I could not help but smirk as I thought about the misshapen couple with the wife wearing the hair curlers and the green face goo having her misshapen husband check for marines in the middle of the night, and their kids scared of a marine under the bed. I don't think the marines were a bad influence, I was always this twisted they just helped hone the humor to a razor edge.

We hoofed it to the village, it was empty and we raced behind a building to get cover. We did our best to use the buildings to block the line of sight to the forest as well, we got low to the ground and quickly went silent. No sounds, not a bird, a bug or an animal for miles. Just the night sky and the stars were out, it was a clear night. Time seemed to drag on, I glanced at my watch that was still running, it was still early 2200. We still needed to get to dawn. We saw no targets in either direction, about a few minutes later. We had a mass of robbed figures charging towards the explosion where the camping area was.

Everyone stayed still, all of our breathing was slowed. As the robed mobb ran past us, some had horses and some were off, the ones off were slightly slower than those on horseback. Their horses were just as deformed, just as disgusting. Their weapons looked vicious, cobbled together bad knock off weapons with angles jutting out all wrong kinds of ways. They looked unbalanced and impractical and their weapons would not be worth picking up.

Thankfully they raced past us. The night slowly turned into an eerily quiet night within the next half hour, we waited another 30 mins just to be sure.

Not making a sound observing everything around us. With the cacophony of insanity behind us. The rest of the night went off without any problems.

The next morning, it was quiet, we got to take shifts mapping out the town, sleeping. Pinpointing the best spot to place the bait. It was odd there were still no sounds, no animals, nothing just the wind and sun. The only positive here was the well had clean water. It was cold for hours and refreshing. Williams found a good spot, it had plenty of long grass that hadn't been cut yet. He had expertly placed our fake mouse. You had to look super close to see the bait.

When the night came, the mouse started squeaking. It was mimicking a mouse pretty close to the real one. We got into position to get the angle on the mouse to watch. With that it was like magic happened. Two owls swooped out of the forest. They both flew over to where we were, I saw the jars open and I could see sergeant Buford slowly turn to stone. With a fluid motion Williams blasted the jars without a thought, he hit both jars at the same time shattering both.As that happened the life and color slowly returned into Sergeant Buford. he looked at us funny and started waving his hands in a weird yet menacing way.

Myself: "Sergeant are you alright?"

The Sergeant looked at us and did not recognize what we said. He looked confused and still tried to wave his hands in a similar way, it looked like he was angrily interpretive dancing in our general direction. Near the fence there was a weird sound and a tiny shadow. Looking at the shadow there was a figure about the size of a toddler.

The toddler looked odd. It was wearing a tunic, pants,the hat was kind of like a winter ones with the poof balls on the top, minus the poof ball but had a brim that ran around the edges. Looking at the clothes closer only got more crazy, it was made up of so many different shades of green. The toddler also had a beard, he seemed to look at us when we mentioned Sergeant Buford's name.

Myself "Well this is kind of weird, but I think Sergeant Buford is in the toddler over there, and the toddler is in the sergeant. I think they switched places like that movie with the mother and daughter."

Doc: "Dang it, this is the last thing we needed."

Causes Safety Briefs: "I would have rather had that mob of those hooded jerks than this."

Myself: "I understand, I have no idea what caused this problem."

Toddler that had Sergeant Buford in it was annoyed that he could not talk. I saw the funniest thing I probably have in a long time. The toddler made a knife hand and pointed towards the trees. It had an angry face as it did it. Sergeant Buford was still dancing around us waving fingers, just less enthusiastic.

Myself towards sergeant Buford, "Ok I hope you can understand me, if you can follow us just be quiet. We need to stay together and help each other. That's the only way we can get you both back to where you need to be. Do you understand?"

Sergeant Buford nodded. I looked at the toddler and explained the same thing, he nodded. Looking at the toddler closer, I started to think, especially with the weird gestures that sergeant Buford was initially doing this had to be a leprechaun. I do not think he was annoyed that we stole his cereal.

From what I could remember about Leprechauns, they were big sticklers on manners and cultural norms. They know every single one and try to use them all for their own benefit and towards your detriment. They loved puzzles as much as they loved using hospitality and manners towards their benefit.

Well started to move towards the forest, the tracker started to vibrate. I removed the tracker from my ruck and it was going towards the forest. We headed in the direction towards the forest. Everyone was doing rather well keeping up even Toddler Buford. We made it closer to the trees and the display stopped on one spot. The tracker disappeared, lucky for me there was a last known spot saved on the device. I really had to give credit to the designers. They deserved at least a beer when all this crap was over.

The trees slowly started to appear, getting larger and closer together. We got almost on top of the last known part. It was still on that spot. The spot itself was right on a hill. It was near the trees. Big Buford waved and pointed at me. I am thinking they switched bodies but they could not talk.

He then pointed at a fox near the hill that was kind of walking, prancing and dancing around the hill. I was hoping the fox would actually understand me.

Myself: "Fox where did the owls go?"

The fox with one paw pointed to the hill.

Myself: "That makes no sense, how did they get there?"

I swear the fox sort of laughed and I think it shrugged its shoulders and started to shimmy a little bit, as it shimmed a door started to grow.

I think I heard in my head you must come back to this same point to come back if not you might be lost forever. My kin might not be as helpful as I. With that he left. The portal itself seemed to bend reality and flail about in two different locations at the same time. When stepping through it felt like my stomach was yanked from my head to my feet back to my head and finally resting where it is supposed to be.

The area around us was almost like an eternal night. The stars that peaked through the trees just seemed to be professionally placed there. None of the stars I saw matched up with any constellation or position I was familiar with. Looking closely the trees seemed to be the same, they all seemed dark shades of green and black mixed together There were leaves but they were not identifiable. In fact the more you look at them the more vague they look. The grass and ground looked and felt like ground. The smell was something off, it smelled like flowers but not near your face. The entire place felt off, it felt like a memory at best.

I quickly marked the point on the tracker, as long as we had the tracker we could get back to where we were before. The tracker had quickly updated to show where the owl went, it flew all over the place and it was hard to track. I was able to figure out the distance to the end tracking point. The owl threw it up. it was on the ground, the only thing different is how it smelled. It smelled and looked like a big owl pellet.

There was a path that seemed to lead through the forest, at one part along the way there was water, the weird thing is the river seemed to be running backwards. It was running the opposite way it was supposed to. The water smell seemed to be distant like someone trying to remember it. I tried to glance at my watch, not a second went by. I did not want to be here any longer than needed.

We followed what would look like a path, there were red eyes here glimmering from branches and the ground. One got close; it was a pure white squirrel. Just like the owls. Big Buford went over and angrily waved his fingers and hands at it. He snarled as it ran away. In the distance a lone harp played, it was light on the wind. Then notes seemed to carry themselves on the wind. They seemed to overpower everything else around, even the songs of the birds took a bow.

We followed the harp music, they seemed to bend towards the notes of sorrow. It felt like blues music. The real blues music, the one where the artist had really gone through life. They got dealt more than a few punches in life but still kept on going. The landscape started to change, it was what someone remembered as a mountain with a cave in the middle. The cave was perfectly yet vaguely carved into the mountain.

In the cave was a roaring fire, the pops and crackles were distant and muted. On a stump inside the cave sat a small old thing. He was mostly hair and a beard. The strands of hair seemed to go for many feet. There was so much hair it seemed that his beard was playing instead of him. Without stopping he blew the hair out of his eyes. For a split second I could see the brightest blue eyes. It was like looking into the ocean around Hawaii. I missed those dark blue waters.

He looked over at our direction, "I never thought I'd have guests at this hour. It has been quite some time since I've last had at least a guest."

We looked at him. I had to carefully listen to what he said to understand. How he spoke felt old, like his words were all antiques, some you knew what they were, others you had no idea. You had to hear each sentence to get the context.

He said, "Please come in, no need to gawk outside, who knows what the weather will bring, you can call me The Harper or just Harper for short."

Myself: "Harper, what is this place?"

Harper as he kept playing that haunting tune, " I thought you would know, this is the realm of the fair folk."

As I processed it, I had that oh crap moment, we are over our heads and we are on their turf. We need to play by their rules. I remembered that story of the man who fell asleep near one of their mounds and woke up an old man.

Harper looked at me as if he could almost read my mind, "No that won't happen here, trust me they are just as mad as you are. What is here is not playing by even our rules. We want you to deal with this threat as much as you do, to be honest there aren't many of us around anymore."

Myself: "What happened?"

While playing the harp, he took out a pipe, somehow lit it, and was smoking it without stopping the current melody.

Harper: "The same thing here as where you were. I know you are travelers from a place that does not believe in us. Truth is there are not too many of us left. I might be the last one."

With that a screech came in from outside the cave. Out of the corner of my eye a white blur flew by. A popping sound like a freshly opened bottle of sparkling wine was heard.

Harper started to slowly turn to stone, as if he were fighting it. "You must stop the person doing this. They will not stop until everyone is like…"

He turned to stone and the music he played slowly stopped. The only thing that remained in the cave was a now dead and cold fire pit. No sound, it was rather somber. No one deserved to have that happen, nor did anyone this happened to before. Just erasing someone's existence for what? Another question just as important: why?

We walked out of the cold cave with Harper's statue still in thought, playing the harp with his pipe in his mouth. The harp and pipe were still made of wood. His stone fingers trapped in the next notes he wanted to play, his face frozen in mid word.

Myself: "We need to figure out where to go after we leave here. We probably need to book it too."

Everyone nodded, especially after I repeated this in the Old Irish for Not Buford.

I looked at Toddler Buford and asked "Are you going to be able to keep up?"

Toddler Buford shrugged.

Causes Safety Briefs opened his pack and started pulling out some pieces of leather. He started to tie it together into a rough harness with a seat. What on earth did he have in his ruck?

Myself: "Causes where did you get that from?"

Causes Safety Briefs laughed, " Don't ask questions you don't want the answers to, Petty Officer. Doc you are going to have to carry the sergeant."

Doc looked weirdly at him and put on the harness, he picked up toddler Buford easily in one hand like he was a shoe box. He sat him in the harness and toddler Buford tied himself in. It looked rather sturdy, almost like a western saddle.

Causes Safety Briefs: "I got a present for you to sergeant" he handed him a small crossbow and bandoleer."

Toddler Buford then had the creepiest toddler grin I had ever seen form on his face. It was like that I got something in my mouth, drawn on the walls and I am running away from you kind of grins.

After we left the cave, the path seemed to carve itself out of the trees to the right, the path stayed to the left. The path that was carved was a very tiny and slight trail. A deer trail. This was one that animals would use not too many people; it was wide enough for one person. However, Doc had to almost walk sideways to keep moving. Toddler Buford kept his head on a swivel looking around with his tiny crossbow on top of the mountain that was Doc. I had to fight from laughing Doc looked like the annoyed dad at an amusement park carrying around his son on a long day.

We made it through the deer trail unbothered somehow. I think it's because we were focusing on the mission, compartmentalizing any feelings for the moment. Surprisingly Not Buford was still in the game, we did however take the firearms away from him, not sure if he would intentionally shoot the only people who could help him. He grabbed a tree branch to use. With a few quick motions he ripped most of the twigs off the branch and snapped it down to about the size of a club. The parts that were twigs were close to the branch and really sharp looking. Not Buford just nodded and followed.

You had to give it to the leprechaun following us along and willing to pick up tools and want to help rather than just get in the way or not help and sit there. It was weird everything I knew about them from the limited stories said that he would short change us the first second he got. That might still happen but we'd cross that bridge when we got to it.

The trail never got smaller or larger; it just seemed to stretch. I think we were making progress towards whatever was at the end of this trail. what seemed like an eternity the terrain started to change, it started turning into a wet woods. woods with standing water not quite a swamp or what someone imagined between the two. It's like this place was put together with the memories of someone half awake and trying to recall something from about 5 years ago.

The trail still refused to open until we started stepping into wet ground. It felt wet but we were not getting wet. The best description I could mention is putting your hands in rubber gloves and putting them in cold water in the middle of summer. You can feel the water, you can feel it being cool and wet but your hands are still dry. We sloshed through the trail and slowly decided it wanted to open.

In the wet woods the trees had a partially rendered moss, like it was from a bad mod for a video game that needed to be updated but still somehow loaded. There were no sounds, just the angry red laser eyes. Our eyes were scanning while moving through this wet sloop, I could hear the sucking sounds on my boots.

With the woods opening up there were lights in the distance, it was a hut. It was odd to see some sort of civilization, possibly another person here that could help us. Harper did say that there were a few left. He did say that no one was supportive to who was doing this. It was odd he mentioned nothing more, not who was doing this.

We were still radio silent, still hand communicating. It was odd for me being in charge yet having the least experience. I know I was leaning on them as much as they were leaning on me. It sucked that we could not speak to Sergeant Buford. We needed to embrace that suck because whoever was doing this was not going to say sure take your time, let me make this easier for you. That's not how combat works, we were as my drill instructor said we were the wolves keeping others away from the door. We were the predators not them. I think sheep dogs would have been better, but hey, it was his analogy. That crazy dude pushed me further than I thought I could go.

Back on point, we made it closer to the hut and started to slow crawl. we all spread out a bit. Doc was still in the back duck walking with toddler Buford. I again had to fight laughing, not sure if that was the funniest thing I had seen now. Toddler Buford had put the camo face paint on his face, he looked like a toddler wearing a halloween costume from this summer's high budgeted medieval fantasy movie. His face had the confidence of one too, as his eyes swiveled through the woods looking for targets.

As we got closer to the hut it started to look like one of those cabins from a 1980's summer camp with the windows with wood that could come down to protect them from winter. Kind of a wood paneling siding. I motioned to go towards the windows. Thankfully one was not locked down. Doc heaved the window covering so quickly it ripped off it's hinges, he quickly ran to the right by the wall, the windows were shattered and two flash bangs were tossed in. Luckily even Toddler Buford had hearing protection. Guessing it was another present from Causes Safety Briefs and his ruck of wonders.

With the glass shattered and whatever inside must have been wishing they wore their brown pants, then we tactically lept in. The insides were vastly different books lined this room, on a closer inspection they were beyond non sequitur, in titles and even one of the books opened on the table. We quickly secured the room. (I believe other military types would say swept.) Then we moved onto the door, Williams pied the door with his shotgun. This place was eerily quiet and the lights were gone.

We had entered what was possibly the main or common room. This place was starting to defy what the outsides were. This room had to be bigger than the hut we saw outside. It was roomy and cozy, a fire crackle was muffled. On the other side of the room one of the creepiest things I had seen was facing us. It was mostly owl but had some feminine features, kind of motherly at a glance. The arms had started shoulder like but ended in elongated feathered fingers, more wing like less hand like. The feet were razor sharp talons. The face was all wrong, it was a combination of a barn owl face with human features.

She screeched, "You, you caused all of this, all of this pain, all of this suffering. It's all your fault. You could have gone easily, quickly and painlessly but you persisted. "Her voice was more of a high pitched screech. One that just hit the wrong notes, kind of like that stupid hearing test we need to take every couple of years. The sound of her voice made me yearn for the dulcet tones of the bosin pipe. I would rather listen to the cover of that epic sax guy being played on a bosin pipe than what I was currently hearing.

We opened fire on her, she was invited to a buffet of all you can eat lead. The bullets just seemed to bounce off the magic shield she conjured. We kept firing as much as we could. We needed something, Not Buford had charged in there I had warned the guys he was running in. He started swinging that branch like a disciplined madman. It must have been an art form akin to sword fighting in the movies. The best one I can imagine is with a princess and a bride. Come to think of it, Doc kind of looked like one of the characters.

The shield around her started to shatter in flakes, kind of like shaving off the ends that give a golfball its spin. With that the owls came in from the windows. It was now guns up, out, and hate on the owls they would swoop around and down towards us. I quickly called out to watch fire and targets. The owls were now treated to plenty of bullets here and there.

Not Buford was baseballing plenty of the owls and getting a pretty mean batting average. More than a few owl chunks were messily attached to the branch. He hit one with a wet thump and it exploded into feathers and pink mist.

While that was happening Murray was still trying to shoot Owl lady. He managed a few hits on her, she had started to wave her arms about in weird gestures, screeching things I could not understand. I am not joking, lightning sprouted from her fingertips and shot into Murray. He stood his ground and kept shooting, she then casted another spell still screeching in pain while trying to cast causing Murray to fly to the other side of the room he hit the wall with full force and hit the ground. He tried to crawl to a place he could get to his feet. She never stopped trying to hit him.

After all this carnage we had turned to the owl lady. Murder and hate fueled our eyes like an out of control bonfire. We started to fire at her, bullets hitting her, hitting the walls and windows, she casted another spell sending us flying out of the hut.

I was pissed, I was done with it. Doc ran to the other side of the house to look for a window, with toddler Buford jerking along for the ride. He was jerking along like he was riding a camel with three feet. Not Buford got to his feet, brushed himself off and looked at me.

Myself towards Not Buford, "We wait here, we leave no one behind."

He simply nodded, picked up his makeshift pain stick and waited.

Doc came back hoofing it, fireman carrying Murray hunched over and Toddler Buford was still bouncing, firing tiny bolts the size of foam darts towards the owl lady. I got to commend Doc for not giving any F's. I could tell the guys were pissed; Murray was like their kid brother. This owl lady had hurt a lot of people, she really messed him up. Doc gently placed down Murray. He was quickly trying to get the bleeding to stop and get Murray comfortable.

I looked at Causes Saftey Briefs and just nodded. I didn't need to say anything. He handed me two flash bangs, two to Williams and two for himself. We all threw them in quickly towards the cabinets in the hut. This caused the owl lady to search and belly flop on the floor. For good measure he drove what he called an RC FU into the hut. The explosions flattened the hut like it was made out of cheap cardboard in the middle of an explosion.

Doc: "QM2, get over here."

Myself: "Doc on my way."

I raced over to where Doc was trying to keep Murray comfortable and triage his wounds. He looked like hell. Doc did his best, but he wasn't long for this world.

Murray coughed, his voice getting low "Petty Officer, I got something for you."

Myself: "Murray hang on, you can give it to me later."

Murray: "Not much time, take it now."

His hands shook as he handed me two jars covered in his blood. These were unused jars. The only two that existed. We had a chance to fix Buford and the leprechaun.

Myself: "Thanks Murray, dang I am sorry bud."

Murray: "It happens, it's part of being a marine. Promise me something Petty Officer?"

Myself: "Of course what is it?"

Murray: "Fix the sergeant, get you a girl and have some kids."

With that he lost consciousness, he then died. It hit hard, I liked Murray, he taught me a few pointers on shooting and moving. He was with us during the banshee incident. And now he was gone, we weren't leaving him here. I offered to carry him, but doc quickly said that wasn't happening. Looking at the jars we had one shot at this and there was no time like the present. We slowly uncorked both jars and both Toddler Buford and Not Buford turned to stone. I thought about how this worked previously with Wililam's shot. He hit both jars at the same time. Williams had one jar and I had the other.

I looked at Williams, "Ok we need to do this one jar at a time, to avoid the problem happened when both jars were shot simultaneously. You go first, on 3."

I counted to three and he shattered the jar on the ground, out came a green glowing light that swirled around the leprechaun's body, then sergeant Buford's. It finally went into Sergeant Buford's body.

Sergeant Buford: "Ok that sucked, I swear if you tell anyone about this, you are all going to do PT until I throw up."

Myself: "Sorry the skipper wants an accurate record, I won't tell anyone but the record will be available to whoever is cleared to read it."

He shot me a murderous look but that would have to do. Truth be told, I was more scared of the old man than him. The old man could make my life miserable for several eternities and for all of my ancestors and descendants at the same time.

I uncorked the jar I had and a green light flew towards the leprechaun's statue, and he slowly came back to life.

He looked at us "Thank you, that was weird being that high off the ground. I am amazed you just did not kill me there."

Myself: "Why, you were just a bad spot like we were.."

Leprechaun: "You can call me Fintan, it was fun causing mayhem with you." When he said that there was a wild sparkle in his eyes.

Myself: "We are not done causing mayhem, there was a warband of misshapen ones attacking a city, care to join us?"

Fintan: "Of course sounds like fun especially with the one with the backpack of presents. Besides, I owe you a few favors. Also it helps I don't like those misshapen ones they used me as their hurley ball. Took me a few days to make it back home from the last time I saw them."

Sergeant Buford was not going to be happy having someone similar to Causes Safety Briefs but with his magic could come handy. Besides, we could use extra people. He actually waved his fingers about. Speaking in words I could not understand.

Fintan: "I can now understand you and you can understand me. I kind of like you so I'll keep you under my protection since all of you saved my life." He had that rich Irish accent, the real deal not that fake movie one.

Doc face palmed and nervously laughed, Sergeant Buford had the oh crap face, and Causes Safety Briefs finally had a friend he could cause mayhem with. The people on the business end of that friendship were going to have a rude wake up call. That wake up call would be the last thing they would experience for the rest of their short miserable lives. I was equally terrified yet on the edge of my seat kind of like those announcers made you feel for those monster truck events on Sundays.

I motioned towards my ruck, checking to see if the tracking console was damaged. Thankfully it wasn't, it was still tracking to the point I had originally placed. I looked up in addition to the stars we had seen. We saw this glowing phenomenon, it was similar to the northern lights. The lights were on going but slowly diming like they were hooked up to a dimmer switch in a fancy house. We kept racing along the swampy trail. Fintan was riding on Doc's shoulders. Doc was fireman carrying Murray's body. Williams was leading the way with Causes Safety Briefs covering us. Fintan had the crossbow in his hands with the branch across his back.

We passed the cave with the muffled crackling of the fire, the faint smell of cherry tobacco from memories long passed. The tune coming out of the cave was a happy one this time. It felt energetic, it felt like heavy metal music was pumping through your veins. I felt like I shotgunned two ripp its and was on my way to PRT. We made it back to the place it dumped us out. I think the same fox was there. He grinned, bowed, and started to shimmy dance again. The waves around the land of the fair folk started two wave and distort. We could see where we first entered on the other side.

Fox spoke into my mind " I am happy to see you, I didn't think you'd make it. You have pretty much lost no time, it's probably only 5 minutes from when you entered. They were kind this time. They consider this your payment for saving them."

He chuckled "I'd hurry if I were you."

Chapter 14
Stupid Games

I still have no idea how one laughs thoughts towards you. When I stepped through I was treated to the same stomach assault as before. I was thinking preparing for it would help but nope. No training in any reality could prepare you for that. That level of stomach inducing madness is something I never wanted to sign up for.

That was a jerk to reality, we could see the village in the distance. We had to hoof it there quick, fast, and in a hurry to see if they were alright in the town. We were starting to make it to the village and Fintan waived for us to slow down.

Fintan whispered "Misshapen ones." He still wasn't sure about our tech or how to use the comms net we had. Now wasn't the time to give the guy a crash course.

Without missing a beat we quickly got into the trees. With that our eyes were on an unsuspecting patrol of around 10 misshapen. The leader had his ear mostly bit off on the one side; the other was comically huge, his face covered with pustules perpetually oozing green puss like a dollar store chocolate fountain.

The rest were various states of disgusting and deformed. They were not going to win any beauty pageants nor were they going to be stealthy with the funk that scouted for them, you could smell them coming. They smelled like a barracks room, ate some expired MRE's and washed them down with bad *Taco Bell*. I am told most of their skin looks like if you were to mix together rehydrated wet dog food with expired turkey ala king mre.

Williams threw in a flash bang, one of the stupid idiots picked it up and tried to look at it when it went off. It blew off the moron's hand.

Causes Safety Briefs whispered over the coms, "Let's meet our next contestant on Play Stupid Games, Win Stupid Prizes." He then mock whispered a crowd cheering sound.

Mentally I chuckled but said nothing over the coms, Sergeant Buford also let it go. I think he wanted to let a little steam be blown off. Another idea it could have been baffling to see someone do something so stupid as to pick up a flashbang. They deserved it and deserved to be mocked. Thinking back on it I could see Causes Safety Briefs as a game show host, he would probably wear a digital camo print suit just to mess with people.

With that, we opened up and cleaned up the mess, taking them all out. Fintan was deadly and a quick learner with the crossbow. He was pelting them from where Doc was standing guard over Murray. We ended up getting on the move again. Made it closer to the town. Another group of 10 was running through the town, possibly getting ready to burn it down. People were in their houses, there were screams shouting and pokes of farming equipment poking and jutting out trying to stab the misshapen ones.

They were not even hiding their features now. They were actively showing them off. The biggest one that looked like a pig that slept on the wrong side of a nuclear reactor. It was squealing and snorting out orders. His deformed face was hideous, one eye was twice the size that a normal one should be and the other was a quarter of what it should be and somehow still functioned. His lumpy misshapen muscles bulged threatening to rip what looked like a cheap cloak from some less than repetitive digital merchant. His tusks one was black, it looked infected the other was broken and looked like it was sharpened with a rusty file. I was starting to conclude that the uglier they were the higher in command they would be.

We crawled to the stone fence, over the coms I pointed out the possible leader. The positive thing about fighting these things is they were easy to describe and they were all unique. We had to get in close to get a good shot. Doc was still holding the weight of both Murray and Fintan. We moved Fintan over to Causes Safety Briefs and put the rigg up on his shoulders. It made sense Causes Safety Briefs was built just like a dwarf.

They ran in, Fintan waving his fingers causing a web explosion to fly from his fingertips and explode centering on the group of them. Fintan laughed while Causes Safety Briefs threw a bottle towards the webbed up enemies.

It shattered causing a fire that greedily licked at the spider webs and those trapped inside. They were making quick work of those chumps. The fires were dying down. That was the last group that was terrorizing the village to the north of the city. Lucky for them we stepped in when they did, the misshapen were set to burn the entire village down.

We needed to talk to the person in charge of the village. We had to make it to the city, if they had 20 attacking the village who knows how many were attacking the city. Quick marching was out of the question. I highly doubt cause's safety briefs had a humvee in his ruck, or even a technical.

I went up to the farmers. They were talking around in the morning discussing how to clean up the village, still trying to clean up from all of the rotten food now this issue.

Myself: "Are you guys alright? I think we got them all."

They all looked a little frazzled, the oldest farmer's hair more grey than brown. His beard went past his belt.

Myself towards the farmer, "Are you in charge?"

Farmer: "I guess, what's it to you?"

Myself: "We need to make it to the city, do you have anything that can help us get there quickly?"

Farmer: "I got a cart, but that's about all I can give right now. You might want to talk to the village leader; he might be able to help with a horse or two."

Myself: "Thank you, we will do our best to bring it back in the same condition you gave it to us."

The farmer pointed to where the wagon was, it was a functional and solid cart. We could easily fit everyone on the wagon. It wouldn't be comfortable but it would work. There was a spot where we could hook up two horses. It wouldn't be pretty but it would work. Now to track down two horses. I walked around asking anyone for a horse or two. I kept getting denied. We made it to the biggest house of the village, things were being thrown out hastily.

Myself: "Hello, we need help getting to the city."

Voice inside: "Not my problem, I am getting out of here it's not safe. You are on your own, and they are on their own."

Myself: "You gotta be kidding me, who do you think cleared out the forces near your village?"

Voice inside: "Does not matter, not safe here. I am going as far away as I can."

I went back to the cart defeated. The guys were getting the gear into the cart. I came back without horses. It was hectic, with the farmers trying to get their families back into the houses, trying to get the village cleaned up after being statues for many days.

Sergeant Buford: "Any luck QM2?"

Myself: "No, the village leader is running, trying throwing everything out and trying to get out himself. "

Sergeant Buford: "What a selfish coward." He looked over at Fintan and Cause's safety briefs. "Make it happen."

With that, Fintan whistled, he then spoke in the same tone that Harper did. I could only catch from him that we need your help. I am with the ones that stopped Mother Owl. Out of the woods, came 2 of the most majestic horses I had ever seen. One was black one was white, both looked like they were beyond perfect and models that would advertise for horse shampoo. What was odd was that both had one horn. Fintan guided them to the wagon and attached them to the wagon.

Fintan: "Sergeant, these guys are the good news, the bad I am out of any magic until I rest, I had one heck of a day."

Sergeant Buford: "Understood, Let's get to the city we got some more fools to force into an early retirement."

Fintan nodded, "I'll drive, they know me and will listen. They will only take us just outside the city. They are fearful they will be forced to pull for the king's chariot."

Myself: "That makes sense, please let them know thank you and we understand."

With that we climbed into the wagon, what happened next only Fintan was prepared for. It felt like we had two muscle cars pulling the wagon.

Thankfully the roads were mostly level a few times. I think I was almost thrown out at least twice. Fintan laughed the entire time. I was starting to think him joining us might not be the wisest decision.

We raced past the camp with the fey, Fintan mentioned that some of the less then nice fair folk liked to prey on unsuspecting travelers here. From there we bounced along the road.

Fintan looked over at the charred remains of the hut along that section of the road. He snorted "Serves her right, she tried luring me to that same fate."

As we passed the charred remains of the hut we were seeing some of the misshapen running towards the city on the main road.

Sergeant Buford: "Pick your targets, fire smartly. We got to save ammo. More we kill here the less we have to later on. If you can swing at them do so."

Rifles were out and we quickly worked on firing angles. Doc picked up Murray's rifle and started to pop suckers too. Bullets slammed into the misshapen causing the black red blood to spay from them. They tried chasing after us once they noticed where the pain and agony came from. We left a few injured and wheezing enemies along the road, they were not long for the world. Causes Safety Briefs purposely left one unharmed.

Myself: "Why did you leave that one unharmed?"

Causes Safety Briefs: "It's been a bit since I have messed with someone like that, besides a confused enemy is a demoralized enemy."

I couldn't fault the logic on that.

The misshapen who looked like a mangled frog human hybrid croaked a sigh of relief, seeing no wounds on its body. It looked around seeing the carnage and shuffled about. Seeing it was one of the few uninjured ones. Some held their legs on the ground, others face down in the dirt.

We raced on until it became nightfall.

Fintan: "They can take us no farther."

They gave one more big boost of speed and simply vanished from the cart. Fintan kept the cart on the road as we coasted to a stop. We were a ways out of the city, it would probably be a good 10 min walk 5 if we hoofed it. We made sure the cart was in a safe spot, geared up quickly, and started to make our way closer to the city. We could see lights in the distance. We got closer to the gates and noticed a lot of fire getting closer to the city.

As we got closer one of the towers for the city gate was fully on fire. With that there was a group of 20 of the misshapen near the gate trying to get in. The gate was not budging but they looked like they were going to try to get through the burned down part of the gate once it happened. They were not expecting anyone behind them. They were not expecting to get the jump on them.

The mayhem commenced, out came the rifles. We had one flashbang left, it was in the hands of Causes Safety Briefs. He readied the flash bang threw it and it landed on its side as it rolled towards a section of the misshapen. They had no time to react. When it exploded they were cut down like wheat with a sickle with riffle fire. The wall with the tower crumbled. In an instant another 30 ran into the city.

The misshapen were yelling, laughing and making all sorts of distorted noises. Think farm animals who figured out pitch shifting, auto tune and wanted to use both at the same time. Truth be told they were unsettling and if one wasn't trained they would want to run away or just give up.

We chased after them, I took out another and I heard a click. I was out of ammo and no spare mag. I slung my rifle on my back and drew my trench hawk. I threw the hawk at the closest one, it went right center mass in his back with a wet thwack. I quickly ran to pick up the ax with one ready with a sword and shield. Their weapons were a bit duller on both the edge and the metal coloring.

This misshapen was almost like a bird; the mouth was a weird misshapen bird beak. Its skin was a combination of feathers, molting and skin that was a fever dream out of a dermatologist's nightmare. It shuffled like a sick bird and it would make a sickening squawk.

Myself: "Hey Bird brain, get over here. I got a bone with you."

Birdbrain hungrily screeched. It was a primal scratch of anger and hatred. It shuffled towards me, an ax with a shield. As it banged its shield with precision, feathers exploded from it with each hit, yet no feathers seemed to disappear from its body. It wildly swung its ax towards me. The swing any closer to my face I wouldn't have to shave ever again. I used my ax to grab onto its shield and punched its ugly face. It screeched in pain and my hand wasn't feeling too much better. Its face was a bit bruised, I hit once more, it brought the ax back to try and hit me with the backswing

Its swing was in anger, not professional or any discipline. I was able to dodge the swing leaving him wide open. My hawk collided with his chest and it made a wheezy turkey gobble. My ax tore into the leather straps of his armor. causing the armor to partly fall off. It went back into a primordial rage. It practically told me how it was going to swing with a fury over and over. It wildly swang left, right left then right again, I felt like I was in a terrible quick time event in a video game. It was annoying me, so I went for the other armor strap.

My ax hungerly bit into the other armor strip. The roughly designed armor flopped down and smashed its thighs. It keeled forward squabbling in pain and awkwardly trying to recover. My ax had gone for the ax arm, I went through the misshapen swollen clavicle, the ax snapped his bone like it was balsa wood. Feathers flew in the air. Its black red blood lazily seeped out of the wound as its left ax arm flopped about.

Its black red blood seeped, the gobbling seemed to hit the in between notes. It was trying to block and hit me with the shield it carried, it looked more like junk metal someone tried to convert into a shield. The blocking was done slower each time, the hits from the shield rang my plate carrier.

A quick feint the to head and then went for the chest, my ax angrily bit into its chest not wanting to let go. I got hit once more upside the head. The world started to spin, I could not hold on anymore. The ground rushed up to meet me.

Doc pulled me to my feet with me in one hand and Murray across his back." We still need you, get back here."

He gave me a little shake, and handed me a rip it. You need this now. I took a big drink of the rip it, I've never been a fan of energy drinks. I got the false energy from the drink, doc looked me over quickly, my guess is for a concussion or other damage.

Doc "Who am I?" He quickly moved his finger from the left to the right. happy my eyes were following them. He snapped his fingers, my head and eyes followed the snapping as he snapped left and right fingers.

Myself: "You're Doc."

Doc: "Good, go out there. "

Myself: "Will do doc, I'm almost on fumes. "

Doc: "Let me tell you a little secret we all are. But who else is around to help?"

Myself: "Point taken Doc."

Doc: "Not too fast, you forgot your vitamin M and earth sauce."

I took the motrin, put it in my mouth and shot gunned the rest of the rip it. I topped off my water and went to help plug the hole. We slashed and used the rest of our ammo until we all went black. We switched to whatever weapons we could get our hands on and started poking at them. The blood splatters were all various shades of black red, a very dark color of red to almost black blood. Something was off with the misshapen.

Something more than just their appearance, their obsession with violence. Getting closer to the King's estate. The guards were doing their best to keep the enemy forces at bay. They would be overwhelmed if we did not intervene. We could not let them take another step if possible. We tried to advance to pincer them between the guards at the front of the Kings estate. We positioned ourselves to prevent them from any possible escape route.

This clearly must have been an elite guard of the misshapen forces. None of them were wearing leather armor. All wearing banded and chain mail. Their swords were dull looking in shine and in sharpness, they seemed to curve in weird angles. Their shields looked roughly and awkwardly beaten. Their armor looked hastily made and roughly thrown on their bent and disfigured frames.

Their leader with the fanciest dullest armor looked like a werewolf with mange, he constantly had flies flying around him. His jaw was misshapen with one part of the jaw longer and stronger looking than the other side. His teeth were all mangled and broken. His laminar armor looked rusted in parts and had dull shine in others. We ran closer to them, closing the gap.

We were all black on ammo, no flash bangs, no grenades. We ran in with knives, clubs and axes. This type of fighting was not something any of us were trained for. The misshapen were charging in with torches in the left hand and weapons in the right. They all used weapons that looked like they were made by a professionally inept smith.

Doc: "Fight smartly, only attack when you have an opening and you know they cannot counter."

Doc was able to pick up a sword, tossed one to sergeant Buford, threw another to Causes Safety Briefs, and threw another to Williams. He grabbed a spear to hold in one hand and threw Murray over his shoulder.

Doc: "Ok keep me protected, keep knocking their weapons aside and I'll start poking."

We all nodded.

Sergeant Buford: "Doc You set the pace, everyone you step forward one pace only on the left foot just like marching after Doc takes a step."

More agreement all around.

Fintan: "I think I can hop up on Doc's shoulders to help keep the balance and keep the weapons off of him too."

Doc: "Sounds good help put him in."

We ended up quickly rigging up Fintan to Doc's shoulders, getting it so Murray was evenly distributed.

Sergeant Buford: "Doc you are going to call cadence."

To an outsider this must have been something to see. Five angry soldiers moving in step with an angry leprechaun ready to lay the beat down.

Doc shouted, "Left."

We moved left, Sergeant Buford moved a sword out of the way, Doc struck with the precision of a scorpion. The Spear dug into the sweet spot right in an armpit severing the artery right under the arm where it would be on a human. It seems even with all of their deformities they might have similar anatomy.

They didn't know what to make of this fighting arrangement. I used my ax to swing the next blow wide on my side of the wall. Doc hit the one whose arm I tossed wide to the left. Doc went right for the head.

Causes Safety Briefs called out like a pool shark "Idiot center pocket."

Doc's spear went cleanly through the beast's head, one that looked like a malnourished cat mixed with parts of a bear. It almost went through to the other side of the helm, his spear coming back and thankfully sliding out of the creature's dome.

They started moving back towards the king's estate.

Doc: "Left, right, left"

We were at their heels they kept moving backwards. They kept chaotically swinging at us. Doc struck again, went for the artery on one's thigh. It quickly bled out. Doc's precision with that spear was scary. Fintan was shouting insults towards them.

One with a snake scale like skin that looked like it was molting tried to go for Williams, he hit the weapon off to the left. Doc's spear went right into the clavicle, splintering it causing its sword arm to slump.

Three were pretty much taken out of the fight from our side and another two from the king's warriors side. This was leaving 5 more. This included what was probably their leader's right hand man, a very misshapen cat, he had no fur to speak of, he looked like a sphinx cat with some serious skin issues, pimples galore and other oozing wounds. Where the whiskers should be were almost like coarse piano wire. They were panicking since they were caught between a rock and a hard place. They got stabbed by the guards then tried to move back to us and got stabbed again. Both sides were taking advantage of their lack of discipline.

Doc: "Left, right."

We were able to knock their weapons wide. Doc went for one try near Sergeant Buford. It was a turtle looking one. Doc stabbed it right in the eye. The spear just scratched above the eye causing it to bleed into its eye. It was partly distracted between the slow stream of that blackish red blood in its eye and us.

We were slowly pushing them into the guards at the door of the king's estate just a few more steps. They looked like they were going to break and run; they kept bouncing between the king's guard at the gates. Doc didn't go for the turtle looking one, his blows started to get really sloppy with the bleeding that was getting into his eyes.

The bigger one looked like a mouse, the fur looked managed ridden with pimples constantly forming and popping, a few festering oozing wounds and whiskers that were bent in several different ways. He waddled more than walked. One leg moved in the opposite direction, and his arms were all wrong, one of its forearms was attached to the shoulder.

Doc went for its arm and shredded the giant forearm causing it to drop its ax looking sword. It clanged to the ground, it went for the weapon and doc stabbed through the middle of its hand. They took another step back, still out of range of the king's warriors.

They were getting closer; this could be good or bad. Backing an enemy or an animal in a corner could be a very dangerous thing. We could only hope that the warriors at the king's estate knew what we were doing and were going to cooperate. They wanted to get into the thick of the combat but they knew that the king and those who made it to his estate needed to be protected at all costs.

Doc "Left, right" His spear went out for the turtle looking one this time it went through the jaw into the eye socket. He had to yank with a decent amount of force to remove it with a wet sucking pop sound the turtle one fell with a slow thud to the ground.

They tried to take a step back and got stabbed from their angle, tried switching from ours and got stabbed again. Both sides made a circle around them to prevent the four from leaving. There was nowhere for them to go. The warriors all had spears. They spread out and it was and all you can stab buffett for the misshapen. Every angle they were at was one that left an opening. Time seemed to slow, we all seemed to easily knock their weapons aside.

With that the ground shook with a bit of a thud. You could hear a man yawn and roar at the same time. This man was easily 20 feet tall. His fiery red hair and beard burned like a raging hot fire. His sword was the cool blue color of the sea and his shield like it was made of sea foam. He entered the battle from the falling wall, quickly slicing through the remaining mishappen, rallying people behind him.

Chapter 15
War and Glory

With the death of what was thought to be the last misshapen, the ground rose up to meet me. I tumbled into a sleep right on the ground. I woke up in the morning with a rather beautiful woman caring over me, using a wet cloth to wipe my brow. Ronan in the corner.

Ronan: "Good to see you alive Tayg."

Myself: "How long was I out?"

Ronan: "I would say 2 Moons. You really ran yourself to rags there."

Myself: "Everyone else alright?"

Ronan: "Yes, I am surprised to be honest, all of you put up a fight. Doc woke up first, he was annoyed that someone was caring for him rather than the other way around."

Myself: "That makes sense, where is Private Murray?"

Ronan's cheerfulness fell from his face.

"He is being prepared for his final send off, we are all saddened by his passing from this life. Your healer was concerned and even tried to fight us off when we tried to get him to his room and start to prepare Private Murray for the next life."

Myself: "I see what about the others?"

Ronan: "Your friends are on the mend, they were exhausted, not as bad as you, but nonetheless needed to recover. What I do not know is how did you get here so fast with a wagon and no horses?"

Myself: "We had some help from a leprechaun named Fintan, is he here?"

Ronan nervously chuckled, "He is a known troublemaker, how on earth did you convince him to help you?"

Myself: "There were two owls close together. They took both of them in a jar and the jars were both broken at the same time. I think the parts of them that went into the jars were sort of confused and chose the wrong body."

He nodded intent to listen to the story to see how this insanity would unfold. Usually the fair folk would be causing the mayhem towards mortals not really allying with them.

Myself: "We realized that they switched their bodies, when sergeant Buford stopped talking and looked at us funny and was wiggling fingers. We found a way to follow the owls."

He kept listening along.

Myself "After that we followed the owls, until they disappeared into a hill, a fox had left us in and we followed into this weird realm. Everything was muted, it was like someone was trying to remember something almost forgotten. We found this owl lady. We blew up her hut after she caused fatal damage to Murray. His last words were to live a good life, get married and have kids."

You could feel the sorrow when I said that. They must have gotten along rather well in his short time staying with him.

Myself: "Doc was trying to help him, tried everything he could to keep him alive. In the end he gave me the last two vials and told me the words I said to you."

Ronan: "We'll do right by him, he went out as a hero. He'll get the proper send off I'll make sure of it. I have some good news for you, you have a thankful visitor waiting outside."

I got out of bed, slowly walked out of the king's mansion. Outside was a tall man with a beard made of flames. He had a commanding presence and had a wild look in his eyes.

Bearded man with a booming voice, "It is good to see the ones who freed me."

Myself: "It was a pleasure to help and thank you for the help a few days ago."

Bearded man: "It was good to see combat again after all this time. I was turned to stone like everyone else. I think I was the first one, my mother was the one behind this."

Myself: "Your mother?"

Bearded man: "Yes, I was going through some grief and it was not getting better. So she tried using magic and it was not working. She kept trying different spells until she figured she could turn me to stone."

Myself: "I am sorry that happened, she caused a lot of pain towards others."

Bearded man: "Thank you, however, I think I should be apologizing for this."

Myself: "You can call me Tayg."

Bearded man: "Some call me McLear."

Myself: "It is nice to meet you, McLear."

McLear: "Likewise, It looks like you might need some help? I can grant you two favors."

Myself: "I will have to think about that, I need to talk to the person in charge of our forces."

McLear: "I understand I will give you 2 days time to decide."

Myself: "How will I find you?"

McLear laughed, "I will find you, I am good at finding anyone or thing in the sea."

He walked towards his chariot, looking like it was blue and made of the sea. His horses were different shades of blue and green and their hair looked like sea foam. He stepped on the chariot and off he raced and he seemed to sink beneath the horizon. With that we helped with rebuilding the city where we could. On the ship we had our debreifing with the old man. We worked with the chiefs, and even attended a briefing in the officers' mess. We headed back to the city since we were summoned by the king for official business. We were told it was to be witnesses for a court case.

It was for the village leader, the one who refused to help us make it to the city. We were there in dress uniforms. We gathered in the king's estate. The tables were arranged like a courtroom. It took a few days to get two bards to show up. One to represent the leader of the village that turned to stone and the other to represent those who died in the aftermath of the misshapen raid on the city and the towns to the south. Two bards, and a druid were summoned. The one bard looked like the old animated Ichabod crane personified, he was lanky and had a huge hawkish nose.

The other one looked more at home on the battlefield rather than in court. The druid looked ancient making Ronan look young, he moved faster and was sturdier than he looked.

Ronan walked up to me and said " Tayg, normally I would be the judge but I declined since I am an involved party. The king was able to get two bards and a druid from outside our kingdom."

Myself: "Ronan I can understand that."

Ronan: "You both have some rather weird looking clothes, these are your best clothes?"

Myself: "Yes we have clothes we wear for ceremonies, they are all worn as a uniform."

Ronan: "So why are yours different from the others?"

Myself: "Good question, I am a different part of our army. Before we came here I was part of our army that was on the ship most of the time."

Ronan: "Very interesting, I look forward to learning a lot more. Knowledge is something to pursue and share, not to hoard. It looks like I will be a witness along with the others and yourself."

Myself: "Thank you for letting me know, so it looks like your druid friend will be the one issuing judgment and the two bards one will be trying to prove him guilty the other innocent?"

Ronan: "Yes, that is pretty much correct."

Myself: "That is pretty similar to where we are from, Do you use court cases in the past to help or hinder your opponent?"

Ronan: "Yes of course, and the bards and druids like myself have to know the history as well."

Myself: "Fascinating, anything else special?"

Ronan: "Remember how when you first made it here, I explained to you how people can go up or down in social standing?"

Myself: "Yes, so this is one of those ways?"

He simply nodded.

Myself: "What could happen to him?"

Ronan: "Well it depends, if proven guilty, he would need to pay those injured or harmed. If they became disabled he would need to pay them for the rest of their lives or as long as he lives."

To be honest this was worse than being ostracized or even executed. The laws made sense and I could see why this was done. They could not afford to lose a person, and a person being permanently kicked out would be a huge problem for a community. Their communities needed everyone to do their best to stay around.

Ronan continued, "I already let the judge know you will need to translate for the others. He did ask for Fintan to just provide his statement written in advance. Something about him not wanting any trouble during the case."

Myself: "Fintan is that bad?"

Ronan: "Not sure there are others of his kind that seem to love to cause mayhem as much as possible."

To me it was not right to do that to Fintan, after everything he did even ran into the city with nothing to gain.

Myself: "I feel bad for Fintan, he actually put his life on the line."

Ronan: "I understand, however it is the Druid Ailill's final say on who can be in the room during the trial."

Lucky for Fintan we got him a place on the ship, he was ecstatic to have so much space for himself, he thought he'd have to sleep in the locker. He pretty much turned his rack into a tiny little house. His biggest challenge was trying to get into the seats on the mess decks. The problem is our chairs were swivel chairs like the old fast food restaurant chairs. MR2 had designed something special for him and it was always available in any of the messes he could have gone to.

The king sat in the center up above where Ailill sat. The two bards, the Icabod looking one and warrior one sat at tables separate from each other. It looked oddly like a modern courtroom. The court case was pretty much similar to your normal court cases. The bards argued back and forth. The larger one was named Ercc and the Icabod looking one was named Muirchertach. Muirchertach was pretty much 10 pounds of anger and passion in a 2 pound bag. There were times where Ailill was telling him to stop. It was weird seeing the linebacker lawyer Ercc, he was calm and rational the entire case.

Ailill had dismissed us for a break. We went out to get some air, some water. Our little group all kind of rallied around each other. We talked about rather being back on the ship or being back out in the field again trying to track down where the misshapen came from. We got shuffled back in, and it was our turn to explain from our perspectives on what happened. I was called to the stand by Ercc.

The interview with Ercc went rather well. He was very respectful, honest and asked questions to show my interest in helping those in the city and villages. I made sure to leave out the goriness but still get the point across. I explained how we had borrowed the wagon from one of the farmers, but he had no horses. The farmer suggested I try to talk to the Mayor for help. He had refused to help and was packing up as many belongings as possible.

Muirchertach was exactly the opposite, he was borderline rude, abrasive. He kept asking me why he was only able to examine me. After continuously explaining in different ways I was the only translator for my unit, he finally gave up. He tried to downplay the horses that we got elsewhere. I had to put my foot down.

Myself: "Yes we got the horses, but it was not easy to get them. It took us time."

Muirchertach: "So how did you finally get them?"

Myself: "Our comrade Fintan had to summon them."

Muirchertach: "Oh the little thief."

Myself: "He's not a thief, he did not steal them if that's what you're implying."

Ercc: "Ailill, that is not a valid question, nor is it fair to a man who cannot defend his reputation."

Ailill: "Muirchertach, you better calm down, that's not right to do that."

I was mistaken, yes it was Ailill's decision to bar Fintan from the courtroom but it was because of the prodding from Muirchertach. It annoyed me when someone thought they were far more superior than another, especially when that person put their life on the line.

Ailill: "Tayg please continue your story and Muirchertach another thing like that out of you and I am not going to be happy. Understood?"

Ah rhetorical questions, always better left unanswered. It was interesting to see him getting grilled. Muirchrtach just nodded.

Myself: "Fintan had to use magic, this is something he could have used later on to help us within the city or make it to the village to the south of the city. He had no magic to use by the time we made it to the city."

Muirchertach: "How are we supposed to know that he's not here?"

Ailill: "Enough, he's not here because you forbade him to be. You were the only one who demanded him to not be here. You cannot have it both ways."

Muirchertach: "But, I want to talk to all of them."

Ailill: "Again enough, you would have to go through their translator, they would be here all day. That is not fair to them, I have heard enough out of you. I've made my decision. Your client is guilty."

Muirchertach: "But Ailill, I haven't stopped interviewing the witness."

Ailill: "Do you want me to fine you too?"

Muirchertach: "No, I do not."

Ailill: "He is guilty, he will be stripped of all titles. He will be put in service to the king until his debts are paid. His belongings will be sold and profits covered to pay for damages to the city. A new leader of the town will be elected in his place. Any questions?"

The former mayor slumped in his chair and started crying.

Ailill: "Tayg a moment of your time if I could."

Myself: "Of course, judge."

Ailill: "Ailill is just fine."

Myself: "Thank you, Ailill."

Ailill: "I am truly sorry about Fintan, it was not right to do. I was hoping Muirchertach would be a bit more kind about it. I got annoyed with how he treated you and wanted to treat the people you serve with. I've known a lot of people in my life and the way you carry yourselves is honorable."

Myself: "Ailill thank you, I'll let my comrades know that."

Ailill: "It's true, the King wanted to talk to you."

Myself: "Thank you, I'll talk to him."

I walked closer to King McGreggor.

King "Tayg thank you for your help with the fight in the city, thank you for the fighting in the villages to keep them safe."

Myself "Your Majesty, it was the right thing to do."

King "I can understand warrior to warrior, The ones who fought with us this day will be treated like warriors of my own kingdom. Yes, even Fintan.I know I cannot convince you to be a mayor for one of the towns."

Myself: "I am humbly honored with this, but sadly I cannot accept the offer to be a mayor at this time. I will make sure the others know."

King: "I want to see if we can get the ones on the metal turtle to come visit, of course it will not be all at once. Also tonight we want to celebrate the life of Murray. The only thing you need to bring is your thrust and hunger."

Myself: "Thank you I will make sure that the Captain knows about that. I know that the captain and the rest of the crew will be happy to know that. I know that he would love to chat with you again."

King: "I would love that. Please feel free to stay here in the city. You will have rooms prepared in my estate."

With that he excused himself. I went over to Sergeant Buford, Doc and the others. We all had a long day. They were all sitting around in the corner, next to Ronan. He was doing his best to translate back and forth. I think between the yelling and Ronan translating they could get the jist of it. I think Ronan being there was enough to keep them from being bored. A bored marine is a dangerous marine.

Sergeant Buford: "So what did King McGreggor say?"

Myself: "We are to be treated, even Fintan, as warriors of his kingdom. He's looking at getting the rest of the crew to come to the city for visits to get off the ship. He also said we would be staying in the city and his estate for the next few days."

That night we stayed in the city, we were given the rooms the warriors were given. Our packs, gear, and clothes fitting our stations were laid out for us in the rooms. We were given the royal treatment. They all knew that we did our best to keep the city safe. Out came the honeyed pork, it was slow cooked and practically melted in your mouth. The mead was flavored with raspberries. There were pastries, honeyed water and tons of food. There was no music nor any storytellers; this was clearly a wake.

That night the universe did not exist beyond the king's banquet hall. The only stories they wanted to hear were about Murray. We went around telling stories of his sacrifice, how he died in the explosion of the owl mothers hut. Ronan told how clever he was at playing table games and how kind he was. The mead flowed like water. I made sure to drink mead then honeyed water each one right after the other.

I stumbled back to my room, closed the door and fell asleep as soon as my head hit the pillow on the couch. This couch was expertly designed. The legs were adorned with animals like foxes, hawks and other animals. The incense that burned was full of herbs like sage and others that aided in a restful and deep sleep. That night no dreams came to meet me, no knocks on my door.

The morning greeted us, the meal provided to us was dried pork, nuts and warmed honey water and plenty of hot water. I shared the remainder of the freeze dried coffee packets with anyone who wanted a cup of coffee and saved enough for my second cup. They all watched and followed along as I made my coffee. It was like some weird ritual to them. I made sure there was enough creamer and sugar to go around.

They took us to the beach, and BM2 Leblanc greeted us. He had the trademarked cigarette in his mouth, the wrap around sunglasses, and the ship's ball cap. He was wearing a flak jacket along with coveralls. He slowed the boat down close to the shore but easy enough to get away without getting stuck.

BM2: "Good to see you QM2, are you guys ready to head back?"

Myself: "Yeah, we are. I think we are expected back in a few days."

BM2: "Understood, what the hell happened? We heard a lot of noise and fires on the shore."

Myself: "We had taken out the creature that was turning everyone into stone, after we did that a bunch of deformed disgusting warriors attacked."

BM2: "Good thing we intercepted about 3 of their ships, they were getting ready to offload a lot more of them. We sank the rest of their ships on the shore."

Sure enough I could see the charred remains of two or three ships along the shore. Their smoldering remains littered the beach. You could still smell the burning wood, cloth and hair along the beach. This war was brutal, and this is the only thing the misshapen could understand.

Myself: "I am glad you did, the rifles we have now are more for show right now than anything else, we had no bullets left when we made it back. Murray died when we took out the owl mother."

BM2: "What was that like?"

I explained how crazy and how we used the tracking unit now defunct and would not power on, what the realm she lived in looked like and how Harper was turned to stone just playing music and talking to us. I explained how we found Fintan and helped, however I left out the part about Sergeant Buford.

BM2: "Dang man, that is crazy."

I nodded. "Yeah it was, positive note the King of this area wants to work with the old man so we can get people to come ashore. I don't know too much and try to keep it on the down low."

I could see him be at ease and tension was a lot less. I had a hunch the crew was being run ragged with all the events. They needed a break; anyone could see that. I had some extra dried meat.

Myself: "BM2, here you guys might like this, I wasn't really able to pick up anything else, it is a lot like jerky but better."

I handed him the dried meat, He took a chunk and ate it, he passed the bag off to the gunnersmate that was always with him when they dropped us off and picked us up.

BM2: "Dang that stuff is good, it's sweet but not too sweet. Is the rest of their food like this?"

Myself: "Yeah, their beer is just as good."

GM3: "QM2, this is good stuff, anything fun to do there? Any beautiful ladies?"

Myself: "GM3, there are plenty. You would most likely want to head to the closest thing they have here called a city. Trust me you will want to pay attention to the safety brief. You do not want to annoy these people nor take advantage of their hospitality. They take these things very seriously."

GM3 nodded, took another chunk of pork and handed the bag back to BM2 as we raced back to the Ashtabula. I never thought I would welcome that hunk of metal. It just occurred to me it was a haven from craziness and a home. We made it back and it was rack time. It was apparent that the crew needed the same amount of rest that we did.

Afterward

In the aftermath of the misshapen attacking the city and surrounding villages. There were burning embers and still fires to put out. Almost every house in the villages lost at least one person, the city lost fewer. There was rebuilding to do. Luckily for them and us, the Ashtabula took out three of their ships en route to where we were. They had long ships that sat low to the water line, they were remarkably maneuverable under sail or oar. However not maneuverable enough to dodge anti armor 50 caliber rounds.

We discovered that the rock near the island was not just an island but a person. That person McLear was a being with immense magical powers. He had offered to basically provide us with food regularly, sort of like how we did the underway replenishments. A merchant marine ship (a civilian run ship) would carry fuel, food and sometimes bullets. We would agree to go the same course and speed. Hook up our ship to theirs via a fuel line and start pumping fuel. They would then send a helicopter back and forth with food (ammunition) to off load. He could not promise anything more than food but he said that he would be able to find us and would resupply every month.

That first month, it was similar to the food that the king ate on a regular basis. He sent the spices and the first-time beer and mead were sent. That quickly stopped after it was relayed and explained we could not drink while we fought, however he did send some for the captain. It was beer at first, but it switched out to whiskey, pretty much on par with what the old man had before our trip through the whirlpool.

It still felt weird being out on patrol with the Marines, I still felt like a tag-along, just along for the ride trying to earn a merit badge or something. It felt equally sad that Private Murray was no longer with us. It crushed a lot of us, he was kind of the kid brother that would always have your back. With that we were gathered at a place just outside the city. It had a wonderful view overlooking the ocean. The skipper was there as was gunny. We were all wearing our dress uniforms. Thankfully the skipper decided on the winter uniforms. The wool had helped to keep me warm, there were a few female wandering eyes towards our direction mostly towards the marines in their dress uniform. In another time or universe that uniform seemed to have the same effect.

It was a big turn out to this location and they had something covered with cloth, it was rather tall as well it was a closely guarded secret and not even Ronan would tell me what it was. Even the day of the event he was there. The old man asked him to say a few words considering we did not have a chaplain on board. We only really had visiting chaplins on the ship, never one assigned. A chaplain is an officer who are ordained ministers of their own religion, they are all officers as well.

Ronan: "We are gathered here today to remember and honor Private William Murray."

I thought so, William was his first name, how did Ronan figure that out.

Ronan: "We are blessed with so many that knew him, that he helped and blessed with his presence, selfless sense of duty, sense of wonderment. We know that life will be a little darker without him to enrich our lives. He died how he lived, trying to protect those alongside him and those who could not protect him. Divine please watch over him, please allow him into the afterlife of his choosing."

I think there was dust in a lot of eyes at that moment, we were all standing at attention. With that the American flag was lowered, next to but lower was the Marine Corps flag and under both that flag but on the same pole as the American flag the Ashtabula flag was lowered. Nearby a group made of sailors and marines lowered the flags. On stand by a group of marines offered the 21-gun salute.

Private Murray was buried in the celtic way, there was a mound dug for him, he was wheeled in by warriors from the city. They pulled the yokes on the cart expertly made for him. The cart was expertly crafted, it told the story of his life and death towards the end with mother owl. In the cart he was lovingly placed in his dress uniform with a rifle placed at his right hand, the barrel was bent to a 90 degree angle signifying his time as a warrior was served with honor.

As he passed I whispered, "Rest easy Murray we have the watch. May we meet on fiddler's green."

The American flag was expertly folded and placed on his chest, he had no loved ones. He had no next of kin to give it to. To me that was the most heartbreaking part of it all. I remember his last words asking me to promise to live a life worth living.

After that we returned to the city and were invited into the king's mansion. Out came the food, that honeyed pork, with herbs, out came the honeyed water drinks, with raspberry sage and other flavors. Out came the mead, beer, whiskey and even the wine. The stories flowed as much as the alcohol. It was a moment of celebrating the life of Murray, all we did. The commander was there and he approached me.

Commander: "QM2, a moment of your time."

Myself: "Of course, sir."

Commander: "I'll be out enjoying some of the night air."

Myself: "Understood, I'll be right out."

It was a peaceful evening, thankfully not the calm in the middle of the storm. You could see for miles the ship off in the distance. She was anchored the second time since we got here. You could hear the insects playfully chirping, the birds settling down for the evening. It was that wonderful summer air.

The commander lit his cigar and took a few puffs. "Wonderful evening, isn't it?"

Myself: "Yes sir, permission to speak freely."

Commander: "Of course QM2. What you and sergeant Buford did is phenomenal. You both along with those under you built a relationship with a foreign nation. It's no small feat."

Myself: "Thank you sir, I will pass the word along."

Commander: "Good, I'm trying to find a way to reward all of you."

Myself: "I am honored and humbled sir."

Commander: "I was talking with Ronan, he seems to think it would be best if he went back with us. Said we could use a doctor and a chaplain on the ship."

Myself: "He is a rather astute man, he misses Private Murray too. They would talk as his hearing healed."

Commander: "I am still flabbergasted by that, who thought that sort of healing was possible. I am sorry about Murray, I know he meant a lot to many."

Myself: "Thanks, sir. He was a good Marine, a good kid."

Commander: "To Murray, to this wonderful land and new friendships."

Myself: "Agreed, sir.

We raised glasses and took a drink. The old man is someone I would follow into hell to raid it. We ended up in a foreign land initially with no allies, just our determination to survive.

Commander: "She is beautiful, isn't she?" He pointed at our ship that was out off the coast of the island.

Myself: "Yes sir, she is."

Commander: "The Grey Lady, she is something special, something to rally behind. After the funeral, one could imagine that just seeing her on the coast brought some hope."

Myself: "I never looked at it that way."

Commander: "I think it's things like that is why both you and I joined."

Myself: "Yes sir, yes it is."

It was something to really think about, the old man was right. It's one of the reasons why I joined, to protect those who would not, do make something of my life. When another person came out, he was holding a long pipe. It could only be one person, Ronan.

Ronan in a heavily accent: "Mind if I join you Commander and Tayg?"

Commander: "Not at all, I think it would be nice to have a chat with you. It would be nice to talk logistics with you. " He then turned to me " Dismissed QM2, please enjoy yourself, but not too much."

Myself: "Thank you, sir, and I won't." I saluted the old man, and he returned the salute.

Ronan: "Tayg, before you go. I am sorry for your loss. Willam was a special man."

With that, he gave me a pat on the back. "I know you need to keep your sense of duty on you but if you, but if you need to talk, let me know."

Myself: "I would like that, thank you, Ronan."

I started to walk back to go into the festivities and as I was walking back I could hear the tail end of the conversation. To me they were going to be talking about stuff above my paygrade, so I mentally tuned out most of the conversation.

Ronan: "I know Commander isn't your first name, and you have me at a bit of a disadvantage."

Commander: "My first name is John. You can call me John if you wish."

That threw me off. I would have never thought the old man's first name would be John. Honestly, it didn't matter if it was. It would always be Commander near him when referring to him, and no one was around Old man or skipper, which was the right way to address him. Military bearing had to count for something. It was interesting that the chain of command had ended with him. We needed to look out for him as much as he looked out for us.

In the coming months, Fireman Moore ended up getting medically retired. He wanted out of the Navy. Moore had a series of family emergencies and was not permitted emergency leave. The Leave chits (paperwork) never made it to the old man. Heck, they never made it to his chief. The old man cut him a break and let him go after he heard why he went overboard.

This allowed a good change for Moore, he always wanted to get into cooking and maybe open up his own deli or restaurant. He was able to do that in the city, for a while he did rather well. However it was a bit counter intuitive to the culture of our friends, the king ended up hiring him on as a full time chef. He had already found a lovely lady and rumor had it they were to be married come spring.

We were getting the port visit guide set up after the fighting calmed down and with help from Moore. One of the villagers was assisting with getting sailors and marines from the village to the city in the same cart we used to get from the village to the city to help save it. The villagers would try to tell that and go over the battle as they went to the city. For others they had a chance to rest and take some liberty, but for me, I was going to head back out there again. I had no idea where I was going, but I knew who would be a good person to start with, Ronan.

That haunting trill came over the 1MC it then stated, "QM2 McDermmont to the Captain's cabin. QM2 McDermmont to the Captain's cabin."

I began my climb from our berthing near the engine room up to the Captain's cabin. She was on my mind a lot more than before I ached for her. It was like I thought I had a puzzle completed, just missing a piece I could not find. I longed to see those steel eyes shine and the warmth of her hands.

I entered the Captain's cabin, and the cigar fragrance danced throughout the cabin. It was clear to see he had mead and whiskey. It took on a different texture here from what I had tried. It was a bit smokier and not nearly as clear as the modern whiskey we were used to. The whiskey here turned into a literally cough medicine, to be honest, HMCS implemented a very watered-down version as cough syrup.

Myself: "Sir you wished to see me?" I stood at attention in his estate room.

The Commander looked up from his desk, cigar in his mouth, he placed it in his right arm. In the chair to the left was Ronan.

Commander: "Yes, at ease and have a seat."

Myself: "Thank you, sir."

I left attention and took a seat to the left. Commander Alvarez stood up and shut the door. He made sure two marines were guarding the door.

They were only provided with the instructions that no one was to enter under any circumstances.

He said to them, "Stop anyone who tries to enter. If they are on the crew have fun, but don't damage them too much."

With that the door shut.

Commander: "Ronan told me about something you need to do. I saw the misshapen ships trying to raid the island. Basically, son, you are going into their layer."

Mentally, I thought well this is something way more than not easy. This is a herculean task; well, I best get to it. I figure someone has to bring them down. It wouldn't be easy to do by myself. I didn't want to risk anyone from the ship going on a possible suicide run.

He continued, "You aren't going alone. We cannot take you closer, and a small force might be better."

Myself: "Thank you, sir."

Commander: "Of course, I hope you made some friends along the way?"

Myself: "Yes sir, more than a few."

Commander: "Excellent, dismissed."

Myself: "Sir, before I leave, might I ask a favor?"

Commander: "Just one?"

Myself: "Maybe two."

The next day at morning muster was something interesting; we were all standing in formation. Fintan was with us. His clothing was switched out to look more like ours. His forest cammo only had shades of green; the more you looked at it, the more green it looked. His fast helmet and gloves had the same pattern. The problem we had was trying to get a firearm condensed down to the size that would be practical for him and still pump out the hurt. MR2 was actually having fun with that puzzle.

Gunny: "Private Fintan, please step forward and stand at attention."

He stepped forward with pristine military bearing and purpose. His military uniform was in perfect shape as if it were brand new. Out came Commander Alvarez. As soon as he saw him, he offered a crisp salute like we taught him. The commander returned the salute.

Commander: "Private Fintan, do you swear to support the Constitution against all enemies, foreign and domestic, while in service to the Ashtabula for the duration of your enlistment?"

Private Fintan: "Yes, sir."

Commander: "Very well then, I welcome you to the crew and to the Marine Corps."

The old man saluted Fintan. "Welcome aboard, shipmate."

Fintan returned the salute. "Thank you, sir. "

At that moment, I had a little bit of pity for those who got in the path and stoked the ire of Fintan and Causes Safety Briefs. I highly doubt that anyone believed a leprechaun would have joined us; maybe it was a person who was in a mascot suit, but it was not a real-deal leprechaun.

With that, some of us were dismissed.

Gunny: "Sergeant Buford and QM2 McDermont, I need to talk to you."

Sergeant Buford: "Yes, Gunny."

Myself: "Understood, Gunny."

Gunny: "Both of you have been tasked to take the hurt to the misshapen; you will start once we start allowing people to go on liberty. You are going to assemble a task force we are calling The Usual Suspects."

We both simply nodded. I internally chuckled; that task force kind of summed us up rather well. I had to fight a smirk with the name.

Gunny: "The old man and I aren't letting you off the hook that easily; he wants to thank you for what you've done so far. We are trying to figure out a way to make sure you are thanked properly."

Gunny continued, "You are going to find and take out their HQ, including their leader. You are going to get an intel briefing from Ronan and some time to plan and gear up. Any questions?"

Myself: "No, Gunny."

Sergeant Buford: "No, Gunny."

With that, we were released to make plans of mayhem against the misshapen on their own turf. May their Divine have mercy on their souls since we will not. Time to start planning and getting intel. Ronan would be the best place to start. I had an inkling we had a long way ahead of us. I can still remember my grandfather's words of wisdom: "Anything worth it isn't easy."

Tayg MacDermott, QM2, USN

About the Author

Thomas is a veteran of the United States Navy, when not reading brewing, writing, and streaming video games on Twitch, he's researching historical, and archaeological topics during the pre-medieval, and medieval ages, and the next concert he wants to attend.

9 7 9 8 3 3 0 5 3 5 6 0 6